Praise for Jenny Hale

"Jenny Hale writes touching, beautiful stories."
—RaeAnne Thayne, *New York Times*
bestselling author

The Beach House

"A charming and intriguing love story."   —Shelf Awareness

Christmas at Fireside Cabins

"[Read] for the grumpy-with-a-heart-made-of-ice coffee shop owner ... This book will bring Christmas joy and festive magic to your life!"   —Buzzfeed

Christmas at Silver Falls

"Hale brings the beauty of the Great Smoky Mountains alive in this heartwarming Christmas romance ... Authentic, dimensional characters enhance the emotionally charged love story. Fast-paced and brimming with holiday spirit, this is sure to please."
—*Publishers Weekly*

Summer at Firefly Beach

"A great summer beach read."   —*PopSugar*

an
island
summer

ALSO BY JENNY HALE

an
island
summer

JENNY HALE

FOREVER

New York   Boston

Forever
Hachette Book Group
1290 Avenue of the Americas, New York, NY 10104
read-forever.com
@readforeverpub

Originally published in 2022 by Bookouture, an imprint of StoryFire Ltd.

First Forever Edition: April 2024

Forever is an imprint of Grand Central Publishing. The Forever name and logo are trademarks of Hachette Book Group, Inc.

The publisher is not responsible for websites (or their content) that are not owned by the publisher.

The Hachette Speakers Bureau provides a wide range of authors for speaking events. To find out more, go to hachettespeakersbureau.com or email HachetteSpeakers@hbgusa.com.

Forever books may be purchased in bulk for business, educational, or promotional use. For information, please contact your local bookseller or the Hachette Book Group Special Markets Department at special.markets@hbgusa.com.

Library of Congress Cataloging-in-Publication Data has been applied for.

ISBN: 9781538756065 (trade paperback)

Printed in the United States of America

LSC-C

Printing 1, 2024

To the team of people who helped to pave my way.

an island summer

PROLOGUE

"Listen," Pappy said to Meghan as he stilled his fishing pole, the two of them rocking gently in the old two-seater skiff out on the Pamlico Sound. The haze that draped the water had begun to burn off, stirring the seagulls above. One of them landed on a tuft of seagrass nearby, flapping its white angelic wings.

Pappy's wise attention moved to the sunrise on the horizon and the stripes of shimmering gold and pink that it had painted on the surface of the water. The boat bobbed in its place, anchored between two patches of marsh. The tall vegetation leaned over in unison with the push of the early morning breeze.

Fifteen-year-old Meghan Gray tucked a wayward strand of her dark chestnut hair behind her ear and sharpened her hearing, honing in on the squawk of another seagull in the distance and the rhythmic lapping of the water against the side of the boat. "What do you hear, Pappy?" she asked her grandfather.

His gaze found her, and he looked at her with a strange sort of awe; something bigger was on his mind. He smiled, his tanned, weathered face creasing along the sides and at the edges of his eyes. "That's calm we hear," he said, his voice breathy like the coastal wind. "It's what we all long for, even if we don't know it."

She closed her eyes, following her grandfather's lead, and breathed in the briny air, noting the thick salt in the wind and the light mist on her skin from the fog that was burning off as the sun climbed higher in the sky.

"If you ever feel like you don't have it," he said, bringing her out of the moment, "come back here and find it." He took in a long, slow breath and let it out. "I can't say that I lived my life perfectly, or that I have all the answers—God knows I've bungled some pretty big things . . ." He looked up at the heavens, an ache she'd never seen before on his face. "But if I do one thing right, it's to teach you that whatever's going on in your life, calm is within you. Sometimes, you just have to wade through the deep waters to find it."

That moment with just the two of them, in the mist of dawn, had been perfect. So perfect that recalling it would bring her to tears, even ten years later.

ONE

With a determined huff, Meghan dumped her red-and-yellow waitress uniform into the trash bin outside her apartment with force, and reached around the trailer full of her things to shut the hatch on the old Honda. Her chocolate Labrador Charlie paced around excitedly beside her, his tail thumping against the side of the packed car whenever she came near.

"I've finally had it," she said to her best friend Tess Fuller, while she wrestled one last bag into the back seat. She ran her hands down her tank top and cut-offs to wipe the perspiration off them, the heat wrapping around her like a fiery serpent.

"I'm surprised you lasted as long as you did," Tess said.

Meghan pulled her hair through the back of her baseball cap to get it off her neck and eyed Tess, her confidante since childhood. Tess, wearing one of her signature sundresses the color of a ballet slipper, and white sneakers, sipped on the watered-down iced latte that she'd been holding when she'd shown up by taxi. Her friend, who'd sold her car for cash and sublet her own apartment, had arrived at Meghan's with two coffees and a small pile of her own bags, all packed for the summer.

"I needed the money," Meghan said.

She and Tess had both worked at Zagos, a prestigious restaurant in New York City. Starting as a hostess and barely scraping by on her meager salary, Meghan had dreams of getting a glimpse of culinary art from the best of the best, climbing the ladder, and finally finding her own place as a famous chef. She wanted to express herself artistically, creating dishes for the rich and famous.

But the last five years had been nothing but frustration and doors slammed in her face. She'd worked her fingers to the bone, waiting tables for an awful boss named Vinnie Russo who'd never once noticed her strengths, barely surviving on the income and not getting anywhere professionally.

"Are you sure you want to go back to your pappy's house?" Tess asked.

On one fateful night when Meghan was only fifteen, her parents had died in a car crash, hit by a drunk driver on their way home from a movie, and she'd gone to live with Pappy. Meghan hadn't let her mind wander to the vacant house where she'd spent those grief-stricken days or to her pappy's worn skiff, the small boat that sat empty on the bank by the shed out back. The old fishing cottage had been willed to her when Pappy had left this earth. For the last ten years, she'd hung on to it like a distant memory, not wanting to disturb a single thing. *Come back here and find your calm*, she could almost hear him say.

"I can do it," she replied with resolve, a lump already forming in her throat and uncertainty slithering through her. No longer able to pay her rent after quitting, that house was all she had left, her only option.

"Do you have the keys and everything?" Tess asked, as she moved from the narrow city sidewalk around to the passenger side and dumped her things in her seat. A car drove by, barely squeezing between the open door and the parked cars on the other side of the street. The driver threw up his hands in annoyance.

"Yeah," she replied, eyeing the manila envelope sitting on the dashboard of the used car she'd just bought for five hundred dollars to make the trip back to the Outer Banks. She prayed the worn vehicle would get them there.

Meghan put her hands on her hips to shake off her heartache, taking in the full-to-the-brim car on the busy city side street in front of her. "Well, that's that," she said to Tess, before turning to have one last look up at her empty apartment. The old building blended into the others beside it, offering nothing to catch the eye of passers-by—just an enormous rectangular brick box with rows of windows as far as she could see.

"You gonna be all right?" Tess asked, stepping back up beside her and draping a protective arm around Meghan's shoulders.

Meghan produced a smile for her friend's benefit. "Yeah," she said. "Let's roll."

Tess tossed her empty latte into the trash before sliding on a pair of bright pink sunglasses, her wild auburn curls drawn into a ponytail. "Looks like we're headed to the coast." Her eyebrows bounced up and down excitedly from behind her glasses as she climbed into Meghan's car.

Meghan opened the back door for Charlie, the dog jumping up into his spot. Without a single look in her rearview, she started the engine and pulled away from her old life, headed for her new one.

The late summer sun came in at a slant through Meghan's open window as they made their way along the edge of the North Carolina countryside, finishing up the second leg of their nine-hour drive, having spent last night at a midway spot. As they entered the thin strip of barrier islands nestled quietly between the Atlantic Ocean and the Pamlico Sound, the rural landscape was now dotted with a mixture of old bungalows and beach mansions. Uncertainty ebbed and flowed through Meghan's mind as she drove toward her destination: the one place she could definitively say had taught her what she needed to survive in life.

Growing up, Pappy had taught Meghan how to cook. Even though he'd spent his life outside, working on the docks as a local fisherman, there was a finesse to his weathered hands when he was in the kitchen, and he could cook a meal worthy of any five-star restaurant. He had a vegetable garden out back, fruit trees in the yard, and all the seafood she could think of—everything they needed for those fantastic dinners they would cook together. Meghan's fondest memories were of her days in the kitchen with Pappy, cooking her favorites like Hatteras clam chowder and orange-glazed mahi mahi.

When Zagos's head chef quit unexpectedly and her frazzled boss had decided to completely revamp their menu to combat sluggish sales, Meghan had had the opening of a lifetime. Tess and the others rallied behind her, suggesting that she immediately offer to fill in. She'd proposed that Vinnie include offerings from her grandfather's own recipes, and one night she'd spent more money than she had, buying the ingredients, and producing dishes like her pan-seared foie gras and her pappy's famous chartreuse hollandaise sauce that her coworkers had all adored. But Vinnie had ignored her dishes, letting them sit untouched until they were inedible.

"You're not a chef," he'd finally told her, when she questioned him. "I need someone who's been in the industry, someone who knows what they're doing."

Vinnie was right. She'd never been a chef—she was just a waitress. She could still hear Pappy telling her, *Your dreams are just your future stretching out in front of you. It's up to you to act on them.* And that was when she knew things had to change if she ever wanted to be happy. When he "reorganized" the restaurant, as he'd called it, shifting directions completely, redecorating and offering a mediocre attempt at a diner atmosphere with a mediocre menu, she'd hit her limit.

She'd lain in bed that night in tears. After a lot of soul-searching, she came to the conclusion that she might not be a chef, but she'd never know until she got out there and tried. Although a storm of inadequacy raged within her, and she didn't know if she had the guts to actually do it. She could take the long route and begin culinary classes, or she could throw herself in at the deep end and open her own place, trying her hand at it—but with very little money in the bank, neither option was really a possibility yet.

With absolutely no idea what she was going to do, and with only her inadequate savings, she'd called Tess to tell her that she was going to quit her job and move into Pappy's house. In an act of sheer rebellion, and relatively consistent impulsivity, Tess had quit with her. They'd spent the morning loading everything they owned into the old car, headed for the summer sunshine on Hatteras Island in the Outer Banks.

"Think we'll find somewhere to work?" Tess asked, pulling Meghan out of her thoughts. Tess sank her hand into the bag of granola she'd brought for the trip and popped a few pieces into her mouth while Charlie stuck his snout between the two front seats, hoping for a nibble.

"I hope so," Meghan replied over the radio. Her number one concern had been getting away from Zagos and clearing her head to figure out what she wanted to do with her life. Tess, on the other hand, had seen it more as an opportunity for a free three-month vacation. Either way, Meghan hoped to have a fresh start in the Outer Banks.

As they entered the town of Waves, Tess turned the radio

down and gazed out the window at the brightly colored sails that floated above the sound, attached to kiteboarders who bobbed and twisted in the air, coming back down onto the water's sparkling surface with the grace of an ice skater. "How long since you've been back here?"

Meghan swallowed, pushing the idea of her grandfather's fishing cottage out of her mind. She'd have to see it soon enough. "Not for a decade," she replied.

"That's a long time." Growing up with Meghan back in Virginia, Tess knew all about Meghan's grandfather and how important he'd been to her, and the empathy in Tess's tone was evident.

"Yes," Meghan said, not having light enough words to fill the conversation, the weight of facing this place without Pappy sitting on her heart like a cinderblock.

"What made you decide to come here now when you could've gone anywhere?"

Meghan glanced over at Tess's compassionate stare before returning her attention to the road. Trying to muster up an explanation when her own understanding of it was murky at best, she said, "I guess I just wanted to feel . . . calm."

"Well, this'll do it." Tess waved an arm out the open window, the blue waters within reach, a massive white sailboat pulling in to dock at the marina.

They'd driven down highway twelve south, through the massive throngs of tourists that had clogged up the northern villages of Kitty Hawk and Kill Devil Hills, and continued on through the town of Waves, the beachfront shops and restaurants giving way to wide expanses of marshland, blue skies, and restless surf. And they'd crossed the low-lying bridge that snaked its way through the waters onto Hatteras Island.

The roads narrowed until they found themselves on a winding path leading to Pappy's little cottage. As she meandered through the marshland, she could see it: the brown shingled bungalow on the edge of the Atlantic. In her side-view mirror, there was nothing but coastline behind her, and her dog Charlie's face out his window, his fur pulling backward with the wind, and the soft, swaying seagrass. She sucked in a steadying breath and fixed her gaze on the cottage.

TWO

"May I go in alone first?" Meghan asked Tess as they stood together in the gravel drive while Charlie loped through the tall grass, delighted to finally be out of the car.

"Of course. I'll take Charlie down to the beach."

Meghan gave her best friend a squeeze. "Thank you."

Then, with the envelope in hand, she turned back toward Pappy's. The sea churned onto the shore, hissing at her back, as she walked the sandy path leading to the front porch steps. Her fingers found the paint-peeled railing, and she stepped up each stair slowly until she arrived on the small front porch facing the water. The two old rocking chairs where she and Pappy had gone to sit on the hardest days without her parents were still there, pushed to one side, one of them toppled over. How those chairs had managed to survive the storms over the years was beyond her. Her hands trembling, she reached into the envelope, past the few other contents, and grabbed the familiar brass key, unlocking the door. She gripped the doorknob and twisted it, pushing it open. The hinges creaked out their warning that she was entering the house that Pappy had left her in his will. It had been all he had besides his fishing boat, which he'd sold off to a neighbor just before he'd died.

The minute she laid eyes on the interior, she sucked in a dusty breath, a wave of emotion overtaking her. She pressed her hands to her mouth to keep the sob from traveling all the way down to Tess and Charlie by the beach. She ran her hand along the battered leather sofa, leaving a trail of prints through the dust.

"I'm sorry I took so long to come back," she said in a whisper, her words jagged.

The floor squeaking under her feet, she walked over to the thermostat and kicked on the air conditioning. Then she leaned on the small dinette table and set the envelope down, unable to look at its contents just yet. She'd had it since the funeral, but it never seemed right to look inside. An ache rising in her throat, she closed her eyes, the sound of laughter and the tinkling of dishes filling her ears.

"*I taught Meghan how to make these here biscuits,*" she heard Pappy telling her mother in that soothingly relaxed drawl of his when Meghan was about ten. He was leaning on his elbows, his fork dangling from his fingers above his plate, a wide smile on his face. "*Did it all by herself.*"

"*Delicious,*" her mother said, her face youthful in Meghan's memory. "*Are they cheese?*"

"*Cheddar cornmeal,*" Meghan had answered.

"*Everything she knows, she learned from you, Dad,*" her mother had said with an affectionate laugh.

Pappy eyed her with adoration. He and Meghan had a special bond that had set them apart from anyone else in the family. "*She'll never need a husband because she'll be so independent, but if she ever wants one, I hope to show her . . .*"

". . . what to look for in a man," she heard herself say out loud, bringing her back to reality. When her parents died and the police showed up at her door, she remembered being curled in a ball on the sofa while the two officers discussed who to call. She cried out, "Call my pappy," tears streaming down her cheeks. Pappy had stepped up, coming to her home in Richmond that very night and bringing her to Hatteras Island. The way he'd calmed her restless, anxious soul was by doing what they used to do for her parents: cooking. It had been the source of so many wonderful memories before their death that cooking had carried her through her grief. Now, she looked around the empty cottage to be sure she was alone, and then gazed at the leather chair where Pappy had sat to watch television in the evenings.

Pappy had taught her everything during her teenage years. From hooking up a boat trailer to a truck hitch, to rigging a live bait on a fish hook, to balancing the delicate amount of yeast and flour when making his famous cornmeal biscuits rise. And he was right about teaching her what to look for in a man. "You don't want someone to take care of you," he'd said. "Find someone who *sees* you, someone who knows the greatness you're capable of before you've even discovered it yourself." The only problem was that Pappy had been the one who could see her, and no one could compare to the high standard Pappy had set.

For an instant, she wondered what she was even doing coming back there. She wasn't ready yet. Even after ten years. What good could come of putting herself through these memories? Pappy was gone.

She knew deep down that the real reason she'd come back was because, without her parents, she needed her grandfather right now. Over the years, Meghan had never seemed to find her way. She loved the arts, sketching, cooking, dancing—none of which she'd ever been able to figure out how to make a living off of.

When her awful boss had completely dismissed her that night, she'd sobbed in her bed and prayed that Pappy could hear her. He'd always made her feel like she was special, when the world had told her otherwise. She hoped being near him would guide her, show her what she was meant to do, because somewhere along the line she'd lost track.

Walking over to the kitchen sink, she turned on the water. It spit and sputtered before letting out a stream. She turned it back off. "How am I supposed to be a chef in the middle of nowhere?" She laughed out loud now at the ridiculousness of her choices.

If she were being honest with herself, there were many more opportunities in New York. There were a handful of culinary schools in the city nearby and she could've researched grants or scholarships, but she'd come to Hatteras Island instead. What was she thinking, planning to build a new life here? She went through the living room and peered out the window at the vast wilderness in front of her, Charlie racing down the beach and Tess holding her shoes, her feet in the surf.

That surf had been a joyous sight during her childhood, when she'd come every summer to visit with her mom and dad, but as the years went on it became more knowing, more comforting, as if it could speak to her.

Meghan let herself back outside. The summer heat hit her like a wet blanket, causing beads of perspiration to form on her skin, the coastal wind immediately cooling them. She picked up the toppled rocking chair and dragged it to the center of the porch, lowering herself into it, leaning her head back, and closing her eyes to avoid thinking about how the outside of the house needed repairs. She took in the unique mixture of the salty scent of the ocean and the old cedar of the house, instantly comforting her whirring mind. Wrapping her hands tightly around the arms of the chair as if it could somehow save her from drowning in her life choices, she pushed back, letting the rocking lull her.

Charlie's bark cut through the moment and she opened her

eyes. He was soaking wet and running up the dock toward the house, Tess not far behind him.

"How are you doing?" her friend asked when she'd reached Meghan.

Charlie bounded up the stairs, shaking and sending water spraying across the dilapidated wood of the porch.

"I'm okay," Meghan replied, not wanting to bring her friend down with her own dilemmas. "We should probably get our bags into the house before they melt in the heat."

They retrieved their luggage from the car, bringing it all in and setting each piece down on the oval braided rug in the living room as the air conditioning unit rattled loudly, working to combat the intense heat.

"Feel like you're stepping back in time?" Meghan asked Tess, as Charlie jumped onto the sofa, sending a plume of dust into the air and making them cough. He jumped back down, sneezing.

Tess wandered around the living area, sliding one of the dated magazines toward her and putting it back before eyeing the mason jar full of fish hooks that sat on the coffee table. "It's like 1975 in here." She picked up the metal coaster where Pappy had always set his drink and turned it over in her hand, swirling more dust on the table.

"Maybe we should leave the bags for now," Meghan said, already needing a mental break, "and find a clean place to eat while we make our grocery list. I'm starving."

Tess spun around, suddenly interested. "Only if there are cocktails involved. My treat."

Meghan smiled despite herself. "Done."

The tiny hut of a restaurant, wrapped in blue clapboard, sat in the sand, twinkle lights on the front and the Atlantic sparkling behind it.

"I'm feeling summery already," Tess said, as she did a little dance on the boardwalk leading to the place, beach music playing on speakers above the roar of the waves as they crashed relentlessly in a foaming spray.

Meghan allowed Tess's energy to soak down to her bones. Meghan had known her best friend since the fifth grade, and without fail Tess could always lift her spirits. After Meghan had moved to Pappy's, they'd kept in touch, spending all their babysitting money on stationery to send each other letters, and they called each other every chance they got.

Regardless of how great or not great her choice was to return to the Outer Banks, this move was about taking chances and living in the moment. She needed to try to relax into it and embrace all the wonderful things that Pappy had loved about this place. They took a seat under the grass roof of the porch out back— a wide space with a bar at one end and tiki torches lining the railings—and ordered a couple of cocktails. The idea of iced rum and coconut mixed with the heat and the sapphire ocean view gave her a buzz before she'd even had a sip.

"So, the house is really dusty and needs a good cleaning," Tess said from over her menu, pushing her pink sunglasses onto her head and making eye contact. "We should probably dive in and give it a good scour when we get back, if we want somewhere to sleep."

"Definitely," Meghan agreed, trying not to think about having to rearrange Pappy's things. "And the water just got turned back on, so we'll need to run it for a while to clear out any old water in the lines."

The waitress returned with their drinks: hurricane glasses full of frosty white liquid with a spear of pineapple and strawberries floating in the top. Then Meghan pulled a notepad and a pen from her handbag.

Tess swirled the red-and-white striped straw in her cocktail.

"We'll need cleaning supplies, so you might want to jot those down. And groceries."

Meghan tried not to think about how much this dinner and all the supplies were going to cost her. "I say we focus on those two things tonight. That's enough to keep us busy until the morning." She jotted down a list of cleaning products.

When the waitress arrived to take their order, Tess tapped her menu. "I'll have the pineapple shrimp and fried green tomatoes."

"Perfect," the waitress said. "And for you?"

Meghan scanned her menu quickly. "I'll have the calamari." She then handed it to the waitress, who sauntered off to put in their orders. Leaning over the brightly painted blue wooden table, Meghan poised her pen above the pad of paper. "What food should we get for the house?"

Tess's gaze was fixed on something above them when suddenly a pair of arms wrapped around Meghan.

"My darling," an elderly man said in a gentle southern accent. His scent of cotton and basil wasn't familiar; nor was his face when he pulled back, his trembling hands still on her shoulders. "Hester . . ."

"I'm so sorry," a smooth voice came from behind the old man, strong hands gently pulling him back. The much younger man shook his head apologetically, two lines forming between his captivating blue eyes. "He's . . . confused. Come on, Gramps."

"No," the old man refused. "It's *Hester*," he said urgently. "I'm not leaving her."

"This isn't Hester, Gramps," the man said with an anxious inhale, running his fingers through his crop of dark hair in bewilderment. "Is it?" He peered down at Meghan.

She shook her head, not understanding what was going on.

"I apologize again."

"It's no problem," Meghan said, feeling sorry for both of them. The old man seemed insistent that she was someone else, leaving his poor grandson to corral him over to his seat. "I'm Meghan

Gray," she said, hoping it might help to clear any confusion. She held out her hand to the younger man.

He took her hand in his soft but firm grip, his mind clearly elsewhere. "Toby Meyers," he said. "And this is my grandfather, Rupert. Come on, Gramps."

"You're not Meghan Gray," Rupert snapped, his eyes unsteady, his lips wobbling, looking disoriented. "Your name is Hester Quinn."

"He stays at Rosewood Manor, the senior living facility down the road, and when he gets agitated there, I take him out for dinner. I thought he might like to go out tonight," Toby explained. "But he's still having trouble. I've never seen him quite this distraught before."

Rupert snatched his arm away from his grandson and tried to sit down in a chair at Meghan and Tess's table.

Meghan smiled uncomfortably.

"He must be having an off night," Toby said, pulling the chair back and attempting to coax the old man out of it, his clear distress making her want to put her hands on his shoulders and assure him that it was okay.

Rupert grabbed Toby's arm and looked up at his grandson, his eyes like daggers. "I'm telling you, it's Hester. Stop treating me like I'm a crazy person."

Other diners had begun to take notice of the scene and Toby was getting more frustrated, his lips worked into a frown as he pulled out his cell phone. "I'm going to have to call your nurse if you don't leave these ladies alone."

"Don't you dare." Rupert swiped at the phone.

"Why don't we all sit *together*?" Meghan suggested, scrambling for some way to put this old man at ease and take the immense burden off of Toby.

Tess joined in, nodding. "Rupert, you can keep your seat across from Hester so you two can talk, and Toby can sit beside her. How does that sound?"

Sweet Tess.

"Oh no, we wouldn't want to impose," Toby said, shaking his head, still unsuccessfully trying to move his grandfather by grasping the old man's arm, but Rupert was already scooting his chair over beside Tess.

"It's fine," Meghan said to Toby. "We only just ordered."

Tentatively, Toby took a seat beside Meghan with a thankful surrender in his gaze.

Rupert calmed down once they'd all gotten settled. He stared at Meghan as if he hadn't seen her in years, a smile lingering on his creased face.

Unsure what the old man was thinking, Meghan caught Toby's eye and wrinkled her nose with amusement. He shook his head as if the whole thing was completely unbelievable. Even though Toby was obviously mortified, it was sweet that Rupert thought Meghan was someone he knew. And she had to admit that it was nice to have him there, grinning at her. In an odd way, he reminded her of Pappy. Toby looked out at the Atlantic, and she wished she could set his mind at ease a bit more. She really didn't object to them crashing their dinner at all.

She leaned over and whispered to Toby, "Who is Hester?"

"I have no idea," he replied, clearly troubled by it. "Probably not a real person." He looked up. "Hey Gramps, how old are you?"

"Twenty."

"See?" Toby turned his attention back to the shore, a storm of some sort churning on his own face.

She smiled, but he didn't see it, so her eyes went back to the old man. He had a faraway look in his gaze as if he were peering straight through her, seeing something that wasn't there.

Toby stood up. "I'll grab the waitress and put in our orders so hopefully they come out with yours," he said, pacing off, his shoulders up near his ears.

Once Toby was gone, Rupert leaned across the table and took

Meghan's hand, his expression intense. "I can give you what you need," he whispered. "You don't have to look anywhere else."

Tess's eyes grew round, clearly enjoying the exchange. "She's definitely on the market."

Meghan kicked her under the table, causing her friend to double over and grab her shin.

Picking up her drink, Meghan swirled it around with her straw, the breeze having its way with her auburn hair, her curls fanning across her face while she fought them off and tried to take a sip of her cocktail.

"So, I'm dying to know . . . who is this Hester?" Tess asked the old man outright, nodding at Meghan.

He gave Meghan a tender look, his eyes glistening. "The love of my life."

When he said it, despite the fact that it was directed at Meghan, who clearly wasn't his love at all, he seemed so sure of himself.

"She's my wife," Rupert continued.

"Who's your wife?" Toby said, returning to his seat with an open bottle of rosé. He poured himself a glass. He offered the bottle to Meghan, but she politely declined, opting for just the one cocktail.

"Hester is my wife, silly boy."

"Ah yes." Toby leaned forward, his forearm on the table, as he took a large drink from his glass. "Do you remember Elaine?" His question was softer, with pain laced through it.

"Of course I do," Rupert barked, getting agitated again.

"Isn't Elaine—my grandmother—your *wife*?"

Rupert looked over at Toby, perplexed. "Yes." His gaze fell to the table as if he were putting together an invisible puzzle. "I'm sorry," he said suddenly. "Yes, Elaine is my wife."

Toby nodded in encouragement, before filling his grandfather's glass with a drop of wine. "We won't tell them," he said with a sad smile.

"About Hester?" the old man said in almost a whisper.

"No, your nurses at Rosewood Manor. We won't tell them about the wine." Toby winked at him and handed his grandfather the glass.

Rupert seemed to dive inward. Then, he surfaced again. "Yes," he replied. "Let's not tell them."

THREE

"That was weird tonight at dinner, wasn't it?" Tess said, finally mentioning their odd meal with Toby and Rupert, as she lugged her suitcase across the living room to the small bedroom opposite where Meghan used to stay whenever she'd visited Pappy. "That poor old man."

"He seemed really confused."

Meghan had thought about their encounter the entire time she and Tess had picked up a few items they'd needed from the store to get them through the next few days. She scooped a cup of dog food from the bag they'd bought and reached around Charlie's excited snout to drop it into his bowl. The dog's tail wagged vigorously as he dove in.

Tess twisted her hair into a bun and wound a hair tie around it. "That's got to be hard for Toby. Rupert didn't even remember Toby's own grandmother. But sweet of him to take him out to dinner."

"He seemed so flustered by the whole thing, didn't he?" Meghan opened the cabinet to put the groceries away. She tried not to focus on Pappy's coffee mugs as she scooted them to the side to make room for Tess's boxes of macaroni that wouldn't fit in the small cupboard Pappy had designated for food.

"He wasn't the chattiest person we've met, that's for sure. He barely said a word at dinner."

"Here's hoping for a less strange day tomorrow."

"Yes," Tess said with a laugh, as she grabbed the last bag of frozen vegetables and put it into the freezer, clapping her hands. "Well, that's that." Folding the empty grocery bags and wedging them between the cabinet and the fridge, she asked, "Want to clean now and unpack after?"

With a deep breath, Meghan put her hands on her hips, ignoring how exhausted she was. "Sounds like a plan." She leaned down and stroked Charlie's head. "What do *you* think, old boy?" she asked. "Ready to clean this place up?" He followed her lead, pacing beside her as she took the cleaning products into the living room with Tess.

The two of them stood silently in the middle of the room. "What first?" Tess asked.

Overwhelmed by the task at hand, Meghan surveyed the cases full of dusty books, the furniture that had needed to be covered for the last ten years and hadn't been, and the line of dead potted plants at the window. *You have to talk to them.* That was what Pappy had told her once about the philodendrons he'd kept next to the dining table. It was all so overwhelming, both physically and emotionally.

Tess draped an arm around Meghan, the gesture causing tears to well up in Meghan's eyes. "Why don't we keep everything just the way it is for right now? All we have to do is clean."

Meghan nodded, trying to keep her emotions in check. Maybe after a good night's sleep she'd be stronger.

As if consoling his master, Charlie nudged Meghan's hand with his snout. She reached down and wrapped her arms around her faithful companion, breathing in the serenity that he gave her. Pappy's words came to mind: *If I do one thing right, it's to teach you that whatever's going on in your life, calm is within you. Sometimes, you just have to wade through the deep waters to find it.* She was lucky to have Charlie while she made her way through those deep waters.

"Where should we start, Charlie?" she asked him with a sniffle. In answer, he pulled away and walked into Pappy's bedroom, sniffing as if on the hunt.

"Your mama might need to start somewhere a little less stressful," Tess called to the dog, making Meghan smile despite the tightness in her chest.

"It's okay," she said. "Let me see what he's doing."

While Tess grabbed the leather cleaner and a rag, heading over to tackle the sofa, Meghan followed Charlie into Pappy's bedroom and clicked on the light. She hadn't allowed herself to go in until now. The covers were still pulled up haphazardly from when he'd made it last, and his plaid slippers were half under the bed where he'd always put them.

"Whatcha want for breakfast, sport?" he'd ask, shuffling into the kitchen in those slippers with the local newspaper under his arm and the patches of hair that had remained from his youth, on either side of his head, wildly out of place. "Pancakes or French toast? Or cookies?" he'd say, wiggling his fingers until they reached her side, making her laugh.

"Cookies!" she'd say, as her bare feet swung above the floor, her little nightgown draped over her legs, not a care in the world about the age she saw on his face or the slight limp in his walk from arthritis. She'd never considered back then that one day she'd be without him.

Charlie, who had been sniffing around the room, sneezed.

"I know. It's mighty dusty in here," she said, trying not to completely fall apart at the thought of stripping Pappy's bed. She took a moment and walked around the room, stopping at the small alcove with shelving by the closet and smiling at a photo of Pappy and Gram. Gram's head was tilted back in laughter while Pappy nuzzled her cheek, his arms around her tiny waist. Meghan looked away, tears surfacing. Her gaze roamed the mustard walls, the old plaid curtains in shades of brown, the braided rug that lay under the bed, covering the warm hardwood floor. Gingerly, she leaned across the bed and took one of the pillows, turning it over and pressing it to her face, Pappy's scent lingering only slightly. How she wished she could feel his warm hug.

"I cleaned the sofa off first since it's getting late, and in case this is too difficult for you," Tess said, taking a step into the room and putting a protective hand on Meghan's shoulder. "If you want, you can sleep in my room instead of your grandfather's and I can take the sofa. I'm stripping the bed and putting sheets on next."

"It's okay. I have to face this sometime," Meghan said, waving a hand around the room. "But thanks. I'm so glad you came."

"Well, when my best friend runs off to be a chef, I wouldn't miss her debut."

Meghan smiled for the first time since she'd been back at the cottage. "Baby steps," she said, unboxing a set of sheets for his bed. "I'm just hoping to find an opening at a bar right now."

"I've had your beef stew in red wine sauce," Tess said. "It won't be long."

FOUR

The morning waves crashed in rough, bubbling spray, splashing up and depositing water spots on Meghan's purple top as she walked along the shore in the surf. Charlie dropped his ball at her bare feet, the toy sliding toward the water in the undertow until she grabbed hold of it. She tossed the ball, barely able to keep sight of it, her eyes stinging from salt and exhaustion.

After staying up late to clean, she hadn't slept well in Pappy's room, memories of him flooding her all night, making her restless. At one point, she would've sworn he'd sat down on the edge of her bed. "I gave this place to *you*, Meghan," she'd heard him say. The dream had been so vivid that she'd sat up in bed with a gasp, causing Charlie to wake and snuggle in by her side. She hadn't really gone back to sleep after that.

"You're up early," Tess called from behind her now, hobbling down the sand dune. She stepped up next to Meghan. "How long have you been out here?"

"Oh, I don't know. About an hour?" When Charlie returned, Meghan picked up the ball again and chucked it down the beach, the Labrador taking off after it like a bolt of lightning. "I couldn't sleep very well."

Tess held her hair out of her eyes in the coastal wind. "Are you sure this was a good idea, coming back here?"

"I've been wondering that myself," Meghan replied, turning back to get a view of the shingled cottage with its wide front porch and working shutters that Pappy used to slam closed before the hurricanes came through. "I don't want to move a thing. I feel like, if I do, it'll dislodge a memory and somehow make it evaporate into thin air."

Tess smiled at her. "Your memories are yours forever. Even though you don't want to disturb anything, maybe the change could be a good thing. I wonder if you'd be able to handle this better if you just went ahead and made the house your own—ripped off the Band-Aid."

Meghan knew she'd have to sometime. Maybe Tess was right. Even though it was so incredibly difficult. "It would force me to move forward..."

Charlie dropped the ball again, the bright red toy spinning in the movement of the water. Meghan tossed it out toward the waves, the dog diving into them and emerging with a wild shake, the ball in his mouth. He trotted down the shore in front of them.

"Why don't we get our mind off it and go into town, have a look around at some of the shops, and get a coffee or something? Maybe we can find a few beachy knickknacks to bring back to make it feel more like you."

Meghan gave her friend an amused grin. Tess never seemed to worry about anything. "We need to find a job."

"Yes, we do. But once we're working, we'll have less time to shop." Tess grabbed Meghan by the arm and hooked hers through it before giving her a lighthearted grin. Then she sobered. "And I think you need to take a minute to come to terms with all this. Let's not jump from the frying pan into the fire, you know? I can cover the utilities for a few months if we don't get jobs right away. After all, I'm living rent-free for the summer."

Meghan sucked in a deep breath of salty air and looked out at the pink and orange sky that was quickly burning off to a vibrant blue, the sun on her face. "Coffee sounds delicious, doesn't it?"

"We deserve a day off, you know?" Tess said, dropping Meghan's arm and squatting down to lift a perfect white ark clam shell out of the sand. "Just one day. Then we'll start looking for jobs. One day won't make or break us."

"All right." Meghan called Charlie in, feeling a little brighter.

Meghan rolled the old bicycles out of the shed behind the house and took a step back to assess them. Surprisingly, they hadn't rusted very much over the ten years they'd sat idle. She ran her fingers along the baskets on the front of them that had been filled with bread, vegetables, and seafood from the local market when she and Pappy used to ride into town.

"The tires look good," Tess said, bending down to press her thumb against one of them. "I think they still have enough air."

"As long as they haven't dry-rotted," Meghan said, checking for cracks. "If we run into any problems, the island's so small that we could walk if we have to, and come back and get them." Meghan hopped onto the deep green bicycle that Pappy had always ridden, wobbling just slightly and working to get her bearings.

Tess's bicycle leaned precariously toward Meghan's until her friend got a hold of it. "Which way?" she asked.

"It's been so long, I have no idea where to go. Let's keep our eyes open for a coffee shop."

They rode together down the single lane, a mixture of wiry grass and sand on either side, and a smattering of spindly palm and pine trees scattered along the lots that were filled with little cottages in different colors, until they came to the four-way stop.

The rough seagrass had taken root on the corner and was blowing in the breeze.

It's always windy here, Pappy would say. *You can't live in the Outer Banks unless you love the relentless wind.*

As she looked both ways, she could almost swear she heard him add, "What is it you want, Meghan?" Holding her breath, she honed in on the sound of the breeze, hoping to hear more.

"Which way?" Tess asked.

"Let's go right," Meghan replied, the sound of the rushing air giving way to seagulls overhead and the hum of a car engine as it neared them. They pedaled along until she spotted a familiar brown bungalow with a neon sign that read Lost Love Coffee. Meghan pointed to get Tess's attention. "There we go."

The two of them pulled in and parked their bikes next to the wooden decking that wrapped around the building, and went inside. The eclectic interior was full of old framed photographs and long glass cases of memorabilia, with a coffee bar at the end.

"Oh, it's a café and a little museum," Tess said, already distracted by a vintage postcard under a glass box. "This says that it was the first postcard to make it to the island from a voyager on the *Titanic*. They'd mailed it prior to boarding," she read.

Meghan went over to it, peering down at the slanting script: *I will return, as we all do, to the sea.* While the writer may have meant that they would return to the island, the eerie irony wasn't lost on Meghan. "Who's it to?" she asked.

Tess shook her head. "I can't read it, can you?"

"It's illegible," the barista said from behind the counter, as she tucked a pen into her salt-and-pepper cropped curls. "But we could make out the second line just before it."

Meghan squinted at the lettering, trying her hand at deciphering it. *I'll meet you at our spot. I'll be early.* "Wow," she said, turning around to face the barista, wondering about who this person had left waiting.

"We have lots of relics—all pertaining to lost loves—from throughout the years." The woman gestured to a wall of black-and-white photos, all of couples. "No one knows who any of those people are," she said, "but we acquired all these things right here on the island."

"Where do you get them?" Meghan asked, so interested that she'd forgotten all about her coffee. An old journal page caught her eye and she walked over to it.

"We find them in old houses or the second-hand store in town. That one there just came in." She waggled a finger at a journal page under a block of glass.

"This one's dated 1942." Meghan leaned over Tess's shoulder, peering through the case as she read the swirling, feminine text of the page that appeared to have been ripped from a book. *New York is terrifyingly large for a girl, but I'm managing. The city is who I am. I am enjoying the lights, the buzz, and the energy. But every now and again, it'll hit me out of nowhere, missing him. It'll punch me right in the gut. I love him. I always will. And I curse the forces that made me choose between my life and his.*"

"That's incredible," Tess said. "I could feel her . . ."

"Me too," Meghan said. "Life can really get in the way of things, can't it?"

"Mm," Tess agreed.

"Let's get coffee," Meghan said, before she started thinking about how life had had its own way with *her*. "Can we get two lattes, please?"

"Of course." The barista hit a few keys on the cash register.

"I love this idea of old letters and things," Tess said. "What if you played off your grandfather's aesthetic and made the cottage retro?"

"I think right now, we need to just focus on making it clean," Meghan laughed. "We still have so much to do . . ."

"Hey, are you John's granddaughter, by chance?" the barista asked, pulling Meghan's attention to her.

"Yes," Meghan replied, eyebrows raised.

"I knew right away when you mentioned his cottage. Word gets around our little island. When the lights came back on, people started talking and we've all been waiting to see who's moving in."

Meghan considered the idea that no one had probably noticed her empty apartment back in New York.

"Your grandfather used to show me photos of you when he stopped in. He came in all the time right after we opened," she said, placing the pencil behind her ear, tucking a lock of hair back with it. "It was my first job and he was so patient with me while I rang up his order. Every time, he got a black coffee with a splash of milk. He never stayed very long. He was always on his way to fish. He had a charter, didn't he?"

"He did," Meghan said. "He took vacationers out on day excursions in the summers."

"Ah, yes! I remember now. He was popular with families—they all knew how good he was with kids."

That filled Meghan with happiness, the memory of Pappy chasing her with Frankenstein fingers all over the yard outside while she squealed running through her mind like an old movie reel. "Yes, he was so great."

With a nod of understanding, the barista smiled. "I'm Chloe, by the way."

"Nice to meet you, Chloe. I'm Meghan and this is Tess."

"Glad to meet you." Chloe pulled two paper cups from the stack beside her and scribbled a note on one of them. "Any flavor in the lattes?"

Meghan peered up at the menu, her mind still on Pappy. "Oh, you have English toffee? I'll take that. Decaf."

"I'll have caramel," Tess said, coming up beside Meghan.

The barista wrote their choices on the side of the cups with pencil, filled the espresso machine, and hissed the frother. "I'll bet you miss him," she continued.

"I do," Meghan said. And something told her that the missing Pappy part was never going to get easier.

FIVE

Meghan mounted her bike outside the coffee shop. Tess pushed off, rolling up next to her, and the two of them headed down the road. Meghan's hair, coarse from the salt in the air, tickled her face, the seaside breeze whipping around them. Island music from shops and cafés faded in and out as they passed by. The beach atmosphere was like medicine for her soul, like a tiny whisper of the hope she'd had when she'd left here so many years ago with her big dreams tucked into her suitcases.

She and Tess had spent their senior year in high school 154 miles apart, the whole time planning their unified escape to the Big Apple, where they'd chase their futures with a vengeance. They'd spent that first year barely sleeping, talking into the wee hours of the morning, catching up on the years they'd lost living apart. Her friend would follow her anywhere. And Meghan was so thankful she'd followed her to the Outer Banks. It felt good to show Tess where she'd spent much of her youth.

The village was very much the way she remembered it. A few of the shops had changed hands since she'd been there last, but they'd kept that small-town feel with their clapboard and shingled facades, decking, and porches. Locals rode by on pastel bicycles, maneuvering around the sand dunes that had inched onto the edges of the road, and surfers, with their bare feet and chests, carried brightly painted boards under their arms as they made their way to the perfect swell.

Meghan stopped on the corner to wait for the traffic light, and Tess leaned toward her. "Hey, Hester, is that Toby Meyers?"

Meghan peered over at the white Range Rover next to her, recognizing the man from last night. He looked at her, his blue eyes causing her to forget where she was for a second. Realizing that it was time to cross, she waved to him and rode to the other side, catching up with Tess.

"Was that him?" Tess asked, parking her bicycle in the bike rack, her eyebrows dancing in suggestion.

"I think so," Meghan said, parking her bike. As she started toward the door to the souvenir shop, Tess bounced up beside her.

"Did you see his car?" she asked, pulling on the sleeve of Meghan's T-shirt, continuing before Meghan could answer.

"His car?" Meghan shook her head, dismissing the comment, but she had seen it. It *had* crossed her mind that she could barely afford a cup of coffee and he was driving around in that. And the frustration that she could hardly manage to buy that coffee swarmed her. Maybe it had been Pappy's doing, for encouraging her to shoot for the stars, but she felt like she was always one step away from breaking through and being something big, yet it never seemed to happen.

"I hope we run into him again," Tess said. "He was so mysterious. Quiet. You know how those quiet ones are . . ."

Meghan shook her head with a smirk. "The very last thing I need right now is another person to worry about."

"You'd worry about me?" a familiar deep voice sailed up from behind them.

She turned around to find Toby's piercing gaze on her. "No," she said, thinking quickly, "I said you're the *last* thing I'd worry about." She gave him a lighthearted look of challenge, to be sure he knew she was only kidding, although his expression was nearly impossible to decipher, his neutral look not allowing her even the slightest hint of what he was thinking. "Are you following me?" she asked.

Tess eyed her, clearly entertained by the exchange.

He didn't crack even a fraction of a smile, but there was something gentle in his eyes. "I was at the stoplight with my blinker on, remember?"

"What are you shopping for?" she asked, looking away at the random parked cars in the lot to avoid the flutter his stare caused her.

He sucked in a breath that made his shoulders rise and his pecs show through his shirt. She forced herself to focus on his face.

"It's my grandfather's birthday tomorrow and I need to find him a gift." He opened the door to the old souvenir shop for Meghan and Tess, letting them enter first.

The store hadn't changed at all. Old Coke signs and vintage advertisements lined the walls, and the tiled floor was full of artfully displayed tables of unique wares—anything from brightly painted metal fish to old books.

"How old will he be?" Meghan asked.

Toby picked up an hourglass, turning it over and setting it on the table, the white sand sliding effortlessly in a single stream to the bottom, his thoughts clearly full, judging by the downward pull of his brows. "Ninety-eight," he replied. "He's obsessed with old movies from the forties and fifties."

Meghan smiled, warmed by the thought.

"How about this one? *Madness and Magic*." Tess held up a DVD, her gaze on the back cover. "It was made in 1957 . . . 'A crime reporter uses all his tricks and a little magic to get the girl he loves.'" She held it out to him proudly.

Toby studied it, turning it over. "Thank you," he said, "but he already has this one." He handed it back to her.

Tess looked back down at the front cover. "Meghan, is there a DVD player in your pappy's cottage?" she asked.

"I think we have one," Meghan replied, putting a table between her and Toby to give him some space. She looked over at him and his gaze fluttered toward her just before he turned away.

"We could have a movie night tonight after we finish cleaning the living room—my treat." Tess waved the DVD in the air, coming over to her.

Meghan couldn't think of a better way to spend the night than escaping with a movie. Perhaps she'd get so wrapped up in it that she'd watch until she couldn't keep her eyes open. Then she'd fall asleep without thinking about anything going on in her life. "That would be fun."

Tess dropped it into her basket happily. "It has Paul Newman in it. He's so handsome."

Lifting a book from one of the tables, Toby turned it around to view the back, giving Meghan a glimpse at it: *Life in the Golden Age of Hollywood.*

Meghan could only imagine what he went through every day, taking care of his grandfather, and she was in awe of the fact that he did so day in and day out.

"What are you doing?" Tess asked, coming into the small living room at Pappy's after the two of them had finished mopping the hardwoods and shaking out all the rugs before running a vacuum over them. She shook her wet hair, toweling it off.

Taking a break, Meghan had pulled out her laptop and settled next to Charlie while Tess had been in the shower, looking for anything that would take her mind off the fact that she was sitting on Pappy's sofa, trying not to let her mind drift back to the days after school when he'd plop down beside her and stretch his arm around the back, listening to her talk about her day.

"Looking for jobs between here and the town of Manteo."

"Anything good?" Tess asked, pulling at her shirt, the old air conditioner no match for the heat outside.

"Nah." Meghan set the computer on the coffee table, trying not to get discouraged.

Tess wadded her soaking hair on top of her head and fanned herself. "It's scorching tonight."

"Want to take Charlie out on the beach?" Meghan asked, to which the dog popped up and stood at attention, his entire focus on his master. "There are lawn chairs in the shed out back and the breeze will cool us off."

"That sounds so much better," Tess said. "I'll get us each a glass of wine."

Meghan hoisted herself off the sofa and retrieved Charlie's ball, wedging it into her pocket while Tess got their drinks. "Okay, boy. You ready?"

Charlie barked, running over to the front of the cottage, his paws tapping on the floor in excitement. Meghan slipped on her flip-flops and opened the door, the dog rushing out ahead of them and barreling along the wooden path that wound through the tall seagrass down to the beach. Meghan went over to the shed and grabbed two chairs, slipping the metal end over her arm to carry them down to the beach.

"I have to admit, I'm a little disappointed," Tess said, striding along beside Meghan, handing her a glass of chardonnay.

Meghan looked over at her friend, shielding her eyes from the blazing sun to get a good look at her. "Why?"

"You haven't cooked us a single thing since we've been here, and I was hoping to be spoiled for the entire trip."

Meghan grinned, hiding that familiar feeling of doubt, the guilt of letting Pappy down that kept creeping in whenever she thought about her failed culinary career. The chairs clinked against each other as they dangled from her arm and she shifted to reposition them.

"I quit my job for your dinners, you know," Tess teased. But then she said, "You haven't even mentioned cooking since Vinnie didn't give you the chef's job."

The coastal breezed pushed past Meghan, cooling her skin in the penetrating heat. "I just haven't felt much like cooking."

"Vinnie's a jerk," Tess said. "You can't let one jerk stop you from living your dreams."

"He's not stopping me. I'm just . . . I don't know. Not in a good place. I don't feel inspired."

Tess held her wine up to the bright blue evening sky and twirled down the boardwalk. "How could you not be inspired here?" she called out over the crash of the waves, Charlie running off after a sandpiper in the distance.

"I think I'm at some kind of a low point in my life," Meghan said. She dropped the chairs onto the sand and they hopped down off the walk, leaving their flip-flops behind them. "I can't explain it. It just doesn't *feel* right." She took a cold sip of wine, the tartness of it biting her taste buds.

"That microwave mac and cheese I bought last night was for emergency purposes only," Tess warned. "I'm ready to sit out on the porch with a margarita and your tomato fattoush or your mango avocado wraps."

The water fizzed up onto Meghan's bare feet before retreating back to the ocean.

"You read cookbooks like my mom reads romance novels," Tess continued. "I haven't seen you pick one up at all since we've been here. Did you even pack them?"

"I think they're in a box in the closet." Meghan bent down and picked up a tiny piece of driftwood, blowing off the sand. Charlie ran over to her and nudged his ball in her pocket. She pulled it out and chucked it down the beach, the dog tearing off after it, kicking up sand. "I feel like I'm in some kind of holding pattern, waiting for . . . something. I just don't know what."

"Maybe it'll come to you over a pot of summer herb soup. A girl's gotta eat, you know."

Meghan laughed despite her mood. "Maybe," she said.

"That's better than a no."

Charlie was still flopped on the hardwoods, exhausted from a day on the shore. Her cheeks pink from too much salty air and sun, and her hair still wet from her shower, Meghan curled up on the sofa in her pajamas.

"Do you put black beans or white beans in that salmon soup you make?" Tess called from the kitchen, the sound of pots clinking.

Meghan got up and went into the kitchen. "White beans, why?"

"I'm going to try to make it from memory."

Meghan laughed. "How can you make it from memory? You've never made it at all."

"Well, you could help," Tess said suggestively, reaching into the cabinet and holding out a can of white beans.

Relenting for the sake of her friend, Meghan took the can. "We need to heat the oil first," she said, taking over in surrender but not feeling great about it. There'd been magic when she'd stood in this kitchen with Pappy that had disappeared now that she was an adult.

"Yay!" Tess threw an excited punch in the air. "I'll get the wine."

Charlie sauntered over and took his new napping place on the kitchen floor.

Meghan poured a bit of olive oil into the pan, swirling it around to coat the cooking surface, and then placed it on the old burner. "You'll need medium heat unless you want to burn the cottage down," she teased Tess, turning the knob to the appropriate temperature. Then she took Pappy's zester from the drawer, her knowledge of his kitchen like riding a bike. She picked up the lemon and got to work.

It felt odd to cook in that kitchen without Pappy. Like the first time she'd driven on her own. She'd only gone to the grocery store, but every mile that she drove felt like a vast distance between her and the comfort of her home. She missed having Pappy leaning over her shoulder. *Don't be shy with the lemon zest. It only makes it better . . .*

"You okay?" Tess asked.

She added in the salmon, stirring, and shrugged. "Yeah, this just makes me think of my pappy."

"I'll bet he's thinking of you too."

She turned to Tess. "You think?"

Tess nodded.

Comforted by the thought, Meghan smiled.

Tess opened the can of beans. "Your grandfather sure does have a lot of tools in the kitchen." She pulled out one of the drawers. "I mean, what are these?" Tess grabbed two claw-like plastic cooking tools and scratched the air like a bobcat.

Meghan squeezed her eyes shut in amusement. "They're for pulling barbecued meat apart. Pappy used to buy an entire beef brisket from the barbecue restaurant downtown, and the rub was so thick that the spices would stain his hands." She dumped the grated lemon into the pan.

Tess put them back. "With all these gadgets, I'm guessing he shared your love of cooking."

"Yes," Meghan said, adding in the beans and a sprig of rosemary. "He told me once that he started cooking when he was in his late teens. Taught me everything I know." She stirred the beans, coating them in the oil, the citrus smell of lemon rising into the air but doing little to make her feel better. Then, she set the spoon down and turned to her best friend. "What if I've lost it?"

"What do you mean?" Tess asked, popping a grape into her mouth from the bunch in the bowl on the counter.

"What if I've lost the passion to cook?"

Tess stared at her as if her question made no sense at all.

"Pappy always made me feel like I could turn raw ingredients into a masterpiece. And he made me feel invincible whenever I was cooking. But somewhere along the line, I've lost the feeling. It's just a series of steps now." She turned the pan down to a simmer. "I want to love it again, but I just can't."

Tess moved in front of her, forcing eye contact. "Don't let Vinnie ruin your dreams."

"Did he, though? Or was he just telling me what I needed to hear?"

"He's a third-rate manager at a second-rate restaurant. He wouldn't know good taste if it bit him where the sun doesn't shine."

"I don't think it's just Vinnie," Meghan said, shaking her head, feeling lost. "I don't know where I'm supposed to go or what I'm supposed to do." She threw her hands up, all those glamorous dreams of being someone bigger than life sliding away with each tick of the clock. "I mean, look at me! I'm sitting in an old fishing shack in the middle of nowhere. *This* is where I belong?"

Tess chewed her lip. "Maybe it's best not to consider this *after* unpacking all our things . . ."

Frustration with herself mounting, Meghan pursed her lips. "I think I'm running back to the past because I found comfort here. But there's no comfort here now. It's gone. And I don't know what to do." Unexpectedly, tears pricked her eyes.

"Aw, don't let it get you down." Tess pulled two glasses from the cabinet. "I do know what to do," she said, opening the fridge and pulling out the bottle of wine they'd started earlier. She took the corkscrew off the counter and popped the cork, pouring the crisp golden liquid into each glass, the scent of citrus mixing with the lemon in the air. "We're going to drink this, eat dinner under blankets on the sofa, and watch a movie. You know why? Because we don't have to have it all figured out tonight." She handed a glass to Meghan. "Maybe this isn't your destiny. Maybe you came back here just to figure it all out and that's it."

"You're right," Meghan said, giving her best friend a hug.

"I'm always right," Tess teased, making her smile.

Tess sighed dramatically. "I loved that movie," she said, looking down at the DVD box. "Old movies are so romantic."

"It was really good," Meghan agreed, her eyes heavy from the wine and the late hour.

"I swear, you look so much like the character Bridget."

Meghan gathered up the dinner plates, taking them over to the kitchen while Charlie followed, hoping for a taste. "Oh no, not again." Tess had only told her every ten minutes during the movie.

"You do!" Tess giggled. "Who is she anyway?" She turned the box over to read the back while Meghan rinsed off the dishes in the sink. "Oh!" Tess threw her blanket off her legs and got up. "I'm not the only one who thinks it!" She ran over to Meghan, waving the *Madness and Magic* DVD in the air.

Meghan flicked the excess water off her fingers and dried her hands on the dish towel.

"Toby said that Rupert was obsessed with old movies, right?"

"Yeah . . . ?" Meghan folded the towel and draped it on the edge of the sink.

"And he already has this movie." She laughed again, pointing to the actress's name on the back of the box. "Hester Quinn."

Meghan bit back a laugh. "He thinks I'm a movie star."

Tess's eyes sparkled with the mystery solved. "Yes. He must also think he's Paul Newman."

"Oh, bless his heart," Meghan said, clapping a hand over her mouth. "We'll have to tell Toby if we run into him again, so he knows."

"*If*? It's a small town. If you want to see Toby again, I'm sure you can." Tess set the empty wine glasses in the sink. "*Do* you want to see him again? He's definitely easy on the eyes . . ."

"Tess, don't start." Meghan grabbed the dish towel and snapped it in the air toward her friend. "Have you seen how distant he is?"

"He's brooding!" she corrected her. "It's so dreamy, Meghan. You're at the beach, a handsome man has walked into your life . . ." She grabbed Meghan's hands and did a dramatic twirl.

"No more romantic movies for you," she said, dropping Tess's hands. "I'm cutting you off." But Meghan couldn't deny that there certainly was something interesting about Toby Meyers.

SIX

Meghan swam out of her sleep, wrapped in the cocoon of her blanket with the faint squawk of seagulls outside her window. The slant of the sun streaming in told her it must be around eight o'clock. Any later and the beam would slide off the bed onto the hardwood floor. She focused on the lamp made of driftwood on the side table next to the bed until the image sharpened. Running her fingers over her face, she attempted to clear her already buzzing mind.

Today, she and Tess would spend the day applying for jobs in the area. While she needed the money, the idea of running plates from a kitchen, counting tips, and soaking her feet at the end of the night didn't make her want to get out of bed any faster.

Charlie stirred next to her. She reached over and stroked his head, turning toward him. He nuzzled her as if consoling her. "You've got it all figured out, don't you?" she said. "You're always content. How do you do it, hm?" She ran her hands over his ears.

She lay there, her gaze roaming the room. A row of Pappy's tattered fishing hats still lined the wall. If she closed her eyes, she could imagine him in every single one of those baseball caps with the fishing hook on the brim. Meghan got up, slid one off its hook, shaking off the dust, and placed it on her head, her long auburn-brown hair flowing out from under it. "How do I look, Pappy?" she asked quietly. With no answer, she changed out of her pajamas, slid on her cut-offs and a T-shirt, and called Charlie to come with her as she left the bedroom.

Tess's door was still closed, so Meghan gave the dog some fresh water and filled his food bowl before making herself a cup of coffee, the nutty aroma tickling her nose. The air in the cabin was sticky and warm, so she settled at the kitchen table near the air conditioning unit, her attention falling upon the envelope that had Pappy's final things in it. The nurse had said that he'd gathered the items himself quickly just before he'd gone into the hospital. He had given the envelope to the paramedic who'd come to the house when he'd first felt the beginnings of his heart attack. It had her name on it, so they'd saved it for her.

Maybe it was because Meghan still had on his faded denim cap, but she felt strong enough to see what was inside. She set her mug on the table and picked up the envelope, looking down into it. Inside, she found the last photo she and Pappy had taken together when she was sixteen. It had been just after they'd gone for ice cream, the two of them leaning against the railing of the public boardwalk leading to the fishing pier, holding dripping ice cream cones. He was pretending to take a bite of her mint chocolate chip and she was doubling over in laughter. How simple things had seemed then.

She reached in and pulled out an oddly shaped metal object—a very small key of some sort—rolling it around in her fingers.

"Morning," Tess said, shuffling in with a yawn. "Nice hat—oh, coffee. Tell me there's more."

"I made a pot," Meghan said.

"You're my guardian angel," Tess said with another yawn, padding over to the kitchen area to make herself a cup. She pulled Pappy's favorite mug from the cabinet and Meghan let her vision blur to pretend it was him who was holding it. Tess leaned across the counter. "Whatcha got over there?" she asked.

"When I received the will with Pappy's cottage, I also got this," Meghan said, holding up the envelope. "It has the house key, this key"—she pinched the small key she'd found and showed it to Tess—"and a photo of the two of us." Curious, she peeked back in to see if there was anything else in the envelope and spotted a small piece of paper. Scratched in Pappy's handwriting on a scrap of paper was a short list:

1. *My favorite photo of us*
2. *My house key*
3. *The key to the box in my closet*

Meghan locked eyes with Tess and the two of them took their mugs into Pappy's room. Meghan opened the two bifold closet doors and caught her breath when she took in Pappy's clothes. Her fingers instantly trembling, she gently grabbed the sleeve of one of his flannel shirts and held it to her face, wishing his hand were there to lift her chin and tell her it would all be okay.

With a deep breath, she slid his hanging clothes out of the way and peered around inside. A small stack of shelves at the right had a few unopened bags of fishing lures, some trophies he'd won in the local fishing contests, and a smattering of books. She scanned the shelves, but there was no box that she could see.

"Check at the bottom," Tess directed, holding her mug.

Meghan got her cell phone off the dresser and shone the light around the base of the closet, illuminating Pappy's loafers and the boots he used to wear in the marshes. Then she checked the top shelf above his hanging clothes—nothing but more books and magazines.

"I don't see anything," she said, trying to hold her breath to stifle the remnants of Pappy's scent that still lingered. *Pappy, where is it?*

Tess leaned in around her, having a second look. "I don't see anything either," she said. "Are you sure it's in this closet?"

"He said, 'my closet,'" Meghan replied, "but we can check the others."

They went out into the small hallway that led to the living area and opened the coat closet. Nothing out of the ordinary. They checked the other bedroom—no box.

"That's weird," Meghan said. "I wonder where it is?"

"We'll find it," Tess told her. "I'm sure it's here somewhere."

Meghan took the key back into the dining area and returned it to the envelope for safe-keeping, wondering what it was that Pappy had saved just for her.

"Maybe it's a box full of his secret stash of cash from a lottery win, and we'll find it weeks from now," Tess said, sitting down across from her at the table. "Maybe I'm roommates with a millionaire."

Meghan beamed at her friend, thankful for the lighter atmosphere that only Tess could provide in times like these.

"I think we should get ready for the day," Tess said. "We have to visit some restaurants today or we're gonna *need* to win the lottery."

Meghan stood up. "Yes, I'm on it," she said, holding up her mug. "Drinking this in the shower."

"Cheers to that," Tess said, clinking her mug with Meghan's.

Starting closest to the cottage and moving northward, all the way to the bypass in Nags Head, Meghan and Tess had stopped in to restaurants to talk to the management at each one, handing out their résumés. By noon, they'd visited nearly every possibility in the Outer Banks.

As they walked to the car at the last one, Meghan didn't feel any closer to finding a job. "I hope we get a call from someone," she said. "I thought for sure at least one of them would offer us something on the spot."

"We'll get a job," Tess said brightly, before noticing a familiar Range Rover at the small shop next door. "Look! It's fate," she said.

"It's inevitable on this island," Meghan countered. "You said that yourself."

Just then, Toby came rushing out holding a small shopping bag, and spotted them right away.

"Everything okay?" Meghan called to him.

Worry etched on his face, he said, "My grandfather keeps trying to leave Rosewood Manor. He's been really agitated ever since we had dinner that night. He wouldn't even eat the cake for his birthday."

Tess elbowed her friend. "Tell him about the DVD," she whispered.

"I don't know if this will help," Meghan said, "but we've figured out who Hester Quinn is."

His eyebrows shot up, creasing his forehead. "Who?" he asked.

"She's an actress who played in that movie *Madness and Magic*—the one you said he'd already seen."

Toby pursed his lips, nodding in thought. "He's insistent that he needs to see Hester. The nurse there called me at her wits' end, so I ran out and bought him his favorite chocolate truffles, hoping to redirect his thoughts," he said, holding up the small shopping bag.

"Is there anything I can do?" she asked.

"No," he said quickly, as if he'd already imposed upon her enough.

"I could go over there with you," Meghan suggested, worried about Rupert. "Maybe he'll still think I'm Hester and I can convince him to stay at Rosewood Manor."

"I'll drive the car home," Tess suggested. "You and Toby can ride together."

Uncertainty showed in Toby's eyes.

"It's worth a try, don't you think?" Meghan asked.

Before she knew it, Meghan was sliding onto the cool tan leather seat of the Range Rover, Toby starting the engine while Tess waved at them through the window. As the vehicle purred, he handed her the bag of truffles. "You don't have to do this," he said.

"I know. But Rupert sort of reminds me of my grandfather, so it's nice to be with him. Even if he does think I'm someone else." She smiled at him. He glanced over at her with that warm look of gratitude she'd seen when they'd had dinner.

"His dementia has gotten worse over the last year, and it's getting very difficult to take care of him," he said, turning onto the main road. "But he's all I've got."

There was an edge to his voice that Meghan understood. He was clinging to the remnants of a family member he loved. She was so thankful that her last moments with Pappy had been strong ones. She couldn't imagine what it must be like to see the man he loved pulling away from him right in front of his eyes.

"Do you have any family that could help?" she asked.

"My parents were killed in a skiing accident last year," he said, his eyes on the sand-covered road. "It was a shock to all of us, and my grandfather hasn't been the same since. For the first six months or so, he kept asking about them and I'd have to tell him what happened over and over. Every time, he grieved, so sometimes I just told him they weren't here at the moment to spare him."

Meghan's heart squeezed. She knew too well what that grief was like, and she couldn't imagine having to relive it for the first time even once, let alone day after day. "Oh my goodness, that's terrible."

"After they passed, he dove into this obsession with old

movies that took over his life. We wonder if this new manifestation of Hester Quinn is his way of coping, sending him into a fictional world to avoid the pain."

"I'm so sorry," she said, nearly breathless. "How are *you* holding up?" she asked, his tension taking on a new meaning for her now.

He shook his head. "I'm okay," he replied with a heavy sigh. "It's just been a lot." He pulled into a parking space at the front of Rosewood Manor.

"So you're his only family member?" she asked.

"Yes."

"That has to be hard. What about you? What about your job—what do you do when you have to stop to take care of him?"

"I can manage," he said, not elaborating.

"I understand," she said, hoping it would help him if she were to open up a little. Maybe she could help in some way. "I lost both my parents at fifteen."

He turned to her, his eyes wide. "Fifteen? I can't imagine that."

"My grandfather helped me through it," she said. "Maybe it's my turn now to help someone else." She took the bag of truffles and opened the car door. "Shall we?"

They got out of the car and walked up to the facility together, checking in at the front desk, and then made their way down the sterile tiled hallway toward Rupert's room. When they got to his door, a nurse sat in a chair just outside, on guard duty.

"He's been a handful today, bless his heart," she said to Toby.

His chest filled with breath as he nodded in understanding. "This is Meghan Gray. Gramps called her Hester Quinn the other night, so we're going to see if he still thinks that's who she is. Maybe Hester Quinn can convince him to stay put."

"You are a lifesaver," the nurse said, throwing a hand to her chest. "Let's pray it works." She opened the door and called in. "Mr. Meyers? Your grandson is here with a friend."

Toby and Meghan walked in to find Rupert pacing, Hollywood memorabilia covering every surface of the room. Movie posters hung on the walls of the small hospital-style bedroom, piles of books about cinema and old Hollywood filled bookshelves, and a small TV in the corner was dwarfed by massive stacks of old DVDs.

Rupert stopped wandering as soon as he saw her, moving over to her and wrapping her up in his arms, his unique scent of old age mixed with cotton and basil hitting her. "My dear," he said with palpable relief. He pulled back to look at her, yearning and happiness spreading over his face. "How long was the trip from California? I'll bet you're exhausted," he said, patting for her to sit on the hospital bed that had been contorted into the shape of a sun lounger.

"It wasn't bad," she replied, glancing over at Toby, who'd sat down in the corner chair, for guidance. He gave her a look of encouragement.

"You're doing your hair differently these days," Rupert said. "More natural. And you're quite casual."

"Yes," she said, holding the bag of truffles in her lap.

"I'm surprised. You usually like to spend so much time getting ready." He sat down next to her, his earlier distress melting away. "Remember the time when we went to the premiere of that movie ... What was it?" He trailed off, his gaze moving to the wall. "Was it *Pretty Girls*?"

"I think so, yes," she said, playing the part.

"You spent so long making yourself beautiful that we almost missed the beginning." He laughed, his old eyes dancing. "But you didn't need to worry so much about how you looked, because you were stunning before you'd done a thing, just as you are now."

She smiled, not knowing what else to say for fear she might offer up some detail that wasn't in his fictional story and send him into a panic. "I brought you some chocolate truffles," she said, holding out the bag as she looked over at Toby in the corner.

"Oh, my dear, that's lovely. Thank you." He took the bag and held it to his chest. "Later. We'll indulge in these another time. Right now, I just want to get a good look at you." He sucked in a breath of excitement as if he could inhale her right into himself. "How I've missed you."

"I'm glad I could come," she said honestly. Even though he clearly wasn't in reality, he was so delightful, and she could tell by the sweetness in his eyes that he'd been a wonderfully kind man. "So how have you been?" she asked, inching her way toward the conversation about staying at Rosewood Manor.

"Not too bad . . . Missing Elise and Matthew," he said, his words breaking on their names.

Meghan shot Toby a glance for confirmation and he gave her a quick nod before looking down at the floor, his forearms on his knees.

"It must have been a shock," she said, glad that he was at least remembering Toby's parents and didn't have to go through the pain of learning about their death again.

His cloudy eyes filled with tears. "It was. I needed you to help me through it. Where were you?"

"I didn't know, I'm so sorry," she said, grasping for an acceptable answer. "I came as quickly as I could."

He took her hand. "Well, you're here now."

"Yes." She gave his hand a squeeze. "I live *here* now."

His face lit up. "You do? I *knew* you'd come around."

"Mm-hm. I came to spend the rest of my years here. And you know what?"

"What?" he asked, his enchanted eyes wide.

"I really like knowing you're here in Rosewood Manor so I can find you."

His gaze was unstill, as if the thought had never occurred to him.

"I'll come to visit every day if you promise to stay right here so I know where you are."

Toby stood up, panicked. "You don't have to do that."

"I want to," she said. She liked Rupert, and it made her feel like she was doing something good to come and see him, like she had purpose.

"Ah," Rupert said, as if the gesture had hit him right in the heart. A tear spilled down his weathered cheek.

"Promise you'll stay?" she asked the old man.

Rupert put his trembling finger to his lips, clearly overwhelmed by the idea of her visits. "I promise. I lost you once and I thought I'd lost you again." He leaned toward her urgently. "You can't get distracted by something and leave me again. My heart can't take it."

"I won't," she said, staring into his blue eyes the color of a stormy sea.

He relaxed.

A few minutes later, Rupert had sunk down into bed and, just before he fell into a peaceful sleep, Meghan reminded him she'd come to see him tomorrow. Then she and Toby made their way out to the parking lot.

"Thank you for doing that," Toby said as he clicked the remote car key, the lights blinking on the Range Rover ahead of them. "You really don't have to come to see him every single day. I'm not convinced it's such a good idea. I'm sure we can think of something to tell him." Toby opened her door.

"Being around him makes me feel good. He's so sweet."

Toby seemed torn about her visiting Rupert, shaking his head as if he were having an internal dialog, which only confused her. Why wouldn't he want her to help his grandfather?

"It's really fine," she called to him, as he went around to his side of the car and got in.

"Where do you live?" he asked, looking over at her with unsaid words.

She fastened her seatbelt and gave him Pappy's address, wishing he'd tell her whatever it was that worried him. But that was the last thing they said until she got out at the cottage.

"Bye," she told him, breaking the silence and stepping down into Pappy's driveway.

"See ya." His words seemed to have some kind of longing, as if he really hoped to see her again, but he kept his thought-filled gaze on the dashboard, so she shut the door. Then he drove off, leaving her in the quiet of the afternoon, with the creak of the rocking chairs against the wind and the ocean shushing at her back.

SEVEN

"How was he?" Tess asked when Meghan got inside.

"Strange," Meghan answered, still trying to make sense of Toby's reaction. He seemed to be wrestling with something that included her. But maybe she was just reading into things . . . She dropped down onto the sofa, and Charlie sauntered up and greeted her.

"Stranger than at dinner the other night?"

"Definitely."

Tess lowered herself down next to Meghan and put a sofa pillow across her lap. "What? Did he think you were Judy Garland this time or something?"

"Hm?" Meghan asked, turning to her friend. "Oh! You meant how is *Rupert*? He was fine."

Tess wrinkled her nose at her friend. "Who else would I be talking about?" Then, with a look of interest, she said, "Toby was acting strange? How so?"

Meghan recounted her time at Rosewood Manor, her exchange with Toby and the ride home. "I don't understand why he would be so uncertain about me being there," she said, stroking Charlie. "I considered letting it go and not seeing Rupert every day, but there's something pulling me to see him. I really think he'd be happier if I came around."

"Maybe it's because you've always wanted to be someone glamorous, and he thinks you are." Tess gave Meghan a big grin.

"Could be," Meghan said, thinking. "I can't put my finger on it. I just like being with him." The idea of not seeing Rupert settled heavily upon her. "But it feels like Toby might not want me to see him. Toby knows him better than I do and if he feels like I shouldn't see Rupert, then I should probably respect that."

"Did you ask Toby if he didn't want you going to see his grandfather?"

Meghan shook her head. "He's not the easiest person to talk to." She fluttered her hands in the air. "Let's talk about something else. Get my mind off of it."

"Well, I have just the thing," Tess said.

Meghan twisted around, shifting the dog. "Really? What?"

"While you were with Rupert, I looked for more jobs online and I found a brand-new place that's taking applications. It's called Mariner's Inn." She grabbed her laptop from the coffee table and pulled up the website.

"It's gorgeous," Meghan said.

"What if we run up there and put in our application?"

"Yes," Meghan said, excited to think about something other than Toby's standoffish behavior. "Let's go right now."

Meghan and Tess drove until they made it to the village of Salvo. They pulled up outside a massive white inn with a wide front porch, nestled in the sand among the palm trees.

"This is incredible," Meghan said, getting out and taking in the manicured walkways of the magnificent structure. Pots of red geraniums adorned the long row of white rocking chairs, and paddle fans above them whirred from a birch-lined ceiling. Two massive stone chimneys flanked either side of the inn, punctuating the red tin roof.

Meghan tipped her head back to view the huge structure as Tess got out of the car. Then she stepped over toward her friend and took the gray-painted steps one at a time, smiling at a few folks who were rocking at one end, playing checkers on a brightly painted wine barrel. She opened the door and they stepped into the cozy interior. Front sitting rooms on either side of a sweeping grand staircase held twin sofas facing each other. They looked like she could sink into them and never crawl out. A driftwood coffee table between the sofas held a vibrantly painted glass vase that was bursting with blooms.

"Where should we go?" Tess asked, looking around.

"Maybe there," Meghan replied, pointing to the back of the inn where the restaurant was bustling with visitors.

They continued on to the large dining area with white-clothed tables and flickering candles, where the view of the blue ocean could be seen from every direction through the large glass doors. A bar trailed along one side of the room, through the glass wall, and out to the deck in back.

"Hello," a hostess said, wearing the staff uniform: a crisp white shirt and black waist apron to match her trousers. "Will you be dining with us today or having a drink at the bar?"

"We're actually looking to apply for a waitstaff position," Meghan said.

"Oh, great! Come this way." The hostess took them to a table next to the glass wall overlooking the Atlantic, which seemed to be showing off its turquoise underbelly—something it didn't always offer. "Have a seat." Meghan sat down, taking in the high, beamed cathedral ceiling and beach-wood chandeliers, the whole place giving her a very good feeling.

"What positions are you two applying for?" the hostess asked.

"Tess and I are looking for waitressing jobs," Meghan replied. "We both have considerable experience in the field," she said, beginning her well-rehearsed spiel. "I've worked in the restaurant industry for ten years now, and we've both held lead positions."

"I'll grab the applications so you can get a head start on them," the hostess said. "And then I'll go get Tabitha Perry. She's our manager and main server and will ask you two some questions. Would you like a cocktail on the house while you wait?"

Meghan looked over at Tess, both of them clearly excited by the possibility of working somewhere like the Mariner's Inn. "Yes," she answered.

"I'll bring you our best-sellers. What's your preference—sweet, sour, or salty?"

"Sweet for me," Tess said, and Meghan agreed.

"All right! Back in a second."

When the hostess had left, Tess leaned forward, her eyes round with delight. "Free cocktails while we wait? I'm sold on this place. Look at it."

"I know. It's stunning. Great job finding it." Meghan surveyed the tables—all full—thinking about how much tip money she could make in a place like this. "Now, we just have to both get the job."

Tess made a face. "What if one of us gets it and the other doesn't?"

"No sense worrying about that until it happens."

The hostess returned with their drinks, setting Meghan's in front of her—a short, chunky glass with whipped cream, a sprig of mint, and an orange slice. "This is the Island Delight: vodka, our house citrus liqueur, simple syrup, and orange juice." Tess's drink was just as beachy. "And yours is the Moonlight Shores: pomegranate and lime juices with orange liqueur and rum." The hostess slid two pieces of paper their way, topping each with an ink pen. "I'm Meredith. Just shout if you need me. Tabitha will be with you in about ten minutes."

"Thank you so much," Meghan said, stirring the small straw to mix in the alcohol before taking a gloriously sweet sip of the citrus nectar. "Well," she said, holding up her glass. "You certainly came through with the opportunity of a lifetime. Cheers."

With a laugh, Tess toasted her. "To new experiences."

"To new experiences!"

"I told you it was fate!" Tess nearly sang as she took Meghan's hands, spinning her around the tiny living room of Pappy's cottage, rousing Charlie and making him bark.

"We start tomorrow," Meghan told her, still completely disbelieving, handing her the uniform secured in a clear plastic package. "You are a star for finding that job for us."

"I'm so glad we both got it!" Tess hugged the package to her chest. "Tabitha seemed so nice in the interview. Aaaand did you see those delicious plates of seafood they were serving? Oysters on the half-shell and that salmon salad? I'm going to spend all my tip money on lunch and dinner takeout. I just know it."

"And we get rotating days off and we don't have to be there until ten every morning. I'll have loads of time to read and relax."

"Yes!" Tess said, tossing the uniform on the kitchen table. "We'll actually have time to take walks, go out for coffee, make friends."

"That makes me think of Rupert," Meghan replied, remembering how happy the old man was to see her.

Tess stuck her face in Meghan's line of view. "By 'friends,' I meant people under the age of a hundred."

"I'd love to be able to stop by and see Rupert. Even if it isn't based in reality, it's probably the best he feels all day when he thinks he's talking to Hester Quinn."

"But what about Toby?" Tess asked.

"Toby doesn't strike me as the most social of people—he's kind of quiet, very different from Rupert. Maybe he simply doesn't understand what it feels like to need that level of interaction."

"True," Tess agreed.

"What if I just decided to visit Rupert on my own? The hospital staff knows I've been there before; I'm on the visitor's list now." She leaned against the kitchen table and folded her arms. "And if Toby gets wind of it, I'll have had more great meetings with Rupert by then and he'll see how it helps him."

Tess stared at Meghan. "Can I ask you something seriously?"

"Sure."

"Are you spending your time in fantasy land with ol' Gramps to avoid facing your own future and figuring yourself out?"

"Of course not," Meghan said defensively, but she hadn't considered it until now. Was Tess right? "I feel good when I can make someone happy," she said honestly.

"Suit yourself," Tess said, evidently letting it go.

"If I'm going to see Rupert, I need to do a little research on Hester Quinn," she said, waggling a finger at her computer on the table. Under Tess's scrutinizing eye, she went over and grabbed her laptop, sank down into Pappy's worn leather sofa, and kicked her feet up on the coffee table.

"So, you're not a chef; you're an actress now," Tess said with a giggle, before plopping down beside her.

"At least for an hour a day, I am," Meghan said with a grin. She opened the laptop and set her fingers on the keys. "Hester Quinn," she said aloud as she typed the name into her search bar. With a few clicks, she brought up an article.

Hester Quinn (June 5, 1922–September 7, 1995) is an American bombshell actress known for her roles in the 1945 movie When the Sun Rises, *which won her an Oscar, and the timeless comedy* Pretty Girls, *starring opposite Cary Grant. Her early career began on stage, where, despite her undeniable beauty, she played countless gritty characters, her most notable, homeless woman Mitsy Bradford in the play* The Olive Branch, *for which she received a coveted Tony Award. Her performances demonstrated her innate ability to tap in to the human spirit.*

She was a sought-after movie actress for only around ten years when roles began to dwindle as she retreated to a life of seclusion in Brentwood, California. She died of natural causes at the age of 73. She never married and has no descendants. The whereabouts of the assets from her estate are unknown, as she kept her affairs out of the public eye entirely, but her contribution to film can still be felt today.

"I wonder what Rupert would think if he read this?" Tess asked. "How would his mind process it?"

Meghan shook her head, considering it.

"Would it sink in that he couldn't be married to her?"

"I have no idea," she said, wondering if seeing Rupert was a good thing after all. But her thoughts went back to the happiness on his face whenever he saw her. That was all that mattered.

EIGHT

The next morning, the sun shone down in beams of early light, as the seagulls squawked for their breakfast, diving into the sea behind Rosewood Manor. Meghan arrived and checked in with ease. "Do you know when Toby Meyers will be by to see him?" she asked the receptionist, hoping not to run into him.

"He usually comes in the evenings unless there's an emergency."

"Oh, all right," she said, playing off the fact that she was thrilled she'd have her mornings with Rupert.

She went into his room to find the old man sitting up in his bed with a blanket and food tray across his legs. He picked at his scrambled eggs until her entrance disturbed him, and he nearly knocked it all over when he attempted to greet her.

"No, no," she said, hurrying over. "Enjoy your breakfast. I'll sit beside you while you eat." Meghan grabbed a napkin and sopped up a little spill of his orange juice.

He settled back down then, picking up his fork, but his dancing eyes were on her.

"How was your flight?" he asked.

"Good," she replied, stepping into his fantasy easily. She tossed the napkin into the small trashcan by his bed and took a seat in the cushioned chair.

"I hope you went back to Los Angeles to turn down that awful role," he said, lifting his juice to his lips as if the two of them were sitting at a bistro table in a café somewhere. "You're better than that movie."

"Which movie was it again?" she asked carefully, snapping her fingers as if it were on the tip of her tongue.

He laughed. "How could you forget? *Cupid's Goddess*," he said, rolling his eyes. "I'm thrilled you've moved on—you can't even remember the name of it, thank God." He scooped up a forkful of eggs and spread them on a triangular slice of toast. "What about the other one? Does that one have any promise?" He took a bite of the toast.

This was proving more difficult than she'd expected. "Let's not talk about movies," she said gently, skirting around the question. "Let's talk about you. How have you been?"

"Heartbroken," he said, taking her by surprise, an honesty that she couldn't deny in his gaze.

"I'm sorry to hear that," she said, as she leaned forward and touched his hand. "Why?"

He stared at her as if she'd lost her mind. "You know why."

"I want to hear it in your words," she said, trying to piece together some semblance of a conversation.

He pulled his hand from hers, tears surfacing. "I don't want to spend our time talking about this."

"Okay, what would you like to talk about?" she asked him.

"There's nothing to say," he said, his voice breaking. "I just want to sit beside my best friend and delight in the fact that she's here, all the way from California."

"I can do that," Meghan said with a smile, relieved to have a moment of silence. She'd have to figure out how to navigate this if she were going to come every day. But as she looked at him— the lines between his distant eyes, the small pout on his lips—she questioned her decision to come. Her presence today definitely wasn't lighting him up as much as it had. Maybe it was just an off day . . .

The two of them sat quietly until Rupert drifted off, his tray of food still sitting barely eaten. After a few minutes had gone by and he seemed to be comfortably sleeping, Meghan looked at her watch. It was almost time to meet Tess at the Mariner's Inn for their first day. Rupert seemed so peaceful lying there. She hoped his restless mind had gotten a break. Gently, she kissed her fingers and placed them on his forehead. "Back tomorrow," she whispered.

The inn's dining area bustled with waitstaff activity when Meghan and Tess arrived. As the sun rose higher above the tranquil water outside, two servers were lifting lids off of silver trays that lined a long table in front of the stone fireplace. Others were stacking glasses and porcelain mugs by a large selection of drinks. The whole place smelled of sage and cinnamon. Dressed in their new uniforms, Meghan and Tess walked up to their manager Tabitha. She directed them behind the hostess's podium.

"This is where you'll look each morning to find your sections," Tabitha explained. "We have them marked here." She tapped the small laminated map of the dining area. "Brunch starts in about ten minutes. It's a buffet, so you'll want to seat them, get their drinks orders, and direct them to the bar." She walked them over to the kitchen. "Come with me. I'll show you around."

After, they headed back out to the main dining room. "Now, you stand at that back wall and keep an eye on your section," she told them with a smile. "Any questions so far?"

"Not yet," Meghan answered.

Tess shook her head.

Tabitha offered a warm smile. "Brunch is pretty straightforward. Dinner picks up the pace a bit more."

When she'd left them, Meghan and Tess settled in to their spots. With brunch not opening for a few more minutes, they had a little downtime before a busy day. Tess gave her friend a knowing look of contentment, Meghan understanding without her saying a thing. With its large staff and efficient kitchen, this was a cake job compared to Zagos, and Meghan could speak for her friend that both were incredibly thankful to be there.

"So, what did Rupert say when you showed up this morning?" Tess asked.

"He thought I'd flown in from somewhere again," she replied. "And he advised me not to take some movie called *Cupid's Goddess*. I've never heard of it."

"Me neither," Tess said, getting distracted by something. "Hey, is that Toby Meyers?" She pointed out the large window overlooking the Atlantic.

Meghan peered around her friend to see Toby shaking hands with two men in summer suits out on the patio. One of them was striking, with jet-black hair, olive skin, and a wide smile; the other was shorter and had a more serious expression. She allowed herself a moment to take in Toby's relaxed stance and the concentration on his face as he listened to whatever the shorter man was saying.

"Wonder what they're talking about out there," Meghan said.

"I don't know, but you sure do look interested," Tess replied.

Then, suddenly, as if he could feel he was being watched, Toby's gaze found hers through the window, questions in his eyes, his surprise at seeing her obvious. Meghan's heart hammered for being caught spying on him, and she gave him an awkward smile. He waved discreetly while the other two men were engaged in conversation. When he turned back to them, she looked away.

When she finally got the nerve to peek out at them again, Toby was heading down the stairs leading to the path that went around to the front of the inn.

Meghan straightened up and tore her eyes from the last

glimpse of him, her gaze fluttering back to the empty path against her will.

"Maybe he's coming around the front to the hostess stand to get his table." Tess playfully elbowed Meghan. "*Maybe* he'll sit in your section."

Her pulse raced at the thought. Meghan twisted around and craned her neck to see if she could spot him coming in the front, but she was met with unfamiliar faces as the guests lined up for brunch.

The two men Toby had spoken with came in through the glass door at the back and made their way to the hostess stand. Tabitha was there to greet them. With a perma-smile and her shoulders back, she showed them to one of Meghan's tables for two, handing them a menu. So that settled it; Toby must not be dining with them today. Why had he come but not stayed to eat?

"Well, Toby almost sat in your section," Tess said. "It looks like he ditched his friends."

Guests began to trickle in and before they knew it, their tables were filling up.

"Off we go!" Meghan said, grabbing a pitcher of water and heading to the table with the men in suits.

When she neared the table, Meghan slowed her pace to catch a bit of their conversation.

"Plot seventy-five is still available, but I don't know how he'll get his hands on it," the shorter of the two men said.

The other man shook his head. "It's a million and change. But ol' Gramps is good for it." His use of the term "ol' Gramps" took her back to the conversation when Tess had used it, and she couldn't help but feel that they were talking about Rupert. The two men laughed before they settled down as Meghan approached their table.

She tried to straighten out any confusion that might have been showing on her face. "Good morning," she said, filling their water glasses. "Will you be having the buffet today, or would you like something off the menu?"

They both ordered the buffet.

As the tables began to fill up and more people had gathered outside the dining area, Meghan found herself so busy that any questions she'd had about the conversation the two men were having had left her in a hurry.

Those busy workdays she'd gotten so good at were beginning again. While it wasn't her dream job, it was a pretty good one for now, and she was thankful for it. Maybe this time of her life was meant to be spent on the beach, *after* work. Maybe she'd find some truth to who she was there.

"I made two hundred dollars in tips today," Tess said as she plopped down onto the sofa back at the cottage, after changing into her shorts and a T-shirt. The sun still blazed in a bright orange sky, defiant of the approaching evening.

Meghan set down the bottle of window spray she'd been using to clean all the interior glass and scooped up a cup of dog food.

"Did Toby ever come to brunch?" Tess asked. "I was so busy; I didn't even see whether he showed up or not."

"No," she said, dropping the food into Charlie's bowl as the dog waited excitedly for it, his paws tapping on the hardwood floor. "It sounded like those guys were talking about some land. They said it would cost 'a million and change.' I wonder what Toby has to do with them."

"Maybe he's buying it! Easy on the eyes and possibly rich?" Tess's eyebrows bobbed up and down. "He has all the makings of a Prince Charming. You should definitely give him a chance."

Meghan squinted at her friend, shaking her head and making a face. "Except he's nearly impossible to talk to and doesn't seem to want me around. Could be tricky . . ."

"Well, at least we have wine to entertain us."

"Yes," Meghan said with a laugh. "And we get a view of the

ocean all day at work," she added. "People were so nice . . . I don't feel nearly as tired at the end of today as I did in the city."

"Everyone's friendly and generous because they're on vacation, that's why." Tess propped her feet up on the edge of the sofa. "I know it's day one, so I'd better keep my mouth shut, but I'm going out on a limb to say it's the perfect job—great staff, wonderful amenities, and high-paying customers. I couldn't ask for anything more."

Meghan sank down beside her. Tess was right, except for that last statement. "As perfect as the job feels, and I'm so appreciative of it, something is still missing for me," she said. "I just don't feel settled."

"Would you rather be cooking?" Tess asked.

"I don't know," Meghan replied. "Truthfully, I'm not sure anymore if that's what was meant for me. I just feel a little lost." Then, she sucked in a breath of air and let it out slowly to settle her nerves over the whole thing. "But enough of this! We got jobs—great ones! I should be happy and enjoy this moment."

Tess swung her legs over the end of the sofa and sat up. "Yes. Live in the moment. And in this moment, we have lots of tip money and no rent. What should we do with it all?"

"Save it," Meghan said.

Tess frowned. "I'd thought I'd blow it all on beachy cocktails and new bikinis."

Meghan shook her head, amused. "I think I'll just enjoy having a good job and spending time with Rupert. Every now and again, he looks at me like Pappy used to. As if he sees so much more in me than I see in myself." Pappy's instruction on finding the right man to marry came back to her and made her smile.

"That's so sweet," Tess said. She pulled the DVD off the table and peered down at the box. "What was that movie he told you not to do?"

"*Cupid's Goddess.*"

Tess pulled her phone from her pocket and typed in the title.

"Let's see if it's a real movie," she said, scrolling. She clicked a link and read. "Aha! Look at this." She handed Meghan her phone.

The 1953 Cupid's Goddess *starring unknown actress Sasha Ford flopped its opening weekend, despite the top billing it was expected to receive. Rumors swirled that front-runner Hester Quinn had turned down the role last minute, sending the production company scrambling for a suitable lead, resulting in the film's demise. In an interview with* Hollywood Magazine, *Quinn said that her management Artists' Alliance had advised her against it, a claim that they denied.*

"Maybe Rupert thinks he's her manager now," Tess said.

Meghan handed the phone back to her friend. "It looks like it." She twisted toward Tess. "You know, I'm already looking forward to playing the part for him again," she admitted.

Tess slipped her phone back into her pocket. "You've always loved the glitzy side of things."

"It makes me feel like I'm different from who I really am."

"Do you want to be *different?*"

Not sure of the answer, Meghan responded with another question. "Why do you like waitressing so much?"

Tess pursed her lips. "I'm good with people," she answered. "It comes easily to me. They feel like friends for that moment and, because of that, they tip well. I can make a good living doing something that I find simple and enjoyable."

Meghan thought about it. She didn't want to downplay Tess's career choice because it seemed to fit her friend perfectly, but she viewed the job differently. There was a circular monotony to waiting on people, putting on a smile when she didn't really feel she was in the right place, and getting them through their meal, only to start again with the next table. She'd always wanted to be on the other side of those dishes, in the kitchen, showing off her creativity and trying new things. There was something brewing in Meghan's heart that told her she wanted to do more with her life. She suddenly needed that calm that Pappy was so good at finding.

"Want to go down to the beach?" she asked, peering out at the pink sky as the sun began its descent.

Charlie popped up to attention and then ran to get his ball.

"It might feel good to sink our feet in the cool water," Tess said.

Meghan opened the door to the cottage and Charlie bounded out in front of them, loping across the seagrass and onto the boardwalk leading down to the water. "He loves it here," she said. "I know just how he feels."

While Meghan slipped into her pajamas for the night, there was a clang in the closet as something fell. Charlie darted out of it, running over to Meghan for cover.

"What happened?" she asked, stroking his head. "Did something fall?"

Charlie panted, inching closer to Meghan, on high alert.

Meghan picked up the small metal box that had been the cause of Charlie's fright. "What did you find?" she asked, fiddling with the latch. It was locked, and then she knew. She held it to her ear and shook it, the contents rattling inside. "You just found the box we were looking for," she said, lowering it so the dog could give it a tentative sniff. "Where was it?"

"What's that?" Tess asked at the door.

"I think it's the box Pappy had mentioned." She could almost hear Pappy's voice: *You found it.* "It fell on Charlie," she said, peering into the closet for anything else that might be out of place, but she was met with only the line of Pappy's clothes and the same items on the shelves at the back. "I guess Charlie nudged something and knocked it down."

"I'll get the key," Tess said.

Meghan looked into the closet again, wondering where it had come from, but she couldn't find anything amiss.

Tess came back in with the envelope, and Meghan pulled out the small key, slipping it right in. "Ha!" she laughed. "What are the odds?" She ruffled Charlie's fur. "You found it—good boy!" Charlie's tail wagged furiously.

Unlatching the small door, Meghan peered inside. She pulled out a black velvet jewelry box and opened it up. "Oh, wow," she said, peering down at a pair of diamond and emerald dangly earrings.

"Now, those are some pretty fancy fishing lures," Tess said, leaning closer to view them.

Meghan only half smiled, the joke not registering as she moved the box in the light to make the diamonds sparkle. "They were my grandmother's," she said, remembering seeing the earrings in her grandmother's jewelry box. Years ago, when she was about twelve, she'd reached for them and her mother had stopped her. *Not those,* she'd said. *They were Nanna's favorites. They're real gemstones.*

"When I was little, I used to dress up in my grandmother's fancy clothes from when she was younger." The memory wrapped her up like a warm hug. She and her mother would pull Nanna's dresses from the back of the closet and Meghan would put them on, wobbling in her high heels while she bunched up the dress to see herself in the mirror. "She died when I was about eight, so I never really got to know her very well."

"They look awfully formal," Tess said. "Hard to believe someone with those earrings would live in this secluded little beach shack on the edge of the ocean."

A swell of happiness rose in her chest. "Pappy was worth it. He was a well-spoken, intelligent man." She toyed with the box. "He traveled the world for about a year. He visited exotic places. I remember him telling me about a secret island off the coast of Croatia that he adored. But at the end of the day, he believed in a simpler life—ten minutes with him and he'd have you completely convinced that this was the only place you wanted to be." She set the box down on the table, the gemstones shimmering between them. "He used to have a saying: *At the end of the day, all we have is the only thing we really need—love.* I haven't thought about that in a long time, but he's so right." In that moment, she knew that was the real thing pulling at her day in and day out. She'd lost the last person to really show her love.

"He must have been a great guy," Tess said.

"He was," Meghan said.

"I wonder where your nanna wore these . . . ?" Tess said as she studied the earrings.

"Mama told me once that my grandmother knew all the wealthiest people on the island, and she and Pappy were known to have attended a fancy dinner party or two." A grin spread across Meghan's face. "Mama said Pappy wasn't thrilled about getting dressed up, but he'd do anything for Nanna."

"What was your nanna's name?" Tess asked.

"Audrey."

"Like Audrey Hepburn," Tess said, batting her eyelashes.

Meghan laughed, but then sobered. She'd had so many family members that she'd never had a chance to grow up with. "I wish I could have known her better." With a deep sigh, she closed the jewelry box.

"What else is in there?" Tess asked.

Meghan peered into the small container once more, an insignificant piece of paper lying at the very back. She pulled it out and unfolded it, revealing three numbers: 34-26-19.

"No explanation?"

"It's smeared," Meghan said, squinting at the words above the numbers to try to make them out. "Pi . . . something. And then a word ending in S. It's probably nothing."

"See? Pi . . . Maybe I was partially correct and it's his Pick-3 Lottery numbers," Tess said. "You should definitely play them."

With a lighthearted huff, Meghan placed the paper back into the box. "It's probably his locker combination at the marina. I'm sure he just wanted me to have the earrings."

"They're sooo pretty," Tess said.

"Yes, they are," Meghan replied, thinking she'd probably never go anywhere that would require gorgeous gemstones like those.

NINE

On her way in to see Rupert the next morning, she met one of his nurses in the lobby. "Rupert has responded quite well since your two visits," the woman said. "He's done everything he's supposed to do."

"That's wonderful," Meghan said, joy filling her right up.

"I'm about to update the doctors on his care. Would you mind sitting in with me to answer a few questions about Hester Quinn and his state when he's in his fantasies? It would be really quick."

She struggled with the nurse's request, the idea that there would be a record of her visit giving her pause, but at the end of the day, the nurse had said herself that Meghan's visits were helpful. "Sure," she said, following the woman.

The nurse clapped her hands together. "Excellent. Why don't you stop by his room and let him know you'll be back with him shortly?"

"Of course," Meghan replied.

"Great. We'll be in room B5."

Meghan split ways and headed to Rupert's room, knocking on the door and then letting herself in. "Good morning," she said, as she made her way to his bed.

"My love, how are you?" he asked with an adoring smile on his lips.

"I'm doing well. I just stopped in to tell you that I have to run out for a quick second, so our daily chat will be a bit later than usual."

His face fell.

"But I'm coming right back."

He brightened. "All right, dear. See you soon."

With a wave, Meghan let herself out and paced down the brightly lit hallway toward room B5. When she arrived, the blood ran out of her face. Toby was seated at the end of the table along with a group of medical staff, his eyes fixed on her, curiously. The nurse gestured her over to the empty seat next to him.

"Thank you two for coming," a middle-aged woman with dark hair and glasses said from the other end of the table. "I'm Dr. Angela Hughes, the lead physician for Rupert Meyers's care."

Meghan nodded, Toby's questioning look as to why she was there tugging at her concentration.

Dr. Hughes opened a file on her laptop in front of her and began reading. "Just to recap, Rupert shows symptoms of delusional disorder, a mental illness in which someone cannot tell what is real from what is imagined, as well as emotional dysregulation, due to his inability to control his behavior in times of stress. We believe both are primarily a result of his dementia." She folded her hands and made eye contact with Toby. "If it were a mild case, we could prescribe a cholinesterase inhibitor, which might temporarily improve his symptoms by slowing down the breakdown of acetylcholine when it travels from one cell to another."

"Can you put that in layman's terms for us?" Toby asked.

The doctor closed her laptop to address him directly. "Acetylcholine is a chemical we have in our brain that is highly involved in our memory, thought, and judgment. With medication, the acetylcholine, which is in short supply in people with Alzheimer's disease, isn't destroyed as quickly."

The doctor went on to rattle off the dosages of other medications they were giving him for anxiety and depression and their strategies for keeping him calm. Meghan thought about the gentle way the old man looked at her, and she couldn't imagine how frustrating the disease must be for him.

"We do feel that regular visits by Ms. Gray are proving beneficial for his emotional state, and we'd love to hear your thoughts. Ms. Gray?"

Toby cleared his throat and shifted in his chair, making Meghan's heart hammer.

"He thinks I'm someone else, but it does seem to quiet him down," Meghan told the team. "He was disappointed today when I told him I had to step out, but seemed relieved when I said I was coming back."

Dr. Hughes opened her laptop again and typed quickly while Meghan spoke. "I think the main thing is keeping him calm, and you're doing that. Obviously, let him lead the conversation, and try not to embellish his fantasies or detract from reality if you can."

"Okay," Meghan said.

"And if you ever feel unsafe, there's a red call button by the light switch in his room," she added.

"Are you sure that perpetuating this . . . mistaken identity is a good idea?" Toby asked. "We don't have any proof that Ms. Gray coming to see him is doing anything at all. He has good days and bad days, and she might be surprised when she encounters him on a day when he's combative."

Meghan remembered the old man's arms around her at the restaurant. "I can feel him relax when I'm around," she said, finally making eye contact with Toby.

"He can get quite distressed," Toby told her, calmer than she'd expected.

Dr. Hughes agreed. "He's never lashed out at a person, but he's thrown chairs, knocked over bookshelves . . . He can get very upset."

Shocked by this, Meghan asked, "Do you know what he was upset about when he did those things?"

Dr. Hughes scrolled on her computer. "Let me see . . . They're usually related to his delusions. At one point, he said he was late for his plane to California. We were causing him to miss his flight. Another time, he needed to pick something up for someone." The doctor took her glasses off and addressed Meghan. "Because you're a reminder of his fantasies about this Hollywood star, he could get agitated without warning."

"All right," Meghan said.

Toby leaned toward her, his proximity and spicy scent giving her stomach a flip, and whispered, "Really, you don't have to do this."

"I promised him," she said under her breath.

"So." The doctor inhaled sharply and produced a professional smile, "If everyone is in agreement, we'll continue with Rupert's current line of care and see where we go from there. Mr. Meyers, shall we list Miss Gray as a contact should we need her?"

"Of course." Toby stood up and reached a hand across the table. "Thank you, Dr. Hughes."

"Yes, sir," the doctor said, giving him a firm shake.

Meghan stood and followed suit. Then everyone trailed out of the staff room, taking their posts.

"So, you want to tell me what's going on?" Toby asked as they walked down the hallway toward Rupert's room.

"I think my coming here helps him," she said, leaving out the part that it seemed to help her too.

Toby stepped in front of her in the hallway, softly touching her arm and stopping her. She held her breath as he looked down at her, invading her personal space. He paused for a second, sending her heart pattering. "I'm worried it could complicate things."

"But how is it complicating anything?" she challenged.

He pursed his lips as if biting back what he wanted to say, and slowly started walking again. Meghan shuffled up beside him.

Finally, he said, "I just wonder if he and I need to get through this together with no other distractions. Maybe he'll come out of this fantasy."

"I hear you," she replied, considering what it would've been like to deal with some stranger butting into her time with Pappy. "But I did promise him I'd come today," she said. "So, let's go in and then once you see how he is, you can tell me to stay or go and I'll do whatever you want."

Toby looked into her eyes, lingering there a moment and then nodded, and the two of them entered Rupert's room.

The old man was sitting in a chair, watching a black-and-white movie. "Come in," he said, beckoning them in. "Hester, this is one of your best films."

"Which one?" she asked, lowering herself down on his bed.

"*When the Sun Rises*. Oh, it makes me cry every time she has to leave. Your performance is just so stunning." His gaze floated back to the screen. "I know you could be disheartened by Hollywood, but you really are magnificent. Toby, tell her how great she is."

"She's really great," he said, glancing over at her tentatively.

"You have time to watch the movie with me, don't you?"

Meghan suddenly worried about what the doctor had said about Rupert's erratic behavior. She had to get to work, but what would he do if she said no? There was only one way to find out. "I can't," she said gently. "I have to work."

Rupert turned his head, sucking in a breath, something flashing in his eyes. Toby took a step forward, but Meghan subtly shooed him away.

"You're doing *Cupid's Goddess*?" Rupert hissed. "For God's sake, Hester, it's a disaster. I thought I told you all this on the phone. Artists' Alliance is crazy if they think you should shoot this movie. It's career suicide."

He knew about Hester's management? *Jeez*. He really did know everything about this woman. Toby took another step toward her, his muscles tensed as if he were ready to intervene at any moment.

"It's not that movie," she said quickly, to defuse Rupert's anxiety over it. "It's a . . . different one."

Rupert's whole body slumped. "Thank God." He smiled. "You had me worried." He blew a relieved breath through his weathered lips. "What's this one?"

"Hm?"

"The movie. What's it called?"

"Uh, it's not named yet. It's a working title right now. And it's not a done deal," she scrambled. "I'm just . . . seeing if I fit the role."

Rupert narrowed his eyes. "You're nervous," he said, causing her heart to slam around in her chest. Then a smile spread across his face. "That means it's a good role. You always get nervous when you get a chance at something huge." He laughed. "Go get 'em."

"I will," she said, relieved as she picked up her handbag.

"Hester," Rupert stopped her. "You'll be back tomorrow, yes?"

"Yes," she replied, not knowing what to say.

She looked over at Toby, his lips turning upward fondly at her but his gaze still unsure.

"I'm sorry," she said to Toby, as they headed out of the room.

"You're good with him," Toby said once they were in the hallway. "I almost believed you too."

"It's intense, isn't it?" she replied, shaking her head, relieved that he hadn't been upset with her response to Rupert. He held the door to the lobby open for her and she passed through. "I think I need to do a lot more research on this Hester Quinn before I see him again, so that I can keep up with him. Did you know he even knew her management company? I just read about that earlier. He nailed it. Does he sit up on the internet all night or something?"

"No," Toby said with a disbelieving chuckle. "He doesn't even have a cell phone. It's probably in one of his books."

"Well, I'd better get to studying tonight," she said as they stepped out into the sunshine.

Toby stopped her, placing his hand on her arm, his gentle touch sending an electric current down her spine. "I still don't know if this is a good idea . . ."

For an instant, she wondered if he meant *them*. But that made no sense at all. She shook the thought free. "I don't know either," she said honestly. "All I know is that your grandfather lights up when Hester comes into a room, and I feel like I'm doing something right when I see the happiness on his face."

In that moment, a glimmer of fondness sparkled in Toby's sad eyes, and she knew he understood. "We'll see how it goes," he said gently. He reached into his wallet. "Here. This is my card. It's got my cell phone number in case you need me."

"Okay," she said, taking it and reading his name across the top: *Toby Meyers, Bridgeway Properties.* She slipped it into her handbag as the two of them locked eyes once more. He opened his mouth as if he were going to say something but then decided against it. "I'll see ya," he said.

"See ya," she replied to his back.

TEN

"Sometimes, Rupert's so convincing I really feel like Hester," Meghan told Tess as they sat outside on the inn's back deck during their break between the lunch and dinner shifts. Seagulls squawked overhead, casting shadows across the hot sand, the restless Atlantic pounding into the shore in front of them.

"That poor old man has nothing to do but read about her," Tess said. "And the whole world has moved on. But on the bright side, if I were stuck in my own head, I'd like to be twenty years old too."

"True," Meghan said. "I wish just once he'd snap out of it and really talk to me."

"Yeah . . . Does he ever talk to Toby? Does he recognize him?"

"He seems to," Meghan said, the mention of Toby causing the thought of his touch to come back to her suddenly, sending a tingling sensation down her arm.

"What's that face?" Tess said, surprising her.

"What face?"

"You weren't thinking about Rupert just then."

"Yes, I was," she lied.

"Oh, I hope not!" Tess clapped a hand over her mouth and laughed. "Not with that dreamy expression I just saw." She doubled over, her back heaving with laughs.

"Was it that obvious?" Meghan asked, mortified. Had that same look surfaced when she was with Toby? Her cheeks burned at the thought.

"Were you thinking about Toby?" Tess asked.

Meghan rolled her aching shoulders. "It isn't like that. I just feel drawn to him. I can't explain it."

"Not everything has to be explained," Tess said.

Meghan didn't respond, the idea whirring in her restless mind.

The wind unrelenting, Tess tucked a runaway tendril into her bun at the back of her head and stood up. "We should probably get back in. Dinner starts in ten minutes."

While Tess set tables with the dinner candles and cloth napkins, Meghan stacked the menus at the hostess podium and cleared the wax pencil from the wipe-off table map while Tabitha leaned on the wall beside her, embroiled in a deep, whispered conversation with Milton, one of the bellmen at the inn.

"Everything okay?" Meghan asked Tabitha when Milton walked away.

"We're working our fingers to the bone, bursting at the seams," Tabitha said from behind a manufactured smile as a group of tourists walked by happily. "And we've heard that the locals are quietly protesting the expansion of Mariner's Inn. They're pushing back on the zoning."

"Expansion?"

"Yeah. The owner wants to expand the inn. It's all hush-hush," Tabitha replied with a suspicious once-over of the room to ensure she wasn't being overheard. "But I'll bet the owner will buy someone off if he has to." She leaned in closer to Meghan. "The rumor is he's worth millions."

"Really?" Meghan asked, soaking in this bit of gossip.

"Well, *he* isn't—yet. But he's about to get a windfall. It's quite the scandal."

"Scandal?"

Eyeing her as if sizing her up, Tabitha seemed as if she were deciding to tell her something. Then, with a line beginning to form for dinner, she took Meghan's arm and led her around the other side of the wall to ensure no one could hear them. "Well, apparently, he had nothing—no income, no home, nothing. He suddenly showed up here, ready to take care of his grandfather and deciding to open the inn. It's rumored that he's funding it with the old man's money."

Meghan became incredibly curious after what she'd heard from the two men in suits yesterday. "Who owns this place, anyway? No one ever told me."

"Well, he doesn't come in much, barely at all really—some guy from Chicago who's renting a house down the road, in Manteo. I've only seen him once. Named Toby Meyers."

Meghan's blood ran cold.

"Rumor has it that he's put on this air of good guy for everyone, but his goal is to build onto the inn, sell it, and take off with the proceeds, leaving his grandfather behind. Someone said he wants to move to the Gulf Coast." She shrugged. "I don't care who owns it as long as I've got a job." She turned toward the waiting crowd at the hostess podium.

Suddenly, Toby's worries about her seeing Rupert came to mind. Was there something he didn't want Rupert to tell her?

As Meghan and Tess got to Pappy's porch after work, Meghan unlatched the door for Charlie to come out and then sat down on the steps, the Atlantic churning softly, the beach quiet, as if the evening had ushered out all the sounds and left only the wind and the shushing of the tide. Charlie rushed up to them, his tail wagging.

"Hey, boy. Did you miss us?" Meghan rubbed his ears and then opened the door wider to let him out.

Tess sat beside her. "You've been quiet tonight."

"I heard something that's been eating me alive all evening." She told Tess what Tabitha had said. "Is Toby stealing money from Rupert?" she worried aloud. "I can't imagine it."

"Are you going to ask Toby?"

"I don't know. But one thing's for sure: If there is any funny-business going on, I'm going to protect Rupert, because he can't protect himself." She leaned against the railing, watching Charlie. "I feel like Pappy's near me whenever I see Rupert. I can't explain it. It's like I'm supposed to be there."

"Maybe you are," Tess said, putting an arm around Meghan.

"I wonder if they knew each other when they were younger—Pappy and Rupert. Pappy never mentioned him."

"I didn't want to say anything until I knew you were ready, but when we got here, I found a photo album full of old pictures of your grandpa in my room. We could see if any of the people in them look like Rupert."

"You did?" Meghan asked, a sudden eagerness to see it welling up. "Where is it?"

"I'll go get it."

Tess raced back inside while Meghan ran her fingers along the sandy step of the porch, watching Charlie as he sped up and down the yard, chasing the shadows of the seagulls. She was glad she'd come here for Charlie. His world seemed to open up here. He had acres of open beach instead of that little apartment, where he'd curled up all day, waiting for her to come home, only to go out to the city sidewalk on a short leash. She wished she could feel that kind of freedom.

Tess returned, sitting down next to her and handing her

a brown binder. Meghan opened it to the first page and touched the black-and-white photo of her young grandfather. He looked to be around twenty-five or so, wearing a loosely fitted shirt, unbuttoned halfway, the sleeves rolled up, with jeans, cuffed at the bottom. His full head of dark hair waved along the top of his head, and he held a fishing pole, a rugged smile on his lips.

"He *was* handsome, wasn't he?" Meghan said, scanning a few more pictures of him holding up a large fish he'd caught. She turned the page. "Oh, look." She tipped the book to avoid the sun's glare. Pappy had on a tuxedo with a black bowtie and Meghan's grandmother was wearing one of the ball gowns Meghan remembered dressing up in as a child, her hair swept into a fashionable updo. "There he is with my grandmother. I think that dress is still hanging in the closet."

"They look so young," Tess said, peering down at it. "Such a beautiful couple. I wonder which one of your grandmother's dinners they were going to that night." She smiled before leaning in to get a closer look at something. "Are those the earrings from the lockbox?"

Meghan gasped. "Oh yes! They are. Look at them. They're so beautiful."

Charlie came running up the boardwalk, greeting them with a loud pant.

"You all done, boy?" Meghan said with a laugh. "Let's go in." With the book under her arm, she stood up and brushed the sand off her bottom with her free hand.

Inside, Meghan sat down on the sofa with the book and continued to look at the photos. There were some taken in town and out on the boat, others with a few people in them, but none of the pictures had anyone resembling Rupert.

"I think I might be losing my mind," Meghan said, shutting the album. She turned to address Tess, who was filling up a glass of water at the kitchen sink. "The only two people I've spent time with outside of us are a possible thief and an old man with no memory. Pappy would never guide me there, so what's going on?"

"I have absolutely no idea," Tess replied, coming over to her and squeezing between Meghan and the dog.

As they sat in the quiet of the evening with nothing but silence between them, they were no closer to having any of the answers Meghan was looking for.

ELEVEN

"Knock, knock," Meghan said, slipping her sunglasses up like a headband and coming into Rupert's room slowly to give him time to process. "It's Meg—Hester."

"Why don't you dress up anymore?" he asked from his bed, without a hello. He was in a much calmer mood this morning as he eyed her work trousers and white button-up. "You always used to dress up."

"Work, remember?" she replied, before lifting his blinds to let in the view of the seagrass swaying in the summer sunlight. She sat in the chair opposite him.

"What movie?"

"Top secret," she said, pretending to button her lips. "I'm a waitress."

The skin between his eyes wrinkled. "In *that*? Shouldn't they have you in a dress?"

She offered Rupert a smile. "You look good today," she said.

He ran his unsteady hands down the blanket over his legs. "Last night was hard on me," he said. "I kept thinking about how much I miss you."

If only she could tease out what was real from what wasn't in his mind . . . "Rupert, can I ask you something?"

"Of course."

"Do you know anyone named Meghan Gray?"

He smiled and tipped his head back in recognition, surprising her. "Yes. I met her once when you and I were at dinner. Lovely girl."

"Did you know she's a waitress?"

"Is that so?" he asked, life in his eyes as he took in this new information.

"Yes. She works at your grandson's new inn. Remember Toby?"

"Oh, wow. I had no idea." His gaze traveled into the distance above her head, that familiar crease of disorientation forming between his eyes.

"I'm going to step out of the room and Meghan's going to come in to chat with you. Is that okay?" she asked.

He nodded, his mind still clearly far away.

Meghan let herself out, her hands trembling and her heart racing. She waited a few seconds and then walked back in, sitting down in the chair. "Hello," she said. "Do you know who I am?"

"Of course I do. Hester. How are you?"

With a deep breath to offset the disappointment that she hadn't been able to reach him, she answered, "I'm doing just fine, Rupert. How are you?"

"Summer has begun," Tabitha said, as she passed Meghan with an overflowing silver tray full of lunch orders balancing on the palm of her hand. The dining area was packed inside and out, with a line waiting at the hostess's station. Tess was across the room, squatting at a table, jotting down orders as Meghan carried a handful of menus over to a table of five, and they'd only just opened.

After getting beverage orders for her new tables, Meghan went back into the kitchen where Tess was now pinning up a table's food order for the kitchen staff. "People are standing at the edges of the deck, ordering drinks because they can't get a table," Tess said, looking tired already.

"It's madness, isn't it?" Meghan replied as she filled glasses, setting them on a tray.

Tabitha popped her head over from the counter where she had grabbed two plates of stuffed crab and linguini. "It's like this from the start of June all the way until September. If Mr. Meyers doesn't expand soon, we're going to explode."

"I hear you," Meghan said. She picked up the tray and headed out to her table, the whole time thinking about this morning with Rupert. If she could just once get him to acknowledge *her*. She'd been hoping to ask him about Toby, but she should've known better than to think he'd be able to come out of his Hester fantasy with her there. The more she thought about it, the more she decided that she wanted to see him again, to hear whatever it was he wanted to tell the movie star.

As she worked, Meghan couldn't help but feel that, while she wasn't sure exactly where she was going, being there felt like the right start. Maybe it was time to begin laying down roots.

By the time they got home from work early that evening, Meghan was beat. She and Tess took their sore feet out of their shoes and socks and strolled along the beach, the soft sand between their toes. The shoreline was rocky that evening, the receding tide causing bits of shells to turn over in the waves, the water depositing them on the powdery sand.

"We're making triple what we made at Vinnie's in tips," Tess said.

"I need the money so bad," Meghan said, tightening her ponytail.

"I feel like I'm actually starting something here, and I'm only staying for the summer." Tess paced along beside her, the two of them leaving footprints in the sand.

"I think you're right," Meghan told her, reaching down and picking up the remnants of a conch shell that had washed up on the beach, turning it over in her hand before looking up toward the cottage. "I'm wondering if it's time to stop treading water." She tossed the shell into the surf, Charlie chasing after it.

Tess stopped and stared at her. "What do you mean?"

"I think I'm ready to make a few changes to Pappy's house to make it my own," Meghan told her. "It's what he would've wanted me to do." She turned to Tess. "With more workdays like this one ahead, I feel okay using my savings to fix it up."

Tess's eyes rounded. "Are we talking a full re-do?"

Meghan allowed a smile at her friend's enthusiasm. "There is a comforter set I'd love to get . . . But for right now, let's focus on just paint. We could start tomorrow, since we've got the day off."

"I'd love to," Tess said enthusiastically.

"Want to go paint shopping?" Meghan asked.

"Definitely."

"We could paint a palm tree mural," Tess said, widening her arms in the air. "A big sun on one wall . . ."

Meghan chewed on a smile. "Or a nice white . . ."

"Bor-ing," Tess teased. "Okay, okay. We'll work you up to palm trees." She hooked her arm in Meghan's. "Whatever you decide, I know it will be amazing."

Meghan smiled at her best friend, so thankful for her.

The little Honda loaded down with gallon cans of paint, Meghan and Tess walked into Lost Love Coffee. The place was busy despite the evening hour, as all the restaurants seemed to be in the summer in the Outer Banks. Tess spotted a table and ran over to it, dropping her handbag in one of the chairs.

"You relax. I'll grab us a coffee," Tess offered. "What do you want?"

"Surprise me." Meghan settled in at the table to relax and decide her plans for Pappy's cottage. She pulled a pad of paper and a pen from her handbag, just the motion filling her with a little thrill. This was the moment everything would begin, she decided. Good things were in the works—she had to believe that. While she waited, Meghan began a list of the things she could do right now that didn't require a ton of money.

Tess returned with their orders. "I got you decaf. I know how you are in the evenings." Tess set her mug down in front of her with a curtsy and sat down.

"Thank you," she said, adding a packet of sugar and stirring the liquid with her spoon.

"So, whatcha got there?"

"I've made a list of everything I can think of so far. I want to keep as much of Pappy's furniture as we can," Meghan said, wrestling with the urge to cry at the thought of hauling *all* of Pappy's things away. She swallowed, pushing it back down. "This is harder than I thought," she said, her emotions bubbling up.

"You have quite an attachment to your pappy, don't you?"

"Yeah." She focused on her coffee, her gaze moving to the boardwalk full of beachgoers out the window. The shop was clearing out as they all headed back to the beach for crabbing and bonfires. She took in a deep breath, trying to ignore the ache in her chest.

"We'll take it one step at a time," Tess said, reaching over and rubbing Meghan's forearm in support.

Meghan looked back down at her pad of paper. "I was thinking we could paint the dining table and chairs a light tan and the bed frames in both rooms could be kept and refinished."

"White walls and kitchen cabinets with a sand-colored table would be pretty for the kitchen," Tess said with an encouraging expression. "We could distress the paint on the table to make it look like driftwood."

"Yes," Meghan agreed, the hope returning. "With a bowl of seashells in the center of the table . . ."

"Oooh, I like that. What else do you think we could keep?"

"I have to keep as much as possible because I'm on a budget," she said. "What if we got a white slip cover for the sofa?"

Tess wrinkled her nose. "A slip cover on leather? We might slide onto the floor every time we sit on it." She chuckled.

Meghan nodded in agreement as Chloe the barista walked past them saying hello, her arms filled with memorabilia. "I can't afford a new couch, though," she said quietly. She didn't want to blame the fact that she couldn't afford a new sofa on her life's choices, but the thought did float into her mind. Her job barely made her enough money to live on, and she didn't even enjoy it. Tess, who lived on the same amount, never seemed to worry, but it was because she was doing something she loved.

"What if we just dressed it up with cream throws and pillows?" Tess offered.

"That's a great idea," Meghan said, distracted by Chloe, who was beside them, shuffling things along the side table that held all the love stories, setting down new artifacts. "What's new for the collection?" Meghan asked.

"Come have a look," the woman replied.

Glad for the distraction, Meghan abandoned the list, and she and Tess took their coffees with them, peering down at the new items. There was a postcard from someone in the navy, telling his love that he'd be home soon. Another new piece was a locket that was open with black-and-white pictures of a young man in a suit on one side and a woman on the other. "These are so wonderful," Meghan said.

Chloe removed the glass box from atop the old journal page they'd seen last time, to replace it with a pair of lace gloves and a wedding photo. "We got these at an estate sale. Aren't they lovely?" she said.

As she carefully set the journal paper down onto the table, Meghan noticed it was actually a few sheets, stacked together.

"Do you mind if I look at the other pages?" Meghan asked, nearing them.

The woman looked around the empty shop. "Go ahead," Chloe replied, "just be careful with them. They're brittle."

Meghan set her coffee down at their table and then returned to the journal pages, picking up another of the entries with Tess next to her.

How did I get myself into this mess? I'm torn between two lives—the one I know I want and the one that I can't live without. Either way, I've lost. There's something pulling me toward the former, some force of nature that I cannot explain, rendering me heartbroken but also liberated . . .

Meghan gently leafed through the papers, looking for who the book pages may have belonged to, but there was nothing. Just the feminine, loopy handwriting and dates.

"A life she wanted and a life she couldn't live without—sounds like quite a choice," Meghan said to Tess. She flipped it over, looking for answers on the back, but the next entry was about something else.

"I wonder what those choices were," Tess said.

Meghan took in the script again. "I'm dying to know myself. I guess we'll have to come get a coffee every day so we can read the rest and find out," she teased.

"You should keep these from under the glass, so people can read the back sides," Tess suggested. "They're incredibly moving."

"We worry about handling the pages over time," Chloe told them. "But I agree. I read through them. They're definitely captivating."

"It seems awfully private to have on display," Meghan thought aloud. "These were the inner feelings of this woman. I wonder what she'd think, knowing that strangers were reading her thoughts."

The barista stared at them, clearly considering this.

"You have a point. I can't imagine if I'd kept a diary and it got into the hands of the public. Good grief," Tess said, returning to the table and picking up her mug of coffee.

"One of the entries I read was a happy one," the barista said. "It mentioned inviting her best friend from childhood and her best friend's husband to a party. She was so excited that she'd found the perfect birthday gift for her best friend. That's love of a different kind..." She sat down on the stool behind the counter. "Maybe I'll keep that page on display since it's less invasive."

"That's a good idea," Meghan said.

Tess put her palms on the table, leaning in toward Meghan. "Right! Back to decorating."

Getting a head start before their day off tomorrow, Meghan stood next to the gallon cans of taupe paint she and Tess had bought on the way home, assessing the interior of the cottage. As she stood there in the purple and orange evening light, she worked to process the mixture of sadness and hope that fought for space within her.

"Let's begin in the bedroom," she said, not wanting to disturb Pappy's living area just yet. "We can clean out the furniture and the closet in Pappy's room first."

"Sounds like a plan."

Meghan and Tess spent the next three hours unloading the room, removing the window treatments, and filling in nail holes. The only thing left was the bed that they'd pulled to the center, and the swirling dust in the air around them. Charlie jumped up on the bed while Meghan opened the windows to let the briny night air filter in.

"It's bigger without all his things in it," Tess said, clapping her hands free of dust.

"Yes." Meghan swiveled around as she sized up all the blank space. "I think I'll keep it minimal in here to highlight the view out of the double window," she said, pointing to the sparkling Atlantic under the moonlight, the seagrass swaying in the night breeze.

"You have an eye for art," Tess told her.

"We'll see," Meghan said with a grin. "On to the closet." With a deep breath, she went over to it, and she and Tess began pulling out Pappy's hanging clothes, lumping them on the sofa in the living room. Meghan gathered up Pappy's favorite flannel shirts that he used to wear fishing when the fall temperatures began to plummet. She ran her thumb over the wooly feel of it, recalling how it brushed her skin when he hugged her. They stacked his dust-covered shoes along the wall by the front door.

Carefully, Meghan began to remove the things from the shelves at the back: more fishing hats, his watch, a couple of belts. She took it all over to the kitchen table and set each one down, handling it as if it could shatter at any moment.

"Hey, Meghan?" Tess called from the room. "You might want to come in here and see this."

Meghan headed back into Pappy's room to find Tess, head-first in the closet. "What is it?" She peered around her friend.

"Well, that's one way to get extra storage," Tess said, as the two of them gazed into the hole in the wall that had previously been hidden with the things on the shelf. From the looks of it, Pappy had cut out a section of drywall and stashed things inside it, behind his shelves.

She gazed into the dark space, full of who-knows-what that Pappy had decided to store there, her nerves buzzing with an electric charge at finding this unexpected surprise. "Maybe that's why Charlie was rooting around in there the other day," she said, reaching in and pulling out a large cardboard box.

Upon hearing his name, Charlie perked up from his spot by the headboard. Meghan took the box over to the bed and opened it up, more dust puffing into the air in the white moonlight coming through the window. Charlie sniffed the edges of it, his tail wagging.

"Oh, it's more of my grandmother's dresses," Meghan said, pulling out the garments wrapped in plastic. She lifted the protective bag and peered down at the stunning 1940s shiny green strapless dress with an A-line skirt, tailored bow at the waist and matching shawl. "I've never seen this one before." She slipped the plastic off completely and inspected the tag. "Triana-Norell," she said, holding it up to her, spinning around in the middle of the room. "It's so beautiful."

"It's just gorgeous," Tess agreed, pulling out her phone and typing in the name. As the results of her search came up, she gasped. "I just typed in Triana-Norell . . . Norman Norell was a famous designer. Until 1960, he'd partnered with Anthony Triana and then he went out on his own. Norell was known for his elegant evening wear." She looked up at her friend in astonishment. "His dresses are on display at the Met."

Meghan looked back down at the incredible garment. "Oh, wow . . . I can't believe Nanna would wad it up in a box and shove it at the back of the closet."

"Unless your pappy did it, not knowing. That dress is probably worth a thousand dollars or more by now, I'd guess, looking at the others on this page." She scrolled, her interest returning to her phone.

"I should take it to the specialty cleaners in Manteo and have it professionally cleaned and stored properly."

"It looks like it could fit you."

Meghan held it up to her, the hem falling just right. "We'll play dress-up later," she teased. "What else is in here?" She pulled out a matching pair of pumps, setting them next to the dresses. Then she grasped a small glass bottle, lifting it from the box. "Chanel Number Five," she said, holding it up to the lamp, the liquid having long evaporated.

"That's fancy," Tess said.

"My grandmother was an elegant woman," Meghan explained. "She was born into money, but married for love." Meghan smiled as she removed the cap and inhaled, a faint scent of perfume still lingering. "That's one of the things I remember about her. She told me that once when I was really little. She'd grown up with money because my great-grandfather worked in the oil industry. He told her that if she ran off with a fisherman, he'd cut her off financially. She married Pappy anyway, telling me that no money in the world could replace the feeling of true love."

Tess sighed. "I wish I could find someone to sweep me off my feet so much that I'd give up my fortune to live out my days by the sea with the man I love."

Enchanted by the thought, Meghan set the perfume in the windowsill. "I'm ready to give up my fortune," Meghan teased. "All $986 of it."

Tess laughed.

Meghan reached into the box once more and pulled out a piece of paper. Confusion swimming inside her, she turned it around to show Tess the message:

One day, I'll come back. I promise.

"Where did she go?" Tess asked.

Meghan ran her finger over the swooping letters. "I'll bet it was when they first met. She said she'd come for a week and fallen head over heels for him, but her father made her go home to Texas. She spent every day after that trying to figure out how to get back to him."

"Dreamy," Tess said.

"The only thing we really need is love," she said, repeating Pappy's sentiment and wondering if she'd ever be so lucky as to find it herself.

TWELVE

The next morning, before taking her grandmother's dress to the cleaners, Meghan decided to go see Rupert. With the early summer sun casting its long shadows along the palm tree-lined street, she'd decided to take the long way, driving with the windows down to let in the salty air.

She felt protective of Rupert, and she hoped to get some sort of explanation from him about Toby, although she wasn't terribly hopeful. She carried the dress into Rosewood Manor, avoiding leaving it in the heat of the car, and pushed Rupert's door open, the plastic rustling against her legs when she entered with the garment.

"Hi, Rupert," she said as she hung it up on the closet door.

"Morning, my dear," he said over his readers, the newspaper spread out on his lap. He folded it and set it aside, eyeing the dress. "What do you have there?"

"It's a dress I'm taking to the cleaners," she said, lifting the plastic to give him a peek.

"Ah, it's lovely."

"It is, isn't it?" she asked, admiring it.

"You should wear that on the plane when you go to the Oscars. It's a charming travel dress."

"Maybe," she said, trying to answer without actually answering.

He peered down at his paper, that confused, glazed look washing over him.

"You okay, Rupert?" she asked.

"Hm?" He looked up. "Oh, hello, dear. What do you have there?"

His question startled her. "It's a dress I'm taking to the cleaners," she repeated slowly, the fact that he'd already forgotten worrying her.

"Ah yes, I recognize it now."

"You do?" she asked, trying not to change her lighthearted tone, and sitting down in the chair in the corner of the room.

"You wore it to dinner with the Baldwins, remember? That producer."

Meghan nodded, wondering if she could somehow talk him back into his real thoughts. Maybe she could challenge that brain of his and snap him out of this delusion. She opened her mouth to ask him about Toby, but decided not to. She could tell by Rupert's demeanor that he needed to stay in this moment a little longer. "How did *we* meet, Rupert?" Perhaps he'd realize that he'd never really met Hester and, like the moment he remembered his actual wife at dinner, he'd remember where he was right now.

"You don't remember?" he asked, looking dejected.

"I just want to hear you tell me," she said with a smile.

He sat back with a satisfied pout. "All right then. You were on the bench near Peabody's Bait Shop, in that yellow button-up dress with the collar, showing off a figure we'd never seen on the barrier islands before." He looked down bashfully and then met her eyes again. "You'd taken off your white gloves and set them beside you, and you were writing a postcard you'd bought. Do you remember?"

She gave him an encouraging nod. "Keep going."

"I sat down next to you and even though you didn't know me from Adam, you gave me that mischievous look of yours. You turned the card around and asked if I'd check your spelling. I remember gasping at the language *a lady* had used." He tipped his head back and chuckled. "It was addressed to your aunt. I still remember it. 'I'm not coming home. My return trip is postponed indefinitely. It's damn near perfect here.' "

Captivated, Meghan broke out into a huge smile, but right then Rupert's faded.

"We only had that one unspoiled year before everything fell apart . . . We were so secluded and Roosevelt didn't say a thing to anyone." He shook his head, clenching his jaw. "The Germans sank a fleet of ships off the coast . . . No one could believe it," he said in a whisper. "That was when you first wanted to leave."

Meghan now recognized the shiftiness in his gaze as he got agitated. Unsure of what to do, she jumped up and grabbed his hand. "I'm here now," she said, all hope of finding out anything about his grandson sliding away. "I'm not going anywhere."

He settled down and stared into her eyes, his tense muscles relaxing. "Do you promise?"

"Yes," she said, and she meant it.

On the way home from seeing Rupert and dropping the dress at the cleaners, Meghan caught sight of the Outer Banks Museum. As she slowed down, Rupert's story about the Germans stayed with her. Suddenly, she found herself pulling in. She sat in her car, staring at the door to the small building. She'd never been there before in all her years of going to the Outer Banks, and she wondered why she was sitting there now. Rupert had been so believable that she was curious to find out what was real and what wasn't.

She texted Tess that she'd be home soon, then let herself out of the car and made her way up the stairs and into the tiny three-room museum, her skin prickling with the hope that Rupert's rec-ollection of a German invasion had been real. Pacing along the edges of the room, she began her search with paintings of Fort Raleigh's colonists that would later be known as "The Lost Colony" and continued on, reading about the war between the states and how they shaped the coastline.

"Hello," the museum curator said, startling her as he came in from another room. "May I help you with anything?"

"I was curious to see if you had any memorabilia from the Outer Banks during World War Two. I'm specifically looking for a naval battle," she replied.

"Well, yes, we do," he said happily, guiding her into another room. "The World Wars begin here on this wall and wrap around."

"Thank you," she said, her attention falling onto a black-and-white photo of a battleship. Meghan stopped to read the plate on the wall that accompanied it.

Unbeknownst to many, in 1942, a battle thundered off the coast of the Outer Banks. The battlefield spanned the Atlantic, all the way to Europe, a massive conflict for control of the sea. Forty boats were sent to a watery grave over that year at the hands of German U-boats in blasts that shook the earth like an earthquake.

Meghan covered her gaping mouth as she read it. "It's real," she said to herself. She continued on reading about the war, but there was nothing else about that particular moment in history. As she left the museum, thanking the curator on her way out, she retrieved her cell phone and Toby's business card, dialing his number.

He answered on the first ring. "Hello?" his smooth voice came through the phone.

"Hi," she said, needing to catch her breath at the sound of his voice. "This is Meghan Gray."

"Hey," he returned quietly.

"I'm sorry to call, but I was wondering, have you ever taken Rupert to the Outer Banks Museum?"

"All the time," he replied. "It's one of his favorite places."

"Oh," she said, slightly deflated.

"Why?"

"He talked about Hester and World War Two, and, Toby, it was so convincing. I want to believe so badly that he's really there in his memories, but I suppose I need to come to grips with the fact that he just isn't."

"Meghan," he said, his voice soft, the sound of her name making her skin tingle, "he's barely ever in reality anymore. It took me a while to come to terms with it too."

His voice didn't sound like someone who'd steal from his grandfather. He sounded truthful and honest in a way that made her curious about who he really was when he let his guard down.

"Yeah . . ." she said, still thinking about it. "Do you ever wish you'd had more time with him before the dementia set in?" she heard herself ask, knowing the question was more for herself than for Toby.

"Of course," he said. "He's all I've got. Taking care of someone who doesn't even always know who I am is tough."

"It's funny how consistent he is with me," she said. "He never falters when he sees me. I'm always Hester Quinn."

"Or, seeing you reminds him of his reality and he slips into the fantasy every single time to get through it."

Her mind wandered to the flicker of hope that Rupert might have known Pappy, since the two of them were from the same town. She hadn't admitted it to herself until now, but deep down, she wished she could sit with Rupert and talk about old times in Hatteras, maybe hear some great stories about her grandfather . . .

"What is the reality that I remind him of, do you think?" she asked.

"I suppose you remind him that life is still moving and he

can't go back because the people in his memory aren't there anymore. He's here now and probably finds himself alone."

There was a pain in his words that made her ask, "Are you sure you're talking about your grandfather?"

He was so quiet that, for a second, she thought the call had been dropped. "Meghan," he said so softly, her name coming out on his breath like a tumbleweed in the wind. She waited, hanging on his words, for whatever would come after. But then he cleared his throat. "I need to go."

His words hit her like a splash of water. "Oh," she said, gripping the phone and suddenly not wanting him to hang up.

"Bye," he said.

The line went dead.

Stunned by the moment they'd just had, for an instant she didn't move. She just stood there in the parking lot of the museum, her mind in a muddle. She didn't know much about Toby Meyers, but what she did know was there was a lot to him, and so many things he needed to say but wouldn't.

Meghan put her purse down and came into the bedroom, grabbing the old T-shirt and shorts she had laid out on the bed for when she'd gotten back.

"You covered everything in plastic—thank you," she said to Tess when she walked into the living room.

Tess gave her a proud smile while stirring the paint. "I'm excited to get going."

"You're putting in a lot of effort for a place you're only staying in for the summer," Meghan said. "Sure you don't want to stay longer?" Meghan didn't want to think about how quiet Pappy's cottage would be without her best friend.

"You never know," Tess replied, but Meghan knew that making long-range plans wasn't Tess's strong suit. "And all the effort is because I just want to do something nice for you. You deserve it."

"I deserve it?" Meghan asked, stripping off her shirt and switching to the old T-shirt. "What did I do to deserve such a great friend?"

"You're the most selfless person I know. I want to be you when I grow up." Tess flashed her a wide grin before tossing her a paint roller. "Suit up, girlfriend. You've got work to do if you want to have a place to sleep tonight."

Meghan poured paint into the rolling tin and then dragged her roller through it, coating the nap with paint. Fighting back the sudden inclination to call off the redecorating, she pressed the roller against the wall, the bright taupe erasing Pappy's presence with every stripe.

First one wall was done, and then another, Meghan and Tess progressing around the room, the steel drums of beach music playing on the radio. Tess happily moved along while Meghan felt increasingly panicked, praying she was doing the right thing. She didn't want to remove Pappy's touches from this place, but if she ever wanted to make it hers, it had to be done.

"Wait," she said, stopping Tess when they got to the last wall that had the alcove with shelves in the center of it. "Let's tape off those shelves and keep them the way Pappy had them."

As they began to tape off the space, there was a knock at the door, sending Charlie into a barking fit. He bounded off the bed and scrambled down the hardwoods, taking his place as protector at the front of the house.

"It's okay, Charlie," Meghan said, opening the door to find Toby standing on her porch. Charlie wove himself around Toby's feet, sniffing madly.

"I remembered the way here," he said.

A warm flush filled her cheeks.

"Oh, hi, Toby!" Tess called from the bedroom, leaning into the doorway so only Meghan could see her what-in-the-world face.

Toby belted an uneasy hello back to her. "I brought dinner," he said, holding up two bags of takeout. He waved the bags, the savory aroma of fresh seafood and butter filling the air. "Although you look busy."

Meghan stared at him, completely baffled but thrilled that he'd shown up. She didn't want to allow the hope that he was letting her in to become a solidified emotion because she might not be able to manage if he pulled away. She wiped her forehead with the back of her wrist to avoid getting paint on her face.

"It's fine," she said. "I'm glad you came. Come in." She stepped aside to let him enter and took him to the kitchen. He went over to the counter, set the bags down, and turned to her.

"The World War Two exhibit is brand new," he said.

"What?"

"At the museum. You said he told you about Hester and World War Two. He doesn't have any books on World War Two, so I called the museum because I didn't remember him seeing anything about the Second World War and the Outer Banks. Which doesn't mean too much in terms of his mental state, but it does mean he could be pulling it from his memory."

Meghan sucked in a tiny gasp.

"What did he tell you about it?"

"The shelves are all taped off," Tess said, coming into the room, eyeing Meghan. "Oh my goodness, you brought dinner? It smells incredible. Is that cornbread?" Tess didn't wait for an answer. She went right over to the sink and washed up, clearly overdoing the nonchalance, the weight of Toby's presence an elephant in the room.

"I was just going to tell Toby what Rupert said about the war," said Meghan.

"Oh, I'd love to hear that." Tess dried her hands and turned her attention to Meghan, who began recounting what Rupert had told her about Hester in the yellow dress and the boats that were sunk off the coast.

"You said it doesn't mean much, but it's something, right?" Meghan asked.

Toby chewed on his lip, his gaze unstill. "I keep wondering when he'll be lucid again," he said. "He didn't tell you anything else?"

Meghan shook her head, wishing there was more she could tell Toby.

"When he remembers little things, it gives me just a tiny bit of . . . optimism. But I suppose the memory isn't as significant as the fact that he seems to—more times than not—remember who I am."

"I know it has to be hard," Meghan said, trying to read Toby. Was he the person that Tabitha had made him out to be? Was this just a good-guy routine, and he really didn't want Rupert to be lucid at all? Had that been why he'd rushed over? "I'll get us three plates."

"Oh, no. I wasn't going to stay," he said. "I got the dinners for Gramps and myself, but when I called to see if he wanted me to stop by the pie shop for dessert, the nurse said he'd already turned in for the night."

Meghan felt a radiating thud of disappointment. "You need to eat too, though, don't you?" she said.

"I'm not hungry. I only got myself a dinner so he'd feel more comfortable. You two can have it all. I'll let myself out."

"Stay," Meghan said, going out on a limb. She wanted to believe that the kindness that showed in his eyes was real.

He shifted on his feet uncomfortably, his blue eyes nearly swallowing her, making her wonder what was running through that head of his. Something in her gut told her there was more going on than she knew, and she wanted to get to the bottom of it.

"I'd rather go. Enjoy the dinner." The words didn't match the indecision on his face.

"Wait," she said, as he turned around to leave. When he did, she could've sworn she'd seen pain in his eyes.

"I need to go," he replied, walking over to the door and letting himself out.

"I've dated those types before," Tess said once he'd left, as she continued unboxing the cornbread muffins, the warm, buttery steam rising into the air and making Meghan's stomach rumble, her eyes still on the door. "He's got issues. It's pretty clear."

"What do you think they are?" Meghan asked, wishing that he would've stayed.

"I'm not a mind-reader," Tess said, getting two paper plates from the cabinet. "But he's so skittish."

"Yeah." Meghan opened the lid to a box of steamed shrimp and dished some out on their plates, along with a dollop of cocktail sauce.

Tess pulled out a container of macaroni and cheese, filling a serving spoon with the soft noodles. "I thought he might be a good catch, but after seeing him now, I wonder what he's hiding."

Meghan's hands stilled and she turned her attention to Tess. "You think he's hiding something?"

"There's definitely something holding him back from being himself. What that is, I'm not sure. But, given what people have said about him, I'd be careful."

How Tess's tune about Toby had changed. There was no playfulness in her voice at all—just warning. And one thing Meghan knew for sure was that Tess was excellent at reading people, so while she didn't want to admit it, Meghan had to believe that starting anything with Toby Meyers could be a big mistake.

THIRTEEN

Meghan held the bunch of daisies she'd gotten at the flower stand tightly in both hands as she lowered herself onto the cool grass under the oak tree, facing Pappy's grave. She set them down next to the gravestone and ran her hand delicately over the words "John William Gray."

She recalled being with him that final day in the hospital. She'd gotten a call early that morning that she should come be with him, and the whole way there, she shook like a leaf because she knew what was coming. It was that day that she'd first understood what it would feel like without him.

When she'd arrived at his bedside, she realized she'd already lost the strapping father figure who'd raised her after her parents' death. He was barely there, the cancer breaking him down to a wisp of a man. He was spouting out things that made no sense at all, having been placed on quite a bit of medication by then for the pain, and everything he'd said had been a jumble of words. Not wanting to remember him in that state, the picture of it came back in vivid detail against her will and she recalled an odd message he'd given her that came back like a scream: *Go to Ricroft*. It was the only thing he'd said to her that day that had given her pause because the intensity in his eyes had caught her off guard. She'd forgotten about it until now. But as she sat across from his grave, she felt peace, as if he were sitting there in the grass beside her, completely content.

"Pappy," she said in a whisper, a lump forming in her throat. "I wish you could tell me what to do. I need you so much right now. I feel like I'm wandering aimlessly."

Tears welling up, she stopped talking and let the words on the gravestone blur in front of her, feeling as though her heart might break right in two. She lay back on the soft grass and stared up at the sky, the billowy clouds floating in the bright blue sky giving her no answers.

You already have the answers, she could almost hear Pappy saying. *They're within you.*

Maybe there was some truth to that. Maybe the answers *were* within her. She just couldn't see them yet.

When Meghan arrived at Rupert's room, it was completely dark, despite the late morning hour. She clicked on the lamps and opened the blackout drapes.

Rupert watched her move around, his eyes clear, his gaze steady.

"You okay?" she asked, wondering why he'd been sitting in the dark.

He nodded. "Just been thinking."

She smiled. "About what?"

"I fell asleep and missed my grandson's visit yesterday. I wanted to talk to him." He shifted in his bed. "Hester, you'd adore him."

"Is that so?" she asked, excited that he understood he'd missed Toby.

"You told me that you wanted me to go on without you, and I have. I've had a wonderful life."

"I'm so happy to hear that."

"Good. But are *you* happy?" he asked, the bed creaking as he leaned forward, the creases deepening between his brows. "Sometimes I wonder about you—*worry* about you." His eyes suddenly glassed over with tears, his lip trembling. "You're my best friend. And while I wanted us to be more—and I know we can't—I still love you."

Meghan sat down on the edge of the bed and took his hand. "I guess happiness is being content in the present moment and not spending too much time thinking about the past or the future," she said, not sure of how else to answer. She definitely couldn't answer for herself *or* for Hester on that one. "So, what did you want to talk to your grandson about?" she asked, changing the subject to something she was better versed in.

Rupert brightened, blinking away his tears. "I think he's met someone, but he won't admit it."

"Oh?" she asked, suddenly interested.

"Yes. He's never talked about another woman since Mary."

Meghan stared at him, wondering if she should take this information as valid.

"You know, when Mary left us," he continued, his gaze so clear that she forgot where they were for a minute, "I thought it had broken him for good." Rupert hung his head, his lips set in a deep frown. "When he asked me if it ever got better . . ." He let out a sigh. "I told him he will go on. Part of him will always be tied to her, but his soul will find a way to live again."

"By 'left,' do you mean . . . ?"

"They were only married a year before the accident," he said. "Her death, along with his parents', was the biggest jolt to our family that I'd felt in a very long time. Not since my own Elaine had passed. It was unbelievable." Rupert blinked, tears falling down his cheeks. "He'd stayed back at the ski lodge and the three of them had headed for the slopes . . ."

Meghan closed her eyes, her fingers finding her lips for a

second to stifle the shock, and she knew in her gut that there was truth in his words. The pain of death that she was so familiar with scratched its way back up into her consciousness, and tears pricked her eyes. She wrung her hands on her knees as she sat on the crisp sheets of Rupert's bed, digesting this news.

This tender moment of what seemed to be clarity coming from Rupert had her mind jumbled with whether or not to believe him, but as she looked at his coherent face now, his message so clear, she knew she probably should. Every glance that Toby had given her now took on new meaning. What did that tell her about the rumors she'd heard? Could this tragedy have hardened him into a man that would steal from his own family?

"I had no idea," she said in a whisper.

"How could you?" Rupert asked. "You've been in California."

Oh yes, I'm Hester. She swallowed, angry at the disease again.

"You remember Elaine?" she asked, yearning for more of the truth.

"Of course," he said. "But *you* remember her?"

"No," she answered honestly, her mind still on their earlier moment about Toby and his late wife.

Rupert nodded, that look of confusion settling in the lines between his brows.

If what Meghan had heard about Toby and his wife was true, she would have to tread lightly. And she wasn't so sure she was strong enough to deal with the pressure of something that heavy. After all, she was still trying to heal herself.

"We're down a person," Tabitha said as she whizzed by Meghan and Tess. "Can one of you take on section two today? Meredith is doing three and seven."

"Of course," Meghan said, grabbing the chock-full wipe-off table map and showing it to Tess. "It's a full house today."

Meredith, who'd just come out of the swinging kitchen doors, stopped at the podium to check her next table. Meghan handed her the table map. "It's crazy. We've got a wait list of an hour. Oh! And Tabitha said she forgot to tell you two. Our big summer party is tomorrow. I hope we can accommodate everyone . . ."

Tess lit up. "Summer party?"

Meghan took the map from Meredith to get her table list.

"It's our annual black-tie Midsummer Night's Dream party for guests and staff. You're invited. Would you like to come?"

"Of course!" Tess said, eyeing Meghan elatedly. "Coincidentally, Meghan just took her fancy dress to the cleaners and everything."

"It's my grandmother's dress," Meghan added.

"Perfect timing then," Meredith said.

It certainly did seem perfect. The idea that she'd actually get a chance to wear a dress that elegant lured her right in. Her mind went back to those days she'd put on her grandmother's dresses as a child. This was Meghan's turn to feel glamorous. Now, she just prayed she could fit in it.

An insanely busy work day hadn't deterred Meghan and Tess from finishing the painting in the living room and kitchen, cleaning up, and getting the rooms back in order. Charlie flopped onto his dog bed right about the time both women fell onto the sofa in exhaustion. The dining table had been pushed back into its spot by the windows, the furniture arranged, the rugs laid.

With the front door wide open to reduce the pungent scent of the paint fumes, Meghan stared at the old television set perched in the corner. "We definitely need to do some updating in here."

"True, but we are blessed with our choices of VHS cassette or DVD when it comes to movie options," Tess teased.

Meghan chuckled and peered out the door at the magnificent view, wishing she had the funds to outfit the porch with cushioned chairs. The tiny slip of blue ocean peeked out from behind the wide expanse of vegetation that bordered the wooden walk on either side, and the deep purple sky was priming itself for the appearance of the first night's stars.

"So do you believe that stuff about Toby?" Tess asked, bringing up their earlier conversation.

"The widowed part or the millionaire-swindler part?"

"They're very conflicting ideas of him, aren't they?" Tess held her hair up into a sweaty ponytail, the heat from outside filling the tiny cottage. "Grieving husband and guy who would rob his family blind."

"Could he be both?" Meghan asked, contemplating the two. "Could one have caused the other?"

Tess dropped her hair and shook her head in response, clearly without an answer. "You could ask *him*. Although I'm not sure the next moment you see him will be the best opportunity."

Meghan gave her friend an inquisitive look.

"He might be at the Midsummer Night's Dream party."

She'd almost forgotten that he could be there. "Whichever of his issues is true—or not true—I'm not ready to deal with any of it right now. I barely have my own life in order . . . Should I back out of the party?"

Charlie got up and sauntered through the open door to the front porch, dropping down on it with a thump and lying on his side.

"You don't have to do anything that drastic," Tess replied. "It's a big party. You can hang out with me and the staff. If he's there, I'll bet you'll barely even see him."

Meghan nodded, thinking. "I came here to have a break from my problems. Not to add to them. But somehow, I have." She turned toward the warm breeze coming in off the ocean.

Tess's normally lighthearted expression downturned. "So will you keep seeing Rupert?"

Her friend's question caused indecision to tug at Meghan. Poor Rupert had nothing to do with any of it. But being tied to

Rupert would mean she'd be forced to see Toby, and she was starting to wonder if it was a good idea to keep running into him. "Maybe I'll shorten my next few visits, tapering off until I finally just stop," she thought aloud, already worrying that Rupert would miss Hester terribly.

"Maybe that's the best thing," her friend said.

Meghan took in a deep breath of the calming, salty air. "Yeah. It probably is."

FOURTEEN

"What do you want to do today?" Meghan asked, padding into the dining area, holding her morning cup of coffee. With the inn's restaurant closed for party preparations, Meghan and Tess had the day off. She pulled out a chair across from her best friend and took a seat.

"Anything you're burning to see that you haven't since you've been back?" Tess asked, already sitting at the table in a T-shirt, her bare legs crossed, wearing glasses that Meghan only saw her wear just before and after sleeping.

Meghan chewed on her lip, combing through the days of her youth to answer Tess's question. Then, suddenly her time at Pappy's grave came back to her. "You know, right before Pappy died, he told me to go to 'Ricroft.' Do you know of it, by chance?"

"No, it's a place?"

"*I've* never heard of anywhere called that, but the way Pappy said it—'go to Ricroft'—it sounds like it."

Tess pulled out her phone. "Let's do a little search and see if anything comes up in the area. How do you spell it?"

"No idea. R-I-C-R-O-F-T maybe?"

Tess typed it in and peered down at the screen, frowning. "Nope. Not a thing."

Meghan shrugged it off. "It was probably nothing."

"Well, since we're at the beach, why don't we bake in the sun until we're crispy like toast, and then go buy all the fixings to make margaritas that we can have while we get ready for tonight."

"That sounds amazing," Meghan said before taking a sip of the sweet, creamy liquid, the bite of coffee just enough to give her senses a jolt. "I have to see Rupert and then pick up my dress first, and then we'll spend the whole day on the beach."

"We'll glow tonight after all that sun," Tess said happily. "Oh! I just thought." She sat up. "You get to wear your grandmother's earrings! That's exciting."

"Yes." She'd get to wear the earrings she'd never imagined she would. In an odd way, she felt like it was Pappy telling her to believe in herself and one day, she'd be someone she was proud of.

Meghan knew that she should save her tip money, but she stopped in to Lost Love Coffee for an iced latte and a little time to herself to get her mind ready for her visit with Rupert. She gave her order to Chloe and then perused the relics. Under the hiss of the latte machine, as Chloe cleaned it for the drink, Meghan stopped at the journal pages that she'd read the other day.

"We think we've found another page of that diary," Chloe said, nodding toward the glass from the bar, where she was dumping the shot of espresso into the cup. "The second-hand shop found it wedged in an old picture frame. It had apparently gotten separated from the others. The owner dropped it by."

Intrigued, Meghan leaned over it and read the entry:

Sometimes I feel like the worst person in the world. I'll never be able to make this better. The guilt of choosing myself over my family is a weight I wish no one to ever have to bear. I still think about those untainted days ... The first day I'd met one of the best people in my life. I'd made him laugh. Just sitting there, in my favorite dress, on a bench by the sea, writing a postcard to Aunt June ...

Meghan's breath caught. Those final words screamed at her. "How long has this journal entry been on display?" she asked, swallowing, her mouth bone dry.

Chloe slid the coffee across the bar. "Just a couple of days. Why? Do you think it's too personal? I was iffy, but it mentioned such a lighthearted moment ..."

Meghan took the cup of coffee on autopilot, not hearing Chloe's explanation, her mind consumed with getting answers. "You know Toby Meyers?"

The machine hissed again as the barista wiped the spout with a rag. "The guy with the inn?"

"Yes, has he brought his grandfather here since you displayed this?"

The barista gave her an odd look. "Not that I know of. Isn't his grandfather at Rosewood Manor?"

"Yes," Meghan answered breathlessly, trying to tell herself that this was all a huge coincidence, her eyes fixed on the journal entry she didn't want to admit to herself was *strikingly* similar to Rupert's story of meeting Hester Quinn.

What if Rupert actually did know her? What if the story was true and Toby had no idea? If Rupert wasn't as delusional as they'd thought, he might be eligible for that medicine the doctor mentioned and his memory loss could be halted for even just a bit more. Or maybe he'd reverted back to his twenties to avoid the pain altogether, and with counseling or something, he could have more memory than they thought. As much as she didn't want to get involved with Toby, Meghan would have to tell him and the hospital staff as soon as she confirmed it.

She snapped a photo of the journal entry with her phone. "Thank you!" she said to Chloe, holding up her coffee cup and racing out the door. She needed to see Rupert right now.

"Hello," Meghan said tentatively, sitting down beside Rupert. "How's your day going?"

"As good as any other," Rupert replied.

She wanted to blurt out all her questions the minute she'd walked through the door, but she knew better. Instead, she asked, her words careful, "Did you know that I had a journal?"

He looked at her, his eyes glazed, a confused look in them. "How would I know? I don't know you."

"What?" she asked, taken aback by his answer.

He kicked off his slippers and put his bare feet under the covers. "Are we having cream pie tonight for dessert?"

Meghan's heart fell into her stomach. "You don't know me?" she asked. The idea of him not recognizing Hester was incredibly more concerning than when he thought she *was* Hester.

"Are you new here?" he asked, busying himself with one of his books—a big, glossy hardback of Hollywood stars that lay open across his lap.

She let his question go and scooted closer to him to see the page he was looking at, all the while trying to keep her disappointment in check. Then, she spotted a picture of a woman with dark hair and a jawline the shape of hers. "Do you know Hester Quinn?" she asked, tapping the page.

He looked up at her with those cloudy eyes for a long moment and didn't speak. But then a tear fell down his cheek.

"What is it?" she asked.

Rupert didn't answer. He closed his eyes and laid his head back on the pillow. "I need to sleep," he said.

She inwardly cursed herself for taking so long at the coffee shop. She'd missed her window and now Rupert wasn't able to converse with her. As he lay there, instantly falling asleep, she willed him to wake up and tell her everything, but perhaps it was all just wishful thinking, a fantasy, and the doctors were right. She pondered why she was so invested, why she cared so much about Rupert and his failing mind. And she knew exactly why. She wanted to save him, give him even a few more days of his life back, something she hadn't been able to do for Pappy.

"What if Rupert became lucid or he's subconsciously decided that he doesn't want us to know that he has ties to Hester Quinn?" Meghan asked Tess, as she hung her grandmother's plastic-draped dress she'd picked up at the cleaners in her closet and plopped down on her unmade bed. "What if he was putting on the fact that he didn't know me?"

"Or what if he has the delusional disorder and Alzheimer's they've diagnosed him with, he was having an off day, and you're just a sucker for happy endings?" Tess countered. She lowered herself down beside Meghan, pulling a pillow across her lap. "They're doctors, Meghan. They know."

"You're probably right," Meghan said, her shoulders slumping as she climbed down next to Charlie, who'd found a sun spot in the bottom corner of the bed. She stroked his thick fur. "But it doesn't explain that page I read in the journal," she said, hanging on to the tiny shred of evidence. "It might prove that Rupert can have the drugs he needs to slow down the Alzheimer's. They've pegged him as completely out there, but I wonder if it's not so far-fetched." What she didn't want to say was that Tabitha's story about Toby was weighing on Meghan, and the medicine could make Rupert lucid enough to give her an answer as to whether Toby was entitled to Rupert's money.

"I wonder where the rest of the journal is," Tess said.

"I was wondering the same thing. From what Chloe said, very recently, the second-hand store found a few more pages and gave them to the coffee shop. I mean, they couldn't sell them—who would want a few ripped pages? But how did *they* get them?"

Tess tossed the pillow aside, a tiny smile twitching at the edges of her lips. "I know you. Something tells me that I'm going to spend my beach day rooting through old relics at a second-hand shop . . ."

Charlie shifted under her hand with a groan, as if he understood.

Meghan gave her a please-let's-do-this smile. "You know I won't be able to sit still in a beach chair until I have the answer to whether the second-hand store has more, one way or another." She leaned over her dog. "Charlie, you can come too."

Charlie sat up with expectant eyes, his tail giving a swish on the sheets.

"Come on, Charlie," Tess said. "Your mom wants to go on a wild goose chase, but not your kind of goose."

The dog jumped off the bed and waited at the door.

"You never know what we might find," Meghan said, feeling optimistic.

"That's definitely true with you: you never know . . ."

With Charlie secured next to a bowl of water on the porch by the open double doors, Meghan and Tess went inside The Memory Box, the second-hand shop in town. Meghan ignored Tess's loaded glances as they followed the owner through the maze of junk piles. Large wooden paddle fans on the high ceilings of the old barn-like space did little to cool the summer heat, but the open doors at the front and back allowed the sea breeze to filter in, keeping them all from overheating.

The old man everyone called Simp, short for his last name Simpson, looked to be about seventy-five, hunched at the shoulders in his button-up cotton shirt with the sleeves rolled to the elbows. "I remember I'd found the pages when I went through a pile of old memorabilia that had sat at the back of the shop for a while," he said, leading them through the showroom as it was called on the welcome sign (if one could call it that) and into a warehouse-style back room. "It must have been sitting here for twenty years..."

Twenty years? "The pages?" Meghan asked.

"The pile," he clarified with a smile.

He gestured to an enormous grouping of random objects, heaped on top of one another—old record players and televisions, wooden furniture, books, lamps, some tin boxes that Meghan had no idea of their purpose... There was so much there, she could hardly imagine where to look for a single journal.

"As the showroom empties out, I add new pieces," he explained, putting his hands on his wide hips.

"So, when people buy things in the shop, you put more out, but until then, it sits here," Tess clarified.

"That's right," he said with a nod, as he began to sift through the pile of junk.

Tess widened her eyes at Meghan.

A loud clatter brought their attention back to the owner, who was head-first in the pile, a large brass urn rolling away from him. Meghan stopped it with her foot and righted it.

"I saw these the other day," he said, his voice muffled from behind the items. With a wipe of his brow, he handed a few more pages to Meghan. "They're yours if you want them."

Meghan peered down at the papers, the same curly script filling them, excitement bubbling up inside. "Yes!" she said, holding them to her chest. "I'd love to have them. Are there any more?" she asked, glancing around where he'd been digging.

The old man shook his head. "That's all I've found so

far. They didn't talk about love, so I didn't bother calling the coffee shop to see if they'd like them." He led them back to the front. "No idea how they got here..." he said over his shoulder. "They must have been shoved in the boxes with other items."

Meghan grabbed a pen and a scrap of paper from her handbag and wrote down her name and phone number. "If you find any more pages, could you give me a call?"

"Of course," he said, filing it away with the rest of the mess on the counter.

With the papers held tightly against her, she thanked the owner and untied Charlie. "I'm glad you came with me," she told Tess.

"What are friends for besides forgoing margarita shopping for a dusty junk shop?" she teased. "Should we at least grab an ice cream cone while we read them?"

"That sounds great." Meghan leaned down and rubbed Charlie's head. "Want some more water and a puppy cone?" she asked. Charlie walked along beside them, an extra bounce in his step as if he'd understood.

They headed along the sidewalk toward the bright pink and yellow umbrella-clad tables of the ice cream shop. Seagulls squawked above them in a bright blue sky, the heat soaking down to Meghan's bones as she held the pages by their corners, trying not to bend them any more than they already were or smear the ink with her hot hands.

When they arrived, Tess got Meghan's order and told her not to read a thing until she returned. Then Meghan took Charlie to the community dog bowl at the back of the shaded outdoor dining area. She sat down at one of the tables and used the heavy salt and pepper shakers to keep the journal pages from blowing away, dying to read them.

After what seemed like forever, Tess walked toward them

with two heaping ice cream cones, handing the mint choco-late chip one to her. Meghan licked it around the base to keep the melting ice cream from dripping down the cone, remem-bering how she and Pappy used to sit there and do the same thing. *Try a new flavor*, he'd always encourage her, though she inevitably got the mint chocolate chip. *But this is my favorite*, she'd say. As she took another crisp and icy lick of her cone, she could hear his words even now: *How do you know it's your favorite until you've tried them all? Just because you're comfortable with something doesn't always mean it's the best.*

"Sit, sit," Meghan said, pushing the memory away, the pages calling to her. "I can't stand the suspense anymore."

Tess pulled a chair up beside her, the two of them huddled over the letters. The next entry read:

> *I'm so glad that I don't have to make movie decisions on my own. I'd have jumped at* Cupid's Goddess *and it tanked on opening night. Thank heavens for good friends. Sometimes I feel like a fraud, a puppet in everyone else's hands, but at the end of the day, I've proved that I can't make my own decisions or my life would be a disaster . . .*

"It is Hester," Meghan said, eyes wide as she looked at her friend in awe. Meghan licked a runaway drip off her cone. "The friend who advised her against the movie has to be Rupert. It matches his story."

Tess took a nibble of her chocolate ice cream. "Unless Rupert thinks he's someone else."

"But the journal entry in the coffee shop also said that she'd met someone on a bench when she was writing a postcard. Rupert knew that too."

"It does seem awfully odd that a man who isn't even aware

of his present surroundings would be able to research that much information," Tess agreed.

"If he did know her, and he seemed to be in love with her, what happened?" She didn't wait for an answer before she began reading the other entries—one per page, just like the rest. Meghan moved the salt and pepper paperweights and held the flapping pages down with her hand to read more.

I've been so busy in production that I haven't had time to think about my wreck of a life, which is good. I've made such a mess of it . . .

As the words made more and more sense to Meghan, she looked at Tess. But before she could say anything, the ball of ice cream fell from her cone into her lap. "Ah!" she squealed, trying to save her shorts. When she did, Tess jumped up, the pages flying in the coastal wind and landing on the other side of the picket fence between the ice cream shop and the road.

Meghan dropped her cone, grabbed Charlie's leash, and ran to the little gate, fiddling recklessly with the latch as the three papers flew upward in swirling motions, blowing across the road. Once the gate was open, they pushed past a few tourists on their way in, sprinting around the fenced-off dining area toward the road, where they had to wait for passing cars.

The pages took flight on the sea wind that carried them over the massive dune toward the ocean. Meghan scrambled across the street as soon as she could, digging her flip-flops into the fiery sand, slipping on the steep incline that sent her sliding backward while Charlie barked on the end of his leash.

Panic in her chest, she tried again, coaxing the dog, but the dune was too high to climb. Out of breath, she turned to find Tess, who was down the road, trying to get up a lower hill with not much success. The nearest public stairway was so far away that she knew the journal pages were gone by now. Even still, she ran down to them and bounded up each wooden stair as quickly as she could until she got to the top. Charlie's tail wagged in excitement as she dropped his leash. He hopped down into the sand and ran down to the water, the leash dragging behind him. Shielding her eyes, Meghan peered down the beach in both directions, but the pages were nowhere to be found.

"Do you see them?" Tess said, her hands on her knees as she gasped for air.

"No," Meghan replied before stepping onto the beach. She checked the seagrass on the other side of the dune, all the way to where they'd been sitting, to see if the pages had gotten caught in it, all the while scanning the beachgoers and the surf. For a second, she was sure they were floating in the water, but when she ran down to it, it was just a reflection.

"I can't believe that just happened," Tess said, catching up to her with Charlie.

"Unbelievable." Meghan sat down on the sand, devastated. The dog flopped down beside her.

Tess threw up her hands but then relaxed. "You know what? No harm, no foul," she said.

"What?" Meghan looked up at her friend, shielding her eyes from the sun, baffled.

"Until an hour ago, you didn't even know those pages existed. And it's only luck that the old man could even find them. I doubt the rest said anything much anyway."

"They proved that Rupert might know what he's talking about," Meghan said.

"But did they?" Tess countered. "I mean, would the hospital really take that as some kind of evidence? I doubt it."

"I can tell Toby, though—with or without the pages."

"If he'll believe you. But, regardless, it did give you what *you* wanted to know—a definite connection between Rupert and Hester. Maybe you can get more out of him another day."

"I guess you're right," Meghan said, standing up and facing the wind to let it cool her off. With a deep breath to calm her nerves, she took Charlie's leash. "Come on, boy, let's get you some water."

FIFTEEN

"What do you think everyone at Zagos is doing right now?" Tess asked Meghan, leaning back on her elbows, her face pointed toward the sun as they lay on the loungers they'd dragged out to the beach, along with a jug of margaritas in the cooler.

Meghan turned her head to address Tess, unsure if her friend's eyes were open or closed behind her pink sunglasses. "Working their fingers to the bone."

Tess rolled over and grabbed her margarita, sipping the tangy nectar from the wide straw that matched the insulated thermos they'd put their beverages in to keep them cold in the heat. "I'll bet not one of them is doing what we're doing."

"Definitely not, in the city," Meghan said with a laugh.

Tess perked up. "You did the right thing coming here."

"You think so?"

"I know so."

Meghan sat up and swung her legs around to face Tess, digging her feet into the warm sand. "You know, when my parents died and Pappy took me in, I didn't want him to think I was mooching off him. I would clean the house and he never once had to wash any dishes."

Tess leaned over and got her drink. "How would he think that? You were fifteen, with no parents."

"I just wanted him to know that I appreciated the work it took to raise me." She looked out at the ocean, the spray of it splashing haphazardly as the waves rolled in. "I feel the same way now. I want him to know that I can contribute somehow. I'm just not sure how to do that."

"You're one of the best people I know," Tess told her, pushing her sunglasses up onto the top of her head. "And if anyone will figure it out, it's you. Give yourself some time and just enjoy where you are right now. This moment is a gift from your pappy because had he not left you the house, you wouldn't have it."

"It's my moment of calm," Meghan said, Pappy's words coming back to her. *Find your calm.*

"It fits you like a glove," Tess said, her hands on the hips of her little black dress, her eyes sparkling with excitement from her bronzed face as she took in Meghan's green vintage strapless gown. "You're putting mine to shame, and this is the dress that got me a date with Alex Tisdale."

Meghan laughed, remembering Tess's one date with the heart-throb D-list off-Broadway actor who played in local commercials around New York.

"I'm still waiting on that second call . . ."

Meghan fastened her grandmother's emerald earrings and took a look at herself in the floor-length mirror on the back of Pappy's door. With her hair swept up and make-up on, in that dress, she hardly recognized herself.

"You look amazing," Tess said. "Like you've just stepped out of another era."

"Do you think it's too much?" she asked, smoothing the A-line skirt as she assessed her reflection. The sound of Pappy's voice filled her ears: *You look beautiful.*

"Not at all. It's perfect."

Even if it had been too much, it was all she had. "The shoes are a little big, but I can make them work." Charlie sniffed them as if he understood and wanted to be included in the conversation.

Tess smiled. "I'll bet your grandmother would be so proud." She took Meghan's hands and twirled her around before letting go with a contented sigh. "We're going to dance the night away tonight."

Toby floated into Meghan's mind. She definitely wouldn't be dancing with her boss in front of everyone she worked with if he showed up, especially after Tabitha had confided in her about Toby's plans. "Why did I agree to go to this again?" she asked.

"Because this party will have all the food we could ever want, and an open bar . . ." Tess grabbed Meghan by the elbow and the two of them headed for the door.

Meghan and Tess walked under the enormous balloon arch in various shades of blue, up the wide steps of the front porch and through the front doors of Mariner's Inn. The lobby was decked out in twinkling white lights, strung in rows along the walls and meandering up the branches of the potted trees, with buckets of champagne and filled glasses bubbling on all the tables. Live beach music sailed toward them from the dining room.

"This is going to be a blast," Tess said, grabbing a glass of champagne before linking her arm with Meghan's as she floated toward the dining room in her black ballet flats.

Tess and Meghan walked past the tables on their way to the bar. Their customary white tablecloths had been replaced by glittery aquamarine linens with enormous explosions of white roses in the centers. "Want a drink?" Tess asked her, holding up her half-finished flute of champagne.

"Hi!" Tabitha sashayed over, barely recognizable without her usual ponytail. "We're all out on the porch if you two want to join us," she said above the music, as she jutted a thumb over her shoulder toward the open doors that were also encased in balloons and white lights.

"Meghan's just getting a drink first," Tess said, grabbing the menu from the bar and sliding it over.

Meghan ordered a rum and Coke to appease her friend and the two of them followed Tabitha outside. Three of the kitchen hands were there, plus Meredith, the hostess, and a collection of waitstaff.

"Everything is so beautiful," Meghan said, peering up at the canopy of twinkle lights that had been erected just for the party.

"Mr. Meyers spared no expense," Meredith said. "By the way, you look gorgeous tonight." She gave Meghan a big smile.

"Thank you," Meghan replied.

"You look like you're ready for the runway," Meredith added, her gaze sliding up and down Meghan, making her self-conscious.

"Meghan, there's Darren Fields," Tess said, interrupting them to point out the inn's chef. "We should go say hello and make sure you get to talk to him."

"Does Meghan have a thing for the chef?" one of the staff members teased.

"Definitely not, but she might have a thing for his food." Tess set down her empty champagne flute and waved a hand at the pathway.

Meghan didn't know what Tess wanted her to say to Darren, but after mentioning it to the group, she figured she should probably at least go say hello. They walked over to the middle-aged man as he stood next to the railing with the sapphire sea at his back.

"I haven't had a chance to really meet you," Meghan said to him, holding out her hand. "I'm Meghan Gray and this is Tess Fuller."

Darren shook her hand and then greeted Tess.

"Are you cooking tonight?" Tess asked, grabbing a glass of lemonade from a tray on one of the serving tables.

"I'm not," Darren replied. "Boss had the party catered and gave me the night off so I could enjoy it."

Tess sipped her lemonade and twirled the straw around, making the ice cubes clink together. "Our Meghan here loves to cook and if you ask me, I think she has the makings to be a chef."

Meghan waved her comment off. "I have a few dishes, that's all. I'm definitely not a chef."

Tess's straw-swirling stopped cold and she looked at Meghan like she'd just blown the opportunity of a lifetime. Darren was pulled toward another partygoer, and after he left, Tess jumped in front of her friend. "What the heck, Meghan?"

Meghan looked around to be sure Tess wasn't making a scene.

"That was the perfect moment to strike up a conversation about your dream job. You could've said anything—asked about where he went to school, what his favorite dish to cook is, how he ended up in the Outer Banks—but instead, you said you weren't a chef."

"I'm not," Meghan said, taking a long drink of her rum and Coke, hoping it would relax her.

"And you won't ever be with that attitude."

Tess had never spoken to Meghan like that before and she didn't know what to say, so she turned toward the wind and closed her eyes, feeling lost. "Let's just enjoy the party," she said, turning back to Tess, who was shaking her head. "I'll have other chances to talk to Darren. We work with him."

Tess squinted her eyes. "What aren't you telling me?"

"What do you mean?"

"There's another reason that you brushed off Darren. What is it?"

Fear crept in, and Meghan locked her jaw, not wanting to say anything. She didn't want to say it out loud because actually telling someone what she'd heard would make it real and she didn't know if she had the guts to do that ... A caterer walked by with shrimp cornbread cakes on skewers and offered them to Meghan and Tess, but neither of them took one.

"I need you to tell me right now."

Meghan sucked in a chestful of briny air. "After I spoke to Vinnie, I overheard him on the phone with someone ..." she said. "He *did* try my chartreuse hollandaise sauce. He said it was 'middle-of-the-road' and that I was deluded if I ever thought I could be a chef."

"He's completely off his rocker," Tess said. "Everyone loves it. Why would you choose to believe him over your friends?"

Meghan fiddled with the bottom of her glass. "Sometimes friends are blind to the facts because they see the person behind it." She set her drink down on the wooden railing.

"Vinnie wanted a big name. That's it. His decision had nothing to do with your cooking. You know how he is—all flash. He'd rather go in a different direction than take on a no-name chef. I guarantee it."

"Sometimes I wonder if I just like to cook because it brings me back to the one place in my life where I didn't feel any pain. What if I got into it and it wasn't what I thought?"

Tess smiled at a passer-by before turning her attention back to Meghan. "Well, I'm not going to talk you into it. It's up to you to know what you want."

"That's just it. I don't know what I want. I don't have a clue."

"Growing up, you used to love everything trendy. You studied all the fashion magazines, had the most up-to-date clothes ... You enjoyed being the center of attention. At parties, you could jump in the middle of a group of people and start talking, making everyone laugh. I used to look up to you because there was always something about you that was bigger than life. But as you got older, you pulled into yourself more, and now you're barely a shadow of who you were. But I can tell you that I still see you.

You're doing a good job of hiding behind that fear of yours, but you're still just as fabulous."

Meghan shook her head, the compliment making her uncomfortable.

"Look at you tonight! You're stunning and everyone is eyeing you. You could command the room in a second. I'll bet if you asked, they'd bring food out for you to cook right here in front of everyone, but instead, you're twisting your hands and shying away from the crowd."

"I had big dreams for New York and I couldn't make it happen," Meghan countered. "That should say something."

"And besides that one night when you tried to cook for Vinnie, what did you do to move your career along?"

Meghan stared at her, unable to come up with an answer.

"You wait, Meghan. You wait, hoping success will find you, but maybe you need to go out there and get it yourself."

"And how am I supposed to do that?" she asked.

"Start with what brings you joy and throw yourself into it. What lights your fire?"

Meghan thought about the days since they'd moved back to the Outer Banks—what got her up in the mornings? "In a very strange way, seeing Rupert lights my fire." She hadn't really let it sink in until now, but the idea that she was going to stop seeing him had been weighing on her, and she didn't want to stop. As unlikely as it was, she felt like she had a bond with him.

"So, you like playing the role of Hester Quinn. Maybe you're an actress."

Meghan laughed. "I don't like pretending to be someone else. I like the connection I have with Rupert."

Tess eyed her. "You're having some sort of odd attachment issues or something, but at least you know what you like."

Meghan nodded, pondering what it was she really enjoyed, but she couldn't quite put her finger on it.

"We'll start there." Tess threw her hands in the air. "It's a gorgeous evening! The band is playing; drinks are flowing; we look like a million bucks. Let's act like it."

"You're right," she said, deciding to live in the moment, just like she and Tess had talked about on the beach today. For one night, she wouldn't think about the past or what might happen in the future. The night was hers, and she was going to enjoy it.

Just as they began walking toward the tray of crab balls, Toby stepped into their path, wearing a light blue summer suit that worked wonders with his azure eyes and the gold flecks in his hair. His gaze slid down her dress and back up to her face, something consuming his thoughts.

"I finally meet the boss of this place," she said, lighthearted but careful given the way he was looking at her, his expression pensive.

Tess huffed out a little chuckle as if in support of her.

When he didn't answer Meghan's comment, she added, "You don't spend a lot of time here." She didn't want to seem confrontational, but it was odd that she'd only seen him outside that one time and he'd never set foot in the inn while she'd worked there.

"It's . . . difficult." He broke eye contact and looked away, letting out a long breath. Then, as if making an attempt to redirect the conversation, he said, "Looks like you two were having a serious discussion. Everything all right?"

"Yes," Meghan replied quickly, to keep her best friend from saying something about her profession that she'd have to explain. "We were just talking about . . . food." She shielded her eyes from the evening sun reflecting off the water, peering over at the vast array of hors d'oeuvres, artfully arranged in a splash of color on a table that extended both inside and outside the open glass doors.

"Ah, well there's no shortage of that tonight," Toby said.

"I'm gonna head over there and grab a bite," Tess said, her words loaded. If she'd been trying to be inconspicuous in leaving them alone, she'd failed miserably. "Want anything?"

Toby shook his head. "No, thank you, Tess."

While she hadn't eaten in ages, and she'd been starving up to that point, Meghan's stomach now felt like it had a boulder in the bottom of it. "No, thanks."

"Suit yourselves," Tess said with a smile, her eyes widening suggestively as if to say, "Be careful." Then she padded off, leaving Meghan and Toby standing there.

"When did you start working at the inn?" he asked, as Tess meandered through the crowd. Meghan suddenly wanted her friend by her side to add lightheartedness to the moment.

"I'm surprised you don't know," Meghan replied. "I'd think you'd know everything that went on."

Her comment hadn't been meant to sting him, but tension showed in his shoulders. "Tabitha manages for me. I let her make staffing decisions."

That didn't seem like someone who had his heart in the business. "The staff barely knows you," she pointed out, trying to get a handle on what, exactly, his motivation was with the inn.

"I'm not really involved with that end of things a whole lot. I've hired great people to do the nitty gritty for me. And I've been busy with plans for expansion."

Did he really plan to sell it and run off with the money? With his hands-off approach, it sure seemed like it. Her hopes were dashed. She didn't want to admit it to herself, but she'd been holding out for Toby, silently convincing herself that he wasn't the person everyone thought he was. "You don't want to be involved?" she asked, grasping for something—anything—to explain his behavior. "Work behind the counter, meet the guests, get to know your employees . . . ?"

He clenched his jaw as if he were holding back the real answer, and her stomach plummeted. He didn't seem interested in even one of the things she'd just listed. Which meant, to her utter disappointment, that the rumors were probably true.

Tess's impression of him the other night came back to her:

He's got issues. "I should go find Tess at the food table," Meghan suggested.

Toby met her gaze. "All right," he said.

As she walked away, she glanced over her shoulder to find him turning toward a tray of champagne. He picked up one of the flutes and downed it like a shot.

"Oh my goodness! I won!" Tess cried, before leaving Meghan at their table and rushing up to the DJ to get her beach gift basket full of starfish-shaped soaps and beachy candles that had become hers when her raffle number had been called. Tess held it above her head like a trophy as she made her way back and plopped down. She set the cellophane-wrapped basket on the glittery table, turning it around so Meghan could see.

"Very nice," Meghan said.

"Next up is the Guest Dance," the DJ announced. "A great way to network, meet new people, or at the very least, get the blood flowing for a two-minute song. Men's numbers are in the bowl to my right and women's are to my left."

"The DJ's got a point. We'll never meet new people unless we put ourselves out there," Tess said, pushing her basket to the center of the table and standing up. "Grab us each a drink and I'll go get you a number."

Tess thought everything had some grand purpose, and they'd magically get a number that would propel them into some kind of fated moment with the person they were meant to connect with. But the truth of the matter was that, deep down, while Meghan didn't really believe those kinds of things were true, she hoped Tess was right.

"I'll probably end up getting matching numbers with *that* guy," Meghan said, pointing to a hunched-over elderly gentleman wiping his nose with his hanky.

"Well, you seem to like hanging out with old guys," Tess said.

"Maybe he'll be your next project." With a wink, her friend got up and nearly skipped to the DJ's table to grab them both a slip of paper with a number. Before Meghan could even get them a drink, she returned and held out both her fists. "Which one is yours?" Tess asked.

"It doesn't matter," Meghan said with a laugh. "Just give me one."

"No." Tess wriggled her fists and closed her eyes. "Think about it. Which one is pulling you toward it?"

Meghan stared at Tess's hands, not feeling anything at all, wondering if she were missing some sort of cosmic connection to the universe. "Left," she said, randomly picking one.

Tess opened up her hand, revealing a slip of paper with the number thirty-two printed on it. Meghan plucked it out of her friend's palm.

Tess opened her own number. "Fifty-eight," she said, looking around excitedly.

"Over the next song," the DJ called into the microphone above the buzzing crowd, "find the other person with your number to pair off for the dance." Then, with the kick of a drumbeat, another song began to play.

"I'll be back with my partner!" Tess hurried into the crowd, holding out her number happily while Meghan hung back, wondering why she'd let her friend talk her into doing the Guest Dance at all. The truth was that Meghan did want to enjoy herself, but it was difficult to do after talking to Toby. She wanted to retreat back to Pappy's, where she didn't have to put herself out there. It was as if she had to relearn how to be social, like some long-lost skill, while Tess excelled at it.

Then, her breath caught as Toby walked onto the dance floor. He seemed slightly less anxious than he had, and he moved through the crowd, shaking hands and nodding in polite conversation. Tess ran over to him and flashed her number, but Toby shook his head before the two of them started talking for a second.

As she watched the exchange, Meghan thought again about how she'd had almost the same life as Tess, the two of them following a nearly identical path, yet Tess was perfectly content, while Meghan's life was a complete mess.

She snapped out of her thoughts as Toby began walking toward her.

"What's your number?" Toby asked tentatively, once he'd reached her table.

"Thirty-two."

He showed her his slip of paper with a thirty-two on it. "Looks like we're dance partners."

All the oxygen left her lungs. She looked over at Tess, just knowing she'd have to endure some sort of comment about how the stars had aligned, but Tess was happily chatting with a waiter named Russ.

"What are the odds?" she asked, forcing a smile to cover her nerves, her heart hammering at the idea that Toby would seek her out, her hopes getting the better of her, despite her concerns over the rumors.

"Pretty bad, actually," he replied. "I traded my slip of paper with that guy," he said, pointing to a man in a three-piece suit who was laughing hysterically at something his dance partner was saying, while wiping the sweat from his forehead. "So he could pair up with the woman he's talking to."

Her hopes fell yet again. She couldn't really think he'd have actually tried to dance with her. The urge to run out of the inn and down the street toward Pappy's was strong, but she knew it would only cause questions from Tess and her coworkers.

Toby looked down at her. "I can always switch back . . ." He turned toward the man, but she stood and caught his arm.

"No! No, that's fine," she said, not wanting to cause any drama with the other man. The dance was probably only three minutes. She could handle this.

The DJ announced the final numbers for people who still

hadn't found their dance partner. When everyone had been paired up, a jazzy, slow song began to play and Toby held out a hand to her. She took it, his warm, gentle touch heightening her nerves, and he spun her outward. Her dress puffed out around her legs, the two of them like an old Hollywood couple with him in his summer suit and her in a vintage gown.

Allowing herself to forget the things that usually got in the way, Meghan let herself savor the moment, the feel of Toby's hand at her back and his fingers intertwined with hers. It was a totally different feeling from the beach dances she'd had standing on Pappy's feet, as he guided her through the steps. Toby's understanding of the dance was clear, his lead easy to follow, his embrace more commanding than Pappy's had been, and his woodsy, spicy scent intoxicating.

"Where did you learn to dance?" she asked, letting her guard slip more than she wanted it to.

"My mother made me take dance lessons as a boy. She said it would help me when I was older." He gave Meghan a spin.

She looked up at him. "And did it?"

"It got me a date with Jeanine Simpson in the tenth grade when I asked her to dance at our school formal. Otherwise, its value has been questionable at best." He offered a small smile, making her wish she could always see that little glimmer in his eye. She wondered if it had helped him at his wedding, but he hadn't mentioned one. Was it fictional—something out of Rupert's imagination—or just too painful to mention?

Toby's phone went off, slicing through the moment, and for an instant he paused, but then he reached into his pocket, silenced it, and carried on dancing, the two of them swaying to the music.

"You can get that if you want to," Meghan offered.

He gave her another twirl. "It's a party. I'm trying to enjoy it."

"What if it's important?" she pressed, thinking of Rupert.

He took a step toward her, invading her personal space and

causing her heart to patter, and then guided her backward, at arm's length. "They'll call back." He wound her up into his arms and dipped her, making her laugh despite herself. But when she saw the eyes of the other inn workers on her, she sobered.

"What if it's Rupert having one of his meltdowns?"

There was an instant of hesitation as he thought it through. But then Toby said, "He has an entire staff devoted to his care. He'll be fine for two more minutes." He pulled her toward him and moved to the music.

His phone pinged with a message.

"Please check it," Meghan urged him, letting go of his hand and standing still in the middle of the dance floor.

The gentle look on his face faded and then hardened. Toby reached into his pocket and pulled out his cell phone, putting it to his ear while plugging the other. He listened for a beat before his face fell, that look of apprehension sliding back into place on his features.

"What is it?" she asked as he ended the call.

"You were right. The call was concerning my grandfather. He's awake and they need him to take his medicine, but he's unresponsive. They're wondering if my presence will help."

"Maybe I should go too."

"I'd hate for you to leave the party," he said, an incredible compassion in his eyes that she hadn't seen before, making her want to put her hands on his face and tell him it would all be okay.

"Rupert is more important than any party." Meghan took Toby's hand and, without another thought, the two of them rushed out of the inn, jumping into Toby's vehicle and speeding off while Meghan texted Tess to let her know what was going on.

Meghan held her phone tightly as the Range Rover hugged the road around the curves, Toby staring straight ahead. She wasn't sure what had prompted her to do it—maybe it was their dance, or the way the worry on his face seemed deeper today—but she noticed his hand gripping the gearshift tightly and she placed hers on his. He glanced over, surprise registering, and then something else she couldn't decipher, his knuckles releasing, his hand relaxing with her touch. She knew then that whatever they faced when they got there, they'd do it together.

SIXTEEN

"Rupert has taken a turn. Since last night, he has completely drawn into himself and isn't responding to staff," Dr. Hughes said from behind her office desk to Meghan and Toby. "There are a few reasons he may have done this. Being alone much of the time can make someone with Alzheimer's withdraw. We've already seen how he's turning inward, indulging in his fantasies."

"I don't know if he *is* having fantasies," Meghan said.

Dr. Hughes regarded her with interest.

Meghan explained about what she'd read in the journal and the information she'd gotten at the museum, and how they compared to what he'd said, Toby looking on with skeptical curiosity. "I think he actually knows Hester, and he's reverting back to his younger years."

"I'm still not entirely sure that's the case. It doesn't make any sense," Toby replied. "His whole life, we've never heard anything about Hester Quinn. Given how much he's talking about her now, wouldn't he have mentioned the woman to me before the dementia had set in?"

"Depression and his emotions over your parents' death could also be affecting him," Dr. Hughes said, typing notes into her computer and then looking back up at them, clearly not giving what Meghan said any further consideration.

"What do we do to snap him out of it?" Toby asked, untying his tie, the knot hanging loose at his neck, and unbuttoning the top button of his collar.

"Let him know you're here, without putting pressure on him to interact with you."

"Would it make any difference at all if he did know Hester?" Meghan pressed, wishing for a magic bullet to pull him out of this. She recalled the tears streaming down Rupert's cheek and felt very strongly that he had something to say, yet he wasn't able to get the point across.

Dr. Hughes regarded her with empathy as if Meghan were grasping for straws. "I think the important thing here is to keep his mind active."

Meghan turned to Toby. "May I go in to see him with you?"

"Of course," he replied.

"Looks like you two were having a nice night," Dr. Hughes said with a smile as she eyed their clothes. "I'm sorry to have pulled you from it."

Toby's gaze fluttered over to Meghan with fondness. "This is more important," he said.

Meghan couldn't help but wonder about Toby's reasoning as to why it was more important, the rumors swirling around in her head juxtaposed with the connection they'd had during their dance. She wanted to believe he wasn't the person people thought he was, but just like with Rupert's fantasies, maybe she was more of a romantic than she thought she was.

The two of them walked down to Rupert's room and found him sitting in a chair, staring off into space, not even acknowledging them when they came in.

"Gramps?" Toby said, turning on the lamp by his bed. "It's Toby. I came to check on you."

"I'm here too," Meghan said, her heels clicking on the tiled floor as she stepped over. When she got in front of him, Rupert's gaze shifted to her dress, his cloudy eyes widened, filling with tears, tugging at her heart. "What is it?" she whispered, but he didn't answer.

Meghan and Toby took a seat on the bed across from Rupert, the buzz of the lights the only sound in the room. As Meghan sat there in silence, she considered again how the man next to her and the one across from her were the two people on the island she knew the best, besides Tess. The irony wasn't lost on her that she didn't really know either of them at all. So why did she feel like there was nowhere else in the world she wanted to be than right there? She looked over at Toby, allowing her thoughts to show and wondering if he could read them.

He locked eyes with hers, questions in his gaze, but neither of them said a word.

After they'd sat in silence for more time than was bearable, Toby finally stood up. "We never got to finish our dance," he said, offering her a warm look that sent a bolt of delight through her. Putting in one of Rupert's DVDs, he skipped to a scene where Cary Grant led Hester Quinn onto the floor of his New York apartment, set her martini down for her, and pulled her into his arms, an old 1950s song playing as the two of them danced around the room.

Toby took Meghan's hands and pulled her up. With her hand in his, he began to lead, the two of them gliding around the hospital-style floor. Rupert's gaze moved from the wall to them, following their steps with interest, filling Meghan with hope that he might snap out of it. She squeezed Toby's hand and he twirled her out and back in, Rupert's eyebrows rising, his set jaw falling slack with awe.

Allowing their movements to speak for them, Toby's hands were soft when they trailed along her body, as if the two of them were in this together, giving her a shiver of happiness. She let her fingertips caress his shoulder, his other hand finding hers and gently holding it. He pulled her in, his cheek grazing her temple, and she feared that he could feel the beating of her heart and know that it was thumping because she'd never felt anything quite as wonderful as being in his arms.

Before she was ready, the song ended, the actors beginning their dialogue, and Meghan and Toby both slowed to a stop. The two of them looked at Rupert, a smile emerging through the old man's downturned features. "Where are the Baldwins?" he asked out of nowhere, his voice croaking from not being used.

Meghan let go of Toby and walked over to Rupert, thrilled that he was back in his Hester fantasy once more. While it wasn't the lucid man she'd hoped to know, there was something comforting about their little relationship.

"And Audrey?" he continued, stopping her cold.

"What?" she asked, the word coming out on a breath of shock.

"You have on the earrings you gave her." His gaze found Meghan, and he waited expectantly for an answer, but she couldn't speak. Her limbs began to shake.

She turned to Toby and pulled him to her, the spicy scent of him hardly registering as she leaned into his ear. "Audrey is my grandmother, and I'm wearing her earrings," she whispered. She spun around and faced Rupert again, thinking on her feet. "Is Audrey here at the Baldwins'?" she asked.

"She's supposed to be," he said. "Why? Has she left?"

"I don't know," she answered, caught, herself, between the past and present. "I'll be right back," she told Rupert, grabbing Toby by the arm and leading him into the hallway.

"There are too many coincidences for Rupert not to be telling the truth," she said urgently.

"Had you mentioned your grandmother's name to him?" Toby asked.

"No," she replied emphatically. "I've never mentioned her."

"Would he subconsciously know you were her granddaughter since he grew up on the island?" Toby asked. "He might have made that connection but can't verbalize it, so it's coming out through his fantasies."

Meghan rubbed her temples. "I don't think so," she said, his suggestion bringing her back around to the thought that the hope she was holding onto, for this to end up being something more than it actually was, might just be her own fantasy. But what if *she* was right? "Toby, I think he's telling the truth."

"Meghan, you've dealt with this for a few days, but I've dealt with it for years," he said gently. "You're taking this one tiny illusion and building it into more than it is. He's unwell."

"I barely knew my grandmother, and he might have known her," she pressed.

"Yes, he may have known her, but that doesn't mean you'll get any kind of factual information from him about her. He thinks you're an actress from the 1950s, remember?"

"What if that's the only thing he's gotten wrong?"

Toby blew air through his lips, clearly thinking. "It just doesn't make any sense."

"How did he know these things?" The question was just as much for herself as it was for Toby.

He pursed his lips and shook his head as if appeasing her and not really planning to hear her out any further, almost as if he were terrified to hear any more. She wondered if it was out of fear that his grandfather wouldn't be the man Toby had grown up thinking he was, or was it because the rumors were true...?

He ran his fingers through his hair and then looked her straight in the eye with surrender. "Could you please stop this? There's no way it could be true, and you even had *me* wondering at times. But I can't deal with the distraction of it anymore." He rubbed his face, looking exhausted.

Why couldn't he deal with it? She had no idea why this would prick a nerve, but it clearly had and, suddenly, she considered everything from a different point of view. She'd let the romance of the island and Tess's rose-colored-glasses perspective of things cloud her judgment. What if she really was standing there, outside a sick man's room, with a guy using his grandfather's money? That would certainly be more probable.

"I wonder if you *want* it to seem crazy," she said, testing the waters.

His face crumpled in confusion. "What?"

"You want it to seem crazy so I'll leave it alone, but I can't find a reason why other than . . . I have to know. Is it because you don't want anyone interfering in your plan?" There. She'd put it out there.

"What plan is that?" he asked slowly, clearly trying to figure out her angle.

"Your plan to use Rupert's money to fund the inn so you can sell it. That's what people are saying."

His head cocked to the side, his brows pulling together, his lips falling slack. "I'm sorry, what?"

"Tell me that's not what you're doing."

He seemed taken aback, looking at her in a new light, as if someone had clicked on a blinding light above them. The romance of the night washed right off him in an instant and, for a split second, she didn't want to move past this moment for fear they would never return to the place they were in on the dance floor just a little while ago.

"That's not your concern," he said in almost a whisper, the words emerging from a heavy weight that had come over him.

So, the rumors were *true* . . . She scolded herself for dreaming when she should've been more level-headed. Suddenly, she found herself on the verge of tears, refusing to believe that this could be her reality. She wanted to run back to Rupert and demand that he tell her that it was not all a fantasy. "I'm going back in," she said, her words breaking on her emotion.

Toby gently took her arm, thoughts evident on his face. "Maybe it isn't the best idea."

Meghan had to do everything she could to be sure that she hadn't misread things. There were too many coincidences . . . She pulled away from him and pushed open the door to Rupert's room.

"I think Audrey went home," she said as she entered, blinking to clear her tears and leaving Toby in the hallway.

"Well, it is late," Rupert told her.

"Would you like to go outside with me?" she asked, suddenly wondering if taking him out of his room would get him talking more. He'd been so animated when they'd first met him at the restaurant.

"That's not a good idea," Toby said, loping in. "It's dark outside." But Rupert was already getting out of bed and slipping on his shoes.

"That's okay. Rupert can take my arm so I don't get lost." She gave Rupert a wink, making him smile. "You're welcome to come with us, Toby."

"I'm definitely coming with you," he said, his shock from their conversation in the hallway still clear, as Meghan hooked her arm in Rupert's.

They made their way out to the main lobby, Toby stopping only briefly to tell the front desk their plans, and then walked outside. They stood on the sidewalk leading to the parking lot of Rosewood Manor and Rupert tipped his head up toward the inky black sky, the stars glimmering above them like a galaxy of diamonds, his bottom lip wobbling. "Stars," he said. "It's been so long since I've seen the stars."

"You sure are chatty tonight," Meghan said with a laugh, her absolute delight overtaking her. "You're still with us, aren't you?" she leaned into him and asked.

Toby stiffened, clearly disbelieving.

"Let's take the path down to the beach," she said, removing her heels and letting them dangle from her fingers while leading Rupert, who was still gazing up at the night sky.

"I'm not sure we should take him onto the sand," Toby said, striding up beside them. "He might be unsteady."

"I remember taking you to the beach when you were unsteady," Rupert said, addressing Toby. "You were three and you kept falling over."

Toby stared at his grandfather, visibly in amazement that he'd said something coherent. "It's good to see you," Toby said, all his previous tension melting away, fondness in his words, and Meghan understood completely.

As Rupert looked back at his grandson, it was actually the two of them with nothing getting in the way. And she prayed that they could have more moments like these. It might be just enough to remind Toby who his grandfather was and change Toby's life choices if the rumors were true.

"You coming or not?" Rupert asked Toby, pulling on Meghan and stepping down the path.

"Who've you got on your arm there, Gramps?" Toby asked, as if testing Rupert's coherence, pacing along beside them.

"My nurse," he answered.

Toby nodded, but Meghan wouldn't allow Rupert's misstep to deter her efforts. She was either going to prove that Rupert's fantasies weren't so far-fetched or she was going to convince Toby to be a better person—whichever reality was true, she was going to get to the bottom of it no matter how long it took.

They walked the path, the moonlight lighting their way, and the shushing of the waves like a distant lullaby. Rupert was quiet but smiling from ear to ear, and, regardless what had transpired between her and Toby, Meghan was glad that she'd come tonight.

"You two should have a drink," Rupert suddenly said from between Meghan and Toby. He turned to his grandson. "You certainly could use one, and she's a stunner."

Meghan laughed out loud, despite the tension.

"Where did *that* come from, Gramps?" Toby asked.

"I just thought it was worth a mention."

They stopped walking, the three of them standing at the opening to the beach, the waves crashing in silver sparkles onto the shore, the moonlight casting a long beam of white light out to the horizon. Gingerly, Rupert slipped off his loafers and sank his feet into the sand.

"Be careful," Toby said as his grandfather took a step, the gesture warming Meghan and giving her shattered heart a little bit of hope.

"It's all right. I've got a hold of Hester," Rupert replied, switching back to his fantasy again.

"Your nurses aren't going to be happy with us if we let you fall," Toby said, grabbing his arm carefully.

"I'm not going to be happy with you either if you let me fall."

Toby really laughed, and it was the first time Meghan had heard it, the sound rushing through her chest like a surge of elation, their issues over things she'd heard about him seeming so far away in this moment. Toby reached out and took his grandfather's hand, helping him across the sand.

Rupert took in a long, slow breath of beachy air. "Feel that?"

Meghan waited for his explanation.

"Calm," Rupert said, and she felt an unexpected swell of emotion as she thought of that day on the water with Pappy. Tears brimmed in her eyes and she blinked them away. "I haven't been here in . . ." Rupert continued. He looked up at Toby. "When was the last time?"

"A few years ago, we took you."

"Who did?" Rupert asked, taking a step toward the water.

"I did. With . . . Mary." His voice broke on the word.

Meghan kept her gaze forward, her pulse racing, her breath leaving her. What Rupert had said about Toby having a wife named Mary seemed very true. She wasn't crazy. And neither was Rupert. He had more memories than anyone realized. But *she* could see it. She could feel it in her gut. This wasn't some romantic thought at all. But what if both truths were real? What would that mean for her and Toby?

"I'm tired," Rupert announced suddenly, his voice low.

Toby put an arm around his grandfather. "All right, then. We'll get you back."

SEVENTEEN

"You're a sleuth when it comes to hunting down the facts. You go to museums, chase journal pages down the street, spend way more time with Rupert than you probably need to ... And you didn't even ask Toby to tell you who Mary was last night?"

"It wasn't the right time," Meghan said, pulling up Pappy's old bedding and following Tess into the kitchen.

Tess hit the switch for the coffee pot and grabbed two mugs. "You should have a drink with him and find out. Isn't that what Rupert said anyway, that you two should have a drink? Listen to the old man. I'm itching to know Toby's story."

"Then *you* go have a drink with him." The memory of Toby's laugh floated back into Meghan's mind, giving her a flutter, so she busied herself with making the coffee. As she opened the drawer to get them each a spoon, a loud *pop* caught her attention.

Charlie's ears went up and he rushed over to Meghan.

"What was that?" Meghan asked, looking around the room.

"I'm not sure." Tess shrugged her shoulders and tipped her head toward the ceiling. "Did it come from up there?"

"I don't know." Meghan opened the refrigerator to retrieve

the cream and stopped. "The fridge light isn't on." She leaned in. "I don't hear it running either."

"We've blown a fuse," Tess said, clicking the button on the coffee pot. "Coffee's not running either. Where's the fuse box?"

"I think it's in the back hallway by the washer and dryer." Meghan led the way to the back of the house and clicked on the light, but nothing happened. She opened the door to the fuse box and checked the switches, clicking them on and off. "Anything working?"

Tess flipped the switch on the wall to try the lights again. "Nothing."

"Did we just lose power for some reason?" Meghan asked, opening the back door and looking outside for a sign of a storm off in the distance, but she was met with blue skies and sunshine. "I'll have to call an electrician." She walked back into the living room, looking around for some indication of what could have happened. Charlie followed, looking around too, as if he could figure it out.

"Looks like it's a ponytail-and-Lost-Love-Coffee day until we get to the bottom of it," Tess said.

Meghan put her hand on the air conditioning unit, nothing blowing out. "I can be ready in fifteen minutes." She peered over at the dog. "How about you, Charlie? Wanna go with us so you can stay cool?"

The dog tilted his head, and turned toward the door.

By the time Meghan and Tess had gotten ready and secured an electrician for that evening, Lost Love Coffee was brimming with tourists, all getting their morning fuel-up before spending the day on the beach. Chloe was at the register with two other people making drinks at warp speed. While Charlie lapped up water on the porch outside, Meghan and Tess joined the line.

"I'm not going to have time to see Rupert today," Meghan worried aloud. "I hope he doesn't get worried."

"Maybe call him?" Tess suggested.

"That's a great idea. Why don't you get us a coffee, and I'll go outside with Charlie and call Rosewood Manor to see if I can get in touch with him."

"Okay. Want a pastry or anything?"

"You choose," Meghan said, handing her friend a wad of tip money. "Meet me outside."

With her phone to her ear, Meghan headed to the outdoor seating area, Charlie jumping up and pulling on his leash to come see her. "This is Meghan Gray," she said as the front desk answered the call. "Is it possible to speak to one of your patients, Rupert Meyers?"

"Yes, ma'am. I'll put you through to his room. One moment, please."

Meghan sat down at the little bistro table next to Charlie and rubbed his head while the phone pulsed in her ear.

"Hello?" Rupert asked.

"Hi. It's . . . Hester."

"Where are you?"

"I have to go straight to work today and I have someone coming to my house this evening, so I might not be able to come by."

Rupert sat, silent, on the other end of the phone.

Unsure of his clarity without being able to see him, she added, "I just wanted to tell you so you didn't worry. I'm going to go now, okay?"

"When are you going to stop, Hester?" Rupert finally said, the words coming out irritated, as if she did this kind of thing all the time.

Meghan sat up straight, pressing the phone to her ear to focus on his answer over the sound of the ocean and the buzz of tourists going in and out of the coffee shop. "What do you mean?"

"You flaunt yourself around, go to parties all day and all night, you fall for anyone who gives you attention, and I've had it. You will never find self-worth in other people. You *have* to trust yourself."

"Where is this coming from?" she asked, baffled by the one-eighty he'd taken.

"You have someone coming over tonight!"

"Oh!" she said. "No, not like that. I have an electrician coming over. I've had an issue with the wiring in my kitchen and I need to get it fixed."

"All right," he said, his tone sounding as though he were unconvinced.

"I promise that's all it is. I'll see you tomorrow, okay?" she said, trying to settle him down.

"I do wish you'd look around at what you have once in a while. It's pretty damn great."

Tess came out, a to-go cup in each hand, the door swinging closed behind her, shutting out the hum of chatter inside and leaving them with only the sounds of the ocean and the wind. Meghan pointed to her phone, making a face.

"I can't wait to see you tomorrow, Rupert," she said. "I have to go."

"Always on the go," he said just before he hung up.

Meghan set her phone on the table, feeling unsettled. "Well, that went well," she said dryly.

"Did he go off the rails?" Tess asked, sliding Meghan's latte over to her, through a beam of sunshine that illuminated the table.

"No, but he seems to think that Hester is quite the social butterfly," she said, explaining how he'd reacted.

Tess sat back in the chair, tipping her face up toward the sun before she said, "It sounds like this Hester Quinn was a handful."

"Indeed." Meghan took a long drink from her coffee, thinking how much she would need the caffeine boost today.

"So, I've found the problem," the electrician said, as he placed his screwdriver back into his bag of tools.

Meghan let out a relieved breath. They were about to roast in the summer heat without the air conditioning, and she couldn't wait to get to the bottom of the issue. "That's great. What is it?"

"The wiring is bad."

"Okay, which area? The kitchen?"

"No. All the wiring in this house is going to need to be replaced, and I'd suggest installing central air as well, as that little window unit isn't going to cut it with the current structure. It's probably what's overpowering the system."

"How do you know there's something wrong with all the wiring?" Tess asked.

"The insulation's deteriorated, leaving most of the wires throughout exposed. If you continue to go on with them exposed, it could burn the house down."

"What's this going to cost us?" Meghan asked, nearly breathless at the thought.

The electrician set his bag of tools on the kitchen table, the dusty bag grazing the corner of Pappy's envelope. Meghan scooted it away, her stomach churning with the situation at hand. "Well, for a house this size, I'd say electrical would run you around two thousand dollars, and if you decide on central air, that would be an additional five thousand, probably."

"Seven thousand dollars?" Meghan sank down into a kitchen chair to keep her knees from buckling.

"Yep," the electrician said, unmoved by her response. "Today, it's just the service fee of a hundred dollars. Are you paying by check or would you like us to bill you?"

"Uh," she said, her mind still on the cost and the money she didn't have to pay it. "Bill me."

"All right." He handed her his card. "Give us a call when you're ready to rewire."

"Thank you," she said, in utter shock.

"I don't have that kind of money," she said to Tess, once the man had left.

"We can sweat. We'll get some fans and open the windows if

we need to. Then, maybe you can get on a payment plan for the two thousand to fix the electrical."

"Maybe," Meghan said, feeling like she had a cinder block in the pit of her stomach. "I shouldn't have bought that paint," she said, shaking her head. "I didn't need it."

"There was no way to know, Meghan. Things like this just happen. Maybe we can work some extra shifts."

"You don't need to take on any of this," Meghan said. "It's my house. I'm not going to let you pay a single cent." She put her chin in her hands, her mind whirring with how to handle it, the stress of the situation overwhelming her suddenly.

"I'll take Charlie out for us," Tess said. "Wanna come?"

"Do you mind if I sit and stew about this a little longer?" Meghan asked.

"Not at all. Come on, Charlie. Let's give your mama a minute." Tess opened the door and Charlie bolted out in front of her. "Want me to leave this open so you can get a breeze coming in?"

"Yeah, thanks."

Once Tess and Charlie were down the walk, Meghan finally let the tears that had been building fall. Her life was a series of bad choices, and she didn't know how to dig out of it. She could've kept working for Vinnie, been thankful for what she had as a waitress, and stayed in her rental apartment where everything that broke got fixed, but instead, she'd left it all and assumed the massive responsibility of home ownership before she was financially ready.

But would she ever be financially ready? As a young girl, she remembered sitting with Pappy on the porch, talking about the day she would be a top chef.

Creativity is in your blood, he'd told her. *It's who you are.*

She was starting to wonder if he'd been right at all. She'd listened to Pappy, taken his words for truth, but did he really know, or had he just been telling her what she wanted to hear?

But then, without warning, what Rupert had told Hester

came into her mind: *You will never find self-worth in other people. You* have *to trust yourself.*

Even though she wasn't Hester, his advice was pretty clear for her life too. She didn't trust herself. She didn't trust that she was a good chef anymore. Or that she deserved anything more than the hand she was dealt. But it was hard to trust a dream that never seemed to get off the ground. Did she have what it took, or not?

EIGHTEEN

"What did the Baldwins say?" Rupert asked, when Meghan found him in the recreation room the next morning.

"I'm sorry?" Meghan came over to the sofa where he sat and lowered herself down beside him. Two other patients were playing cards at the table in the corner and entertainment news was on the television hanging on the wall.

"When we left early to go to the beach the other night, what did they say? Were they okay with it?"

"Oh, uh, yes," she said, dropping her handbag beside her feet and wriggling into a comfortable position.

"And Audrey was all right? I know she sometimes feels a bit awkward in those situations. Did she manage okay?"

"Ye-es," she said, trying to keep her composure at the mention of her grandmother's name.

"Well, I suppose she had John to get her through it without you."

Meghan stifled her gasp with a cough. She peered over at the card players, but they were deep in discussion about the ace of spades. "John?" she asked, an electric current shooting up her spine when Pappy's name rolled off her lips. *He did know Pappy.*

"How did you meet Audrey and John?" she asked, while Rupert leaned over and tidied the stack of magazines on the coffee table in front of them.

"What are you talking about?" His hands stilled and he looked over at her, confused. "Audrey is your best friend. How could you forget how we met? Have you lost your mind?"

"No, I just…" She scrambled again to get a foothold in this odd ping-pong game of past to present, her mind spinning with this new information. Was it true or made up? Did Nanna really know Hester Quinn, the actress? "I just wanted you to tell me again. I like to hear you recount our history together."

He settled, leaning back on the sofa, his cloudy gaze landing on the television, although it was clear that the information wasn't permeating his thoughts. He ran his unsteady fingers down his disheveled shirt. "We all met the same day," he began. "Audrey had traveled with you and your cousin from Texas to Hatteras Island. On the bench that day, when I met you, you asked if I'd show you where to get an ice cream float, remember?"

Meghan nodded, dying for him to keep going.

"John was inside, buying a Coke, and when he came out, I told him we were taking you two to the ice cream parlor in town."

So that was how Nanna had met Pappy.

"And you flirted with John the entire time." The old man rolled his eyes, shaking his head. "Always a flirt. But John wasn't a stupid boy. He caught on right away, which only made you try harder, chatting him up."

The hair on her arms stood up. That sure sounded like Pappy. "What did he do?" she asked with a grin.

"He smiled politely and gave you his usual nods and 'yes, ma'ams,' but he spent the rest of the afternoon making small talk with Audrey. They had a lovely friendship for some time. They didn't develop feelings for each other until later." He gave her a knowing look as if she had some insider information. "But their bond began as partners in keeping you on the straight and narrow."

"What brought us to the Outer Banks? Do you remember?"

"Your cousin Ian was an archeology student at that fancy school. He wanted to finish out one of his projects here. He was so busy all day that you girls were left to entertain yourselves, so you sent regular postcards to his mother to let her know how everything was going. While you sat on the bench, writing your postcard to your aunt, Audrey was inside the shop, buying a cream soda with the nickel Ian had given her to spend that day." Suddenly, a smile spread across his face.

"What is it?" Meghan asked, riveted.

"John and I had just worked all day on the fishing boat. We were dirty and hot. The two of you looked like rare flowers sitting there, giggling and happy, and when I asked what you were doing in the Outer Banks, you answered, 'Having an island summer,' as if the area were more than a patch of sand along the road." He chuckled. "It still makes me laugh."

"Thank you for sharing the story with me," she said, feeling as if she were meant to have met Rupert because he could tell her what Pappy had never had a chance to. In a way, she, too, was having an island summer with her best friend, although hers wasn't quite as rosy so far.

"Hello," a familiar deep voice came toward her from behind. Meghan turned around to find Toby striding in. "I was on my way to Mariner's and thought I'd stop in to see you for a quick minute, Gramps. How are you today?" he asked, giving Meghan an uneasy glance.

"Never better when I have the company of this lady," he said. "I was just telling Hester about meeting her that first day. She wanted to hear the story again."

"That's nice," Toby said, but the sentiment didn't really show in his eyes. He sat in the wingback chair opposite them.

"You know, with all that's gone wrong in my life, the good

things still shine through." Rupert put his hand on Meghan's and gave her a tender smile, their moment still lingering.

Right then, she felt like she could actually see the man he'd been, and she wished she had more time with him before he slipped away again.

Then, she looked over at Toby and his face dropped as if he were pondering a comment of his own, and not quite sure of the validity of it.

Suddenly, Meghan checked the time on her watch. "I need to go," she said. "I have to . . . get to work early today and it's so beautiful out that I walked here, so I need to go home and get my car." She also needed to check on Charlie. With no way to keep him cool, she wanted to make sure he was going out to swim through the back door they'd left cracked and to give him fresh water as the temperatures began to rise. The problem was that she had no idea what to do if he didn't go out and it actually was too hot for him in Pappy's cottage. But the other option was to turn on the AC and risk burning the place down, as well as putting him in harm's way. She considered searching for pet daycares in the area, but she'd need a minute or two to find one.

"Always working," Rupert said. "Are you shooting a movie in the Outer Banks?"

"It's top secret, remember?" she said with a grin. "I'll be back tomorrow," she told him with a gentle squeeze of his hand.

"Stay for just a bit more," Toby said, surprising her. A little thrill tickled her insides. "I'm on my way to the inn. I can drive you if Tess can take you home."

Meghan would have to ask him to drop her by the cottage, and she didn't want to have to explain herself. But without a reason to say no, she said, "All right," sitting back down. After all, he was the boss. "Let me text Tess so she knows," she said, pulling out her phone, texting her friend about what to do with Charlie.

"You're going to watch Hester shoot a movie?" Rupert asked, disorientation showing in the creases between his brows as he waded through their conversation, clearly trying to make sense of it.

Before Toby responded, Rupert nodded as if he understood some sort of insider information and leaned forward toward his grandson. "Good boy, making up a reason to take Hester in this heat so she doesn't swelter," he whispered.

What neither of them knew was that, with no air conditioning at home, she'd nearly acclimated to the heat outside and it actually felt nice.

"I'm tired," Rupert abruptly announced out of nowhere, as he did.

"We'd better get you back to your room then," Toby told him, standing up.

Meghan picked up her handbag and followed him over to Rupert, where they helped him stand and make his way back to his room. Then, Meghan and Toby walked out into the sunshine, the warmth of it settling on her skin.

"I have to admit something to you," he said, stopping at the Range Rover and not getting in. "I was headed to the inn to find *you*, but I thought you might actually be with my grandfather, so I came here first."

Meghan looked up at him, the gold flecks in his eyes sparkling in the sun.

He clicked his key chain and the back hatch of his vehicle raised, revealing an antique French Provincial style dressing table. Meghan walked over to it and peered in at the cream-colored paint with gold piping and little pink roses on the drawers, next to the circular brass drawer pulls. "This is stunning," she said, turning back to him to figure out what was going on.

"Do you recognize this at all?" he asked.

Confused, she turned her attention back over to it, running

her hands along its slick finish, admiring the glamorous French design. "No," she said, captivated. "Why do you ask?"

His gaze shifted back over to the piece of furniture with a strange mix of confusion and interest evident. "I was hoping you'd have seen it before."

"Why?" she asked again. "What is this?"

"I was talking to Gramps last night, and he told me a story about Hester and how she used to write at her dressing table. He said that she had *this*—he described it exactly, down to the engraving in the drawer that said Côté Frères. I don't speak French, so I had him write it down for me because I didn't understand what he was saying. I checked online and Côté Frères doesn't exist anymore, so it would be a little difficult to find." He pulled out the empty drawer and, engraved into the side of the wood, was the Côté Frères logo. "I thought perhaps you'd told him about it or something."

"No, I've never seen it in my life. Where did you find it?"

"Simp had it over at The Memory Box."

"You shop there regularly?" she teased.

He allowed a smirk through his usually sullen features, her stomach whirling at the sight. "Gramps told me it was there, along with more of Hester's things. He said Hester had tried to move in with him and she'd shown up out of nowhere, with a driver who'd filled a truck with her furniture—the pieces still full with her things, her personal items in all the drawers—and driven all the way from her house in New York. When he got home, she was unloading it all right there in his front yard."

"New York?" she asked, remembering the journal entry in Lost Love Coffee. *New York is terrifyingly large for a girl, but I'm managing.*

He nodded. "He said he had to turn her away because, by the time she finally came back, he was married."

"To your grandmother," she said, piecing the story together.

"She left everything right there in the grass, got into the truck in tears, and drove away. She never came back. After a few years, he took it all to Simp's dad, who ran The Memory Box."

"How do you know it wasn't your grandmother's, and he's confused?" she asked, surprised and delighted by his willingness to believe.

"Because when I spoke to Simp about it, he remembered his father telling the story about Hester and your grandmother. It's quite the local folklore. He said that my grandfather had a crush on her when she first arrived on the island. He also said that years later, Gramps dropped all this off, telling him it was Hester's and he could probably get good money for it."

Meghan pressed her fingers to her lips in utter shock. "Rupert's not delusional," she said through her hands. "It's all true."

"It makes you wonder, doesn't it?" Toby asked, visibly wrestling with the idea, his gaze unstill. He gestured to the dressing table. "Do you have anything you can do with this?"

"You want to give me Hester's table?"

"I bought it because I couldn't let it go to just anyone, but I don't know what to do with it. I thought maybe you might have a use for it." The kindness in his eyes made it hard to breathe. He'd thought about her.

"Let me buy it from you," she offered, knowing good and well that she didn't have the kind of money it would take to buy a stunning piece of furniture like that.

"Absolutely not. It'll be my gift to you for bringing out this piece of my grandfather's history for his family." He stared at it, unmistakably stunned as the reality of it set in. "It's . . . unbelievable."

"I've never taken a gift this large before," she said, the beauty of it making it very difficult to say no.

"I insist," he said, pulling out his phone. "Let me call Mariner's and tell them that you'll be late today." He dialed the number, putting the phone to his ear. Before she could protest about how she didn't want the other servers to have to absorb her tables, he was already speaking to Meredith, telling her that Meghan would be late.

He was quick to leave them shorthanded and she wondered again about his plans for the inn and whether both sides of the story could be his truth.

"Want to take this to your house?" he asked, sliding his phone into his back pocket.

Well, at least she could check on Charlie . . .

Hester's ornate dressing table looked out of place in Pappy's old bedroom. Meghan stared at it, trying not to think about the fact that a pile of her folded clothes and undergarments were sitting on the chair over in the corner. There was something so intimate about having Toby in her bedroom unexpectedly.

He seemed to read her, an uneasy smile playing at his lips, the sound of Charlie lapping fresh water in the other room keeping the moment in check for her.

"I'd planned to paint the bed frame a cream color," she said, trying to divert the focus. "This will go perfectly with it."

"Is your air broken?" he asked, wiping beads of perspiration off his forehead.

"The cottage doesn't have central air," she said.

He pointed to the box fan she'd been using. "Want me to lift that and put it in the open window? It would draw in a draft and move the stagnant air."

"That's a good idea," she said, "but we've just found out that all the electric wires need to be replaced so we're only running the refrigerator right now." When Toby peered down the hallway, considering this, she discreetly tugged at her shirt to keep it from sticking to the perspiration that had built on her skin.

"When are you getting it fixed?" he asked.

"I'm not sure," she said.

"You're not sure?"

She bit her lip, not wanting to tell him, but given how honest he'd been with her today, she figured she should just say it. "I'm still trying to figure out the best way to pay for it."

"I can help," he said.

Her face burned with mortification. "Oh, no. Definitely not. It's fine," she said, waving away his offer. She didn't need any charity, especially if the money were possibly coming from Rupert without his knowledge.

"You can't live like this for any extended period of time. It's going to be a hundred degrees today."

She looked down at Charlie, who'd sauntered in and plopped down, panting, his four legs spread out on the floor, trying to stay cool. He'd finished his third bowl of water today. She'd kept him wet this morning and let him out every minute that he'd asked, giving him ice-cold water from the fridge as soon as she got home, but it wasn't even midday and she was getting worried.

"Hang on." He took out his phone and made a call. "Tabitha, it's Toby Meyers. Do we have any free rooms available today?" He listened for a tick and then with a pout, said, "All right, thanks. No problem." He slid his phone back into his pocket. "I'd give you a room at the inn, but we're completely booked for the entire summer."

"That's very kind of you to offer."

"Wait," he said, waving a finger in the air, still thinking. "I have a few friends who manage rentals in town; I'm sure we could find something that isn't rented for a few weeks. Why don't you let me make some calls for you to stay somewhere air conditioned and we can get the work started on the house?"

"I can't afford that," she admitted, gritting her teeth in humiliation.

"Well, you can't live *here*." He waved an arm through the air. "It's uninhabitable."

"I'll figure it out," she said, knowing she didn't have the first clue how to do that. She peered over at Charlie, feeling helpless.

"How will you figure it out, when you said yourself that you can't afford it? Let me, at the very least, loan you the money for somewhere to stay. We'll work out a way that you can pay me back in payments or in service at the inn—something."

Meghan had a millionaire offering to give her a place to stay, and all she could think about was how awful it felt. Yet she knew Charlie would be too hot, and she was completely backed into a corner.

"What are you thinking about?" he asked, studying her curiously.

She shook her head, not wanting to say it out loud.

"What is it?" he asked, his voice soft as if he could tell how hard this was for her. She looked up at him and, for the first time, she saw vulnerability in his eyes. He was letting his wall down right in front of her.

"It's easy for you to offer when you have the money to do it. But it's much harder for me to accept it, when I don't have any way or means to repay you. Even working extra won't put the money back into your account." Her voice broke on the words and she turned away so he didn't see the tears welling up in her eyes.

His gentle, tentative touch on her shoulder startled her. "I don't care about any of that," he said. "I just want to do something for you . . . I haven't been myself, and I'm sorry."

She closed her eyes, her back still to him, not knowing what to say.

"Please, let me do this."

Begrudgingly, she turned around. It wasn't like her to ask for help, but she was desperate. "All right."

"Give me a second to call around, and I'll see what I can find."

While Toby made his phone calls, Meghan took Charlie outside to let him run in the waves again and cool off. She motioned to Toby that she'd be down the walk and then set out toward the beach, the sparkling sea pawing at the shore as if beckoning her.

As she walked, she thought about Rupert's story and how Hester had just left everything when he'd turned her down. Where had she gone? Could that be why she'd died in seclusion back in California with no family to speak of? Meghan could relate to the isolation. While she was so thankful for Tess's support and for Toby's kind offer, she couldn't help but feel alone. So many times, she'd willed herself to think like Tess and be completely comfortable in her own skin, but something always felt amiss and she didn't know what she needed to fix it. That dressing table felt a lot like her: out of place and not really fitting in its surroundings.

Charlie dove into a wave, splashing around, overjoyed that she'd come home to let him out. As hot as he'd been, even he was completely content where he was. He ran along the surf, barking happily at the waves as they crashed around him.

"You're in luck," Toby said, coming over the dune. "I found you somewhere to stay for two weeks."

As thrilling as the idea sounded, she knew that cottages in this area, during peak summer months, had a base price of $4,000 a week. While he'd offered to initially cover it, she'd still have to pay back a two-week stay on top of the repairs. She'd be working forever.

"What's wrong?" he asked as he neared her.

"It's . . ." She didn't want to have this conversation. She was a grown woman. She should be able to pay her own bills. Unexpectedly, tears of frustration sprang into her eyes again. She blinked them away, looking over at Charlie. "It's very kind of you," she said instead. She'd figure out how to pay him back.

The compassion in his eyes told her that he could see through it, and she looked away again, focusing on the crash of the waves at Charlie's paws instead. "Can I tell you something?" he said. "I know what you're going through."

She had no idea how he could possibly know about her life,

but just the acknowledgment made her feel weak in the knees, so she sat down on the edge of the boardwalk.

"I've been where you are financially." Toby sat down next to her, the coastal wind whipping between them and up the walk. "I was married," he said, turning his head to look at her. "I worked in the finance department of a large corporation back in Boston, and I was completely unhappy in my job. Mary convinced me to quit. She said we could move to the Gulf Coast where it's always warm, open an inn—that was her dream—serve cinnamon rolls and coffee in the mornings, and listen to people tell us their stories . . ." He took in a tense breath. "I quit. I had no job—nothing. We started to look for places, living on her wages and our savings. We were surviving, but we both knew we couldn't do it forever."

Meghan could definitely understand what it was like to leave a job—money or no money.

"And then, last year, Mary had the accident." He swallowed, his lips tightening with his emotion.

Meghan could guess what he would say next, but she stayed quiet, her heart already breaking with the truth of what Rupert had said.

"We were skiing in the Rockies. I'd stayed back to look for a heavier coat in the ski shop. The one I'd brought was too light for the heavy snowfall." He stared out at the Atlantic, but she knew his thoughts were on that fateful day. "An avalanche buried my wife and my parents."

"Oh my god," she said, unable to stay silent anymore.

Toby's eyes glistened in the sunlight, the tension that she'd seen showing in his features before now completely explained. "We'd lost my parents but when they found her, Mary was still holding on. She was rushed to the hospital with severe head trauma and internal bleeding, and remained in intensive care on a ventilator."

Meghan reached out and put her hand on his, speaking that silent language of loss. He turned his hand under hers, her palm now resting in his, and he looked down at it as if it were a rare relic he'd found.

"I'm so sorry," was all she could say.

"Her insurance covered a lot of it, but without a job, her care wiped us right out. When she finally passed, I had nothing." He gripped Meghan's hand, and she let him.

"I can't imagine what you went through," she said, the sadness of losing Pappy and her parents right on the surface. For months, every time she'd thought about losing Pappy, she'd crumble. "How did you get to where you are now?"

"My grandfather gave me the money." There was a finality in his tone that told her he was answering her concerns about where he got the money to fund the inn.

She didn't want to consider it, but had Rupert actually *given* him the money? "I would think that would be a lot of money," she said, unable to fathom how Rupert had enough to completely get Toby back on his feet *and* build the inn.

"We knew he had off-shore accounts, and inheritance from our family overseas, but we had no idea just how much until our legal team and advisors gave me full access to his books." He shook his head and let out a sigh of relief. "Thank God for his savings. I can't imagine what I would've done without them." Then, he turned to Meghan. "But all that's to say that sometimes, we do everything right and still, nothing seems to go our way."

"Why are you offering me this?" she asked suddenly.

He allowed a small smile. "Two reasons, really. The first one is to thank you for bringing out something in my grandfather no one else could, and the second is because you're the first person since the accident that believes there's good in things. You make me think about life outside of my loss."

She wanted so badly to believe the kindness that she'd seen in him today. Spending time with Rupert was the first thing she'd done in a long time that had felt good, and she wouldn't be able to live with herself if Toby wasn't being truthful.

"We'd better call your dog in and get you back to work," he said, letting go of her hand and standing up. "We can let him stay in my office at the inn."

"Thank you," she said, rising and brushing off her bottom. No matter what his motives were, she was definitely grateful for the help, and while she'd always guessed there was more to Toby Meyers, she was certain she hadn't even scratched the surface.

NINETEEN

"You missed the entire lunch shift," Tess said as she untied her apron after work, tossing it onto Pappy's kitchen table. "We were so busy . . ."

"Sorry," Meghan said, pouring a bowl of water for Charlie. The dog was beat after spending the day in a new location, dropping onto the floor and closing his eyes. "But it was worth being shorthanded. I've got a lot to tell you. Follow me." Meghan led Tess into Pappy's bedroom, filling her best friend in on her time with Toby.

Tess sat on the bed and rubbed her feet, her eyes on the dressing table. "So, it's all real . . ."

"Apparently." Meghan couldn't help the fizzle of excitement over the whole thing. It was such a relief to know that, while Rupert struggled with what year it was, most of what he was saying was true. It made her feel like he'd been granted some dignity in all this. "I hope the heat doesn't ruin the wood or anything," Meghan worried aloud as she touched the painted pink flowers on the front of the table.

"It should be fine," Tess said. "After all, it's been at The Memory Box this whole time."

"You have a point." Meghan walked over to the closet and pulled out her suitcase. "So, I guess we should pack. Our rental is ready whenever we are. Toby told me it has a pool . . ." She wiggled her eyebrows at her friend.

"Then we'd better get packing right now!" Tess took Meghan by the hands and spun her around, making her giggle.

Meghan and Tess stood, dumbfounded, in the large half-circle of a drive, staring up at the massive mansion in front of them, with a curving staircase leading to a sprawling two-tiered porch that wrapped all the way around the house and its forty front windows. They were hot and sweaty from moving Pappy's furniture into the center of each of the cottage's rooms and covering it all with plastic to get it ready for the central air guys and the electricians. Then they'd packed up all their valuables and put them back in the car.

"Are you sure this is the place?" Tess asked, wide-eyed.

Meghan looked back down at the text on her phone. "This is 62 Starfish Way, right? The Seabreeze."

"That's what it says." Tess bounded up the immense staircase, Charlie following, and put her hands on her hips when she got to the top. "You can see the entire sound from up here." She put her hand to her forehead to shield her eyes from the sun as Meghan made her way to the top to view the glistening body of water, tranquil, reaching out to the edge of the world, it seemed.

Meghan punched the code on the lock and opened the front door to the marbled tile, two-story entryway, the ice-cold air from inside cooling her. Charlie's claws clicked along the shiny floors, past the enormous iron fish sculpture in the center, to the back where the living area stretched along the entire house, with a wall of windows showing off the bright blue pool and surrounding Atlantic.

They left the bags they'd grabbed for the first trip up in the front entryway, and Meghan walked over to the champagne-colored stone kitchen counter and dialed Toby's number. "There's no way I'll be able to pay him back for this. I can't imagine what a house like this costs to rent."

"I've never been in anything this nice before in my life." Tess twirled around, opening kitchen cabinets and dancing from room to room as Toby answered Meghan's call.

"Did you find the house okay?" he asked.

"Uh, yeah. But, Toby, it's enormous. How much will I owe you for rent?"

"Don't worry about it. I traded the owner for a prime holiday spot on the calendar at the inn. We're letting him have his annual Christmas party there free of charge."

A swell of happiness floated up inside her at the gesture he'd made to ensure she had somewhere to stay. "I'll work it for free as well," Meghan said, relief flooding her.

"Of course," he said. She could almost feel him smiling on the other end of the line.

Tess tugged on her elbow to show her the massive windows at the back of the room. "I will. Thank you so much," she said, feeling like the words weren't even scratching the surface of her gratitude.

"Go. Unpack. Enjoy the house."

Meghan smiled. "All right."

When she ended the call, she stared wide-eyed at the stunning space.

"Toby has to have a thing for you if he got you this place," Tess said, grabbing both of Meghan's arms and shaking them playfully.

"Why are you excited by this? You said he has issues," Meghan teased back.

Tess ran over and dove onto the white, oversized sofa. "I think I could look past his issues if my crush could get me this."

"It's not about the money, Tess," she said with a laugh. "Although, I cannot *believe* we get to stay here," she said.

Tess hit a button and suddenly, all the glass on the back of the house began to fold in on itself, opening the entire wall to the pool. Charlie walked out to one of the navy-and-white striped loungers under one of the large umbrellas and hopped up on it. "This house has everything!"

Meghan looked up at the vaulted ceiling and its huge chandelier of driftwood and glass before turning to peer down the hallway. "What else does this house have?" she asked, walking into the master bedroom, Tess following. Meghan ran her hand along the pearl-colored duvet on the king-sized bed.

"There's even a brass safe in the wall," Tess said. "Look. 'Proudly secured by Pinetop Securities.' You could put your grandmother's earrings in there, just because you can." She opened the safe's heavy door, revealing a blank velvet interior.

Meghan laughed. "Right now, I need to call the electrician and discuss the repairs for Pappy's cottage." She reached over and shut it.

"All right, but then you're going to sit by the pool and drink cocktails with me. That's an order."

"Maybe it's this lavish house, or Toby's generosity, but I was wondering," Meghan said as she rolled over on the lounger outside, beads of water still on her skin from her evening swim, and sipped her piña colada made at the house's complimentary wet bar, "would you be okay if we have Toby and Rupert over for dinner? I could cook something."

Tess sat up excitedly, sending Charlie to his feet. "You want to *cook*?" she asked, her eyes rounded in surprise. "I thought you'd never ask!" She slipped her sunglasses on and swung her legs toward Meghan. "Have you decided what you're making?"

"What if I did my cavatelli with shrimp and asparagus?"

Tess rolled her eyes and fell back onto her cushioned lounger dramatically while her hand went to her belly, the bright orange sunlight on her face. "Yum."

"I should probably call Toby then. We'll need to hit the local market before it closes." Meghan stood up and wrapped the towel around her waist as the breeze rippled over the infinity pool's glassy surface, making it difficult to tell where the pool ended and the ocean began.

While Tess changed clothes, Meghan pulled out her phone and called Toby. He answered on the first ring.

"Hi, it's Meghan," she said. "I was wondering if you and Rupert would like to come over for dinner tonight."

"That would actually be amazing," he said, filling her with happiness. "Gramps could do with seeing you and being somewhere other than Rosewood Manor. He's totally torn up his room, looking for something. None of us know what it is."

"Oh no," she said, putting her hand to the skin on her chest, the warmth of it making her wonder if she'd gotten a little evening burn out there by the pool. "I have to run out to get supplies, but if it would help him, maybe you two could meet me at the market."

His silence gave her pause. "I . . . can't imagine going through this anymore without you. You're such a big part of his day," he said, his unexpected comment stopping her cold. For the first time in her adult life, someone needed her, and the idea of it gave her a rush of excitement like nothing she'd ever experienced before. "You still there?" he asked when she didn't respond.

"Yes," she said through her smile. "I'm here."

"I need to find the paper," Rupert said for the third time, wringing his hands as he shuffled along beside Meghan and Toby, the grocery cart full of fresh vegetables and pasta.

"We'll find it," Meghan told him, placing a comforting hand

on his shoulder. "Can you help me choose a lemon?" she asked. "I'm looking for just the right one."

Rupert lifted a few, inspecting them, not entirely with them tonight, his clarity as unsteady as the tide. He held out a lemon. "How's this one, Hester?"

"That one looks good. Thank you," she said. "Can you find me one more really good one?" She placed the lemon in the cart and turned to Toby. "What paper is he looking for?" she whispered.

Toby shook his head. "No idea."

"It's *your* ledger paper, Hester. For God's sake," he said, evidently overhearing them. He handed her a second lemon.

"I have all my papers," she said, trying to calm him.

His unsteady gaze found her. "Oh," he said as his brows pulled together. "Are you sure?"

"Yes. It's at home," she lied just a little, hoping he didn't ask where it was when they got to The Seabreeze.

"What else do we need?" Toby asked.

"Just a bottle of white wine," she replied, running back through her mental list of ingredients.

"When did you start drinking white wine?" Rupert asked her. "You always preferred red."

His question stopped her and made her smile because she actually did prefer red to white, but then she realized that he didn't know that and was referring to Hester. "I'm cooking with it," she replied.

"Ah yes," he said, as if just now arriving at the conversation. "What are we having?"

"Cavatelli with shrimp and asparagus."

He smiled. "Do you remember when you learned to cook that dish?"

His question surprised her. "I do." She actually did remember. It was one of the first real dishes Pappy had taught her how to make.

"It was one of the first dishes you learned to make," he said, repeating her thought.

She sucked in a breath. "That's right," she said, stunned. That was a fact about *her*, not Hester. "How did you know?"

"You told me."

She grabbed a bottle of wine from the shelf and placed it into the cart, recounting their time together, but coming up empty as to when they'd ever talked about that dish. "I did?" she asked, racking her brain for even the slightest mention of it.

"It was the first dish you taught John how to make too, remember?"

"No, he taught *me*—" She stopped. *Wait.* Rupert thought he was talking to Hester ... right?

Rupert laughed. "He didn't teach you a thing. *You* taught *him* everything he knows."

Hester taught Pappy how to cook.

"You okay?" Toby asked, the intensity on his face giving away the fact that he understood what was running through her mind.

"Yeah," she said, her moments with Pappy in the kitchen making their spiced fried flounder and the peach tarts he liked to make for dessert flashing before her. She pushed the cart toward the checkout, wondering what else Pappy hadn't told her.

Meghan added garlic and thyme to the oil in her pan and stirred, the earthy aroma of it spilling into the air around them. Then she filled a pot with water, sprinkling in some salt and warming it to a boil.

"So, your grandfather learned to cook from Hester Quinn?" Tess asked, peering over at Rupert, who, after refusing to believe that this was Hester's house, was walking down the hallway, admiring the brushed glass sconces.

"I had no idea," Meghan said, chopping the asparagus before Toby distracted her from the conversation when he popped the cork on a courtesy bottle of champagne they'd found in the fridge when they'd gotten there. "Can we drink that?"

"I'm sure it's fine." He opened cabinets until he found the one stocked with champagne flutes, and he pulled down three, setting them on the counter and filling them while Charlie looked on from his side. "For a year, I thought he was completely losing it," Toby said. "And just since you've been here, I'm beginning to wonder if anything he says is untrue."

Meghan smiled, feeling like she'd been able to add something to their lives by her visits with Rupert.

Suddenly, Toby looked around. "Where did he go?"

Tess grabbed her champagne and handed one to Meghan, who turned down the burners to a slow simmer so as not to burn the food while they went to find Rupert. When they located him, he was standing in the master bedroom staring at the safe, not even flinching, as if they'd all been standing beside him the whole time.

Rupert turned to Meghan. "I'm sorry I didn't believe you," he said.

"Believe me?"

He nodded. "This is definitely your house."

Unsure of why the room safe would've convinced him of this, Meghan nodded anyway. "Would you like to sit out by the pool while I finish dinner?"

"I'd like that," Rupert said.

"I'll sit with him," Tess offered. "You two work on the cooking."

Meghan took one more look in the empty safe and then went into the kitchen while Tess led Rupert out by the pool. He settled in one of the chairs at the table, the waves of the bright blue Atlantic gurgling in billowing foam behind him. Tess sat opposite him, asking him a question and talking with her hands. Rupert answered, but his face had fallen to that still look he had when he'd retreated inward.

"What was Rupert like before the dementia?" she asked Toby, watching Rupert through the window.

Toby stepped up next to her, his arm brushing hers, the proximity unleashing a pack of butterflies in her stomach. "Gramps was always making us feel good," he said. "If things went wrong, he found a way to make us laugh."

Meghan zeroed in on the creases around the old man's eyes and tried to imagine the smile she'd seen in the restaurant that first night. What it must have been like when his soul was young and alive behind those eyes . . .

"One time, when I was about twelve, a few kids and I were playing baseball out back of his house and I hit the ball through his window. I felt awful and I ran into the house, explaining how I'd use my chore money to pay him back for fixing it. He laughed and said, 'I've got a better idea.' Then, he knocked out all the glass, swept it up, and took the entire window from its frame. The rest of the day, we played catch through the open space."

Meghan smiled, imagining Rupert throwing a baseball.

"All day—when we weren't even expecting it—he'd say, 'Heads up!' and out would come another ball." Toby shook his head, happiness lingering on his lips. "I miss him . . ." He turned away, his chest rising with a steadying breath. "So. Cooking. Show me what to do."

Leaving the view of Rupert as he sat outside, Meghan heated oil in another pan, then chopped onions, the slices hissing as she dropped them into the oil.

"You cook like a professional," Toby said.

He noticed her double-take, but she kept going, adding the garlic and thyme before zesting one of the lemons Rupert had picked out.

"What was that look?" he asked, his gaze swallowing her in interest, as if he could see right down to her soul, finding all the inadequacies that were strewn about at the bottom of her consciousness.

She picked up the pan, giving the ingredients a shimmy. "What do you mean?" she asked, tensing, although she knew exactly what look. It was the slight flinch, that moment of impostor syndrome when he'd thought she was anywhere close to a professional. She reached around him and grabbed the wooden spoon to stir the vegetables.

"I can just tell that you cook a lot," he said. "That was all I meant."

"It's fine," she replied, the sudden focus on her making her uneasy. "Can you hand me that?" she asked, pointing an elbow toward the pepper mill.

He didn't move.

"The pepper," she repeated. "Over there."

He stared at her as if he were contemplating something.

"You don't want me to use pepper?" she asked.

"No, I just . . . It's been a long time since . . . What's your story?" he asked in that gentle way of his, as he did whenever he was letting his guard down. He handed her the pepper and her fingers brushed his when she took it, making her suddenly nervous. She busied herself with turning the crank and cracked some in.

Cooking had been something intimate for her, a way of channeling her feelings, and suddenly, sharing that moment with Toby made her feel like she was standing on the edge of a canyon, looking over it, wondering if she could make it to the other side if she jumped. "There's not much to tell of my story, apart from my pappy's house falling down around me." Opting to step back from the canyon, she offered a less personal answer. She dared not say what she was really feeling, how unsure of her own life choices she was.

He took a drink of his champagne and then scooted his glass toward her, that mind of his seemingly whirring, making her anxious. "I get three questions and you have to answer them," he said unexpectedly.

Meghan stopped stirring and regarded him. "All right."

"Why did you move to the Outer Banks?"

"I hated my job in New York, so I quit."

He cocked his head to the side in interest, his blue eyes on her, making it difficult to breathe. "What's your favorite sport?"

"Mini golf." Her lack of pause before the answer made him laugh, the sound of it sending an unexpected plume of happiness through her, and she focused on the food to get herself together, taking one mental step back toward the canyon.

"Is that even a sport?"

"Don't look down on mini golf," she teased, adding in more wine and then a couple of handfuls of cheese, trying to ignore the flutter she felt when his eyes sparkled like they were.

He took a step closer to her. "Last question. Why do you feel like you don't deserve better for yourself?"

She stopped stirring, his waiting eyes telling her that he wouldn't let her avoid an answer. "I don't know what you mean," she replied with her standard response, trying anyway. She took in a breath to steady herself, the fact that he could read her so easily unnerving. She wasn't ready to go there yet—with him or herself. But as she thought about having something better for herself, she couldn't deny the urge to have his arms around her, those eyes of his that seemed like they'd been hers, just waiting for the moment when they could see right into her soul. When he challenged her with his stare, she said, "You're out of questions."

"If I didn't push myself to be better, I'd have crumbled into a million pieces after losing Mary." He leaned into her view to force her to look at him. "Every day is a struggle to uncover the person I am without her. But the more I push myself, the more I uncover what was meant for *me* in this life."

She cut off the heat and plated the cavatelli with shrimp and asparagus, the spicy scent of it floating around them, as she considered what he'd said. He'd faced far more than she had, and yet he seemed to have figured out what to do. Why was she still floundering?

"I'm just saying that if I tell you that you cook well, you're allowed to take the compliment." He grabbed a fork and speared a shrimp with a piece of asparagus and pasta, putting the bite in his mouth. His face was unreadable as he chewed and swallowed, and Meghan's heart pounded with anticipation. She hadn't cooked for anyone other than Vinnie and her friends, and suddenly her entire self-worth hinged on this moment, when she knew that was preposterous. But it was because, deep down, cooking was part of her, a passion, and if she couldn't do that well, she wasn't sure what she was supposed to do in life. Then, finally, he said, "This is incredible."

"Thank you," she said, trying to heed his advice and take the compliment when her mind was screaming at her that he was just being kind.

"I'm serious," he said, coming closer, making her heart pound. "It's really delicious. One of the best dishes I've ever tasted outside of a restaurant."

She stared at him, silent, unsure of whether to cry in sadness for the lost time of doing what she loved, or tears of joy for finally getting acknowledgment from someone other than her friends and family.

"Why don't you own it and say, 'Why yes, I'm great at it'?" He leaned toward her, his woodsy scent of sandalwood and cotton filling her lungs. "Why are you afraid to admit it?"

She forced herself to look him in the eye. His guard was down completely, and he seemed to actually want to know about her, about why she was nearly trembling standing there in front of him. She peered out at Tess and Rupert, searching for a view of the water to give her calm. "I wanted to be a chef at one time, but I was turned away in my last job. I don't have the credentials . . ."

"That doesn't matter," he said.

She didn't counter, but she did feel like it mattered. Everything in her world until this moment had told her it very much mattered. Before the familiar feeling of dread at having no purpose in life washed over her, she switched gears and picked up the dish. "Could you get the plates and utensils for me, please?"

Pensively, Toby followed, taking them outside and setting them onto the table. He went back in and returned with their drinks. Charlie followed him out, finding a spot in the setting sun on the patio.

"I've been waiting for this since we got to Hatteras Island!" Tess said, serving Rupert a plate while the old man looked on, beaming and seeming completely content as he scooped up a forkful of his dinner.

The ocean breeze, the setting sun, and the wide-open house cooled the patio, and Tess had lit the tiki torches and candles, the surround lighting clicking on—all of it offering the most glorious of settings. Tess went in and got Rupert a glass of water.

"It's been entirely too long since I've had your cooking, Hester," Rupert said, digging in. "I've missed it so much." He took another bite, his eyes dancing in the light of the candles.

"She really should cook more often, shouldn't she?" Tess asked him with a wink at Meghan, as she came back outside.

Rupert's eyebrows bobbed up and down happily. "I'd take her cooking any day."

Meghan couldn't help but beam, Rupert's delight warming her. Despite the fact that he wasn't really with them mentally, she felt an unspoken bond with him that she couldn't shake. "I'm so glad you could come," she said, meaning it.

"I've said it before," Rupert said, taking the glass from Tess and sipping a small drink of his water, "you've picked the wrong line of work with the acting. You should've been a chef like your father."

Meghan became still as she regarded Rupert with utter surprise. *Hester's father was a chef?*

Tess's eyes rounded at Rupert's comment, a smile twitching at her lips.

Toby leaned over and whispered in Meghan's ear, sending tingles down her arm, "Maybe you're more like Hester than you think?" He gave her a wink.

"Tell Tess and Toby about my father," Meghan said to Rupert, as she filled her fork from the steaming dish in front of her.

"Hester's father was a very well-known chef in Dallas, Texas," Rupert told them. "He had dreams of going to New York and making it big, but instead, he put his own dreams aside to further Hester's career. He was such a selfless man . . ."

Meghan thought about how, even now, her own dreams of being a chef had been put on hold while Hester took center stage. Ever since Hester had entered Meghan's life, it had been as though the woman had been right there with her, still, in death, larger than life.

"It's much more rewarding to help someone else," she said, her mind on helping Rupert more than the subject of Hester's father. She suddenly wondered if Hester had never had a chance to figure that out about herself. She'd been so wrapped up in her own life that she hadn't been able to experience the feeling of doing things for others. Perhaps she'd have been less troubled if she had . . .

"You should open a restaurant or something," Toby suggested, nearly half his dinner already gone, giving her a thrill of accomplishment. "Think about how many people you could help."

"How would that help anyone?" she asked, hearing the rattling of the last bit of change in her bank account. There was no way she could ever open a restaurant. And what she hadn't admitted until now was that something about it just didn't feel right, which only made her more confused.

"You'd give them a big table and good food—the necessary ingredients for making memories."

Rupert looked on with awe. "Are you seriously considering this, Hester?"

"No," she said, shaking her head.

Rupert's face dropped and he took another bite as a seagull squawked overhead.

"What's wrong?" she asked.

"You spend so much time proving yourself—to *yourself*—and spinning your wheels. The fame doesn't make you feel any better about who you are. You have to find it in here." He tapped his chest with an unsteady hand. "You're a talented actress, but you know what? You're talented at anything you put your mind to. What you have to find out is what will make your heart soar. And I'm not so sure it's acting."

"Sometimes I feel like I can't make my dreams happen," Meghan said, forgetting for a moment that Rupert didn't really know who he was talking to. "So many things get in the way and I don't know how to take the first step."

Rupert broke into a wide grin. "Ah, my dear. That part's easy! Take any step as long as it's the first one. And then take another one after that. The time will pass, whether you do it or not. Wouldn't you rather spend your days walking than sitting still?"

"That sounds like something my pappy would say," Meghan said to Tess, considering the old man's advice.

Rupert's eyes clouded over at her comment, his confusion clear.

Just then, Meghan's ringtone inside interrupted them. She set her napkin on the table, scooting her chair out to get the phone. "I'll be right back."

After finishing the call, she returned, sitting back down. "The electrician asked if I could completely clean out the closet in my room so he can access the back of the house. They'll begin repairs at around ten in the morning tomorrow."

"I can help," Tess said. "Why don't we do it before work, on the way?"

Meghan turned her focus to Rupert. "I won't be able to stop by in the morning."

He brightened as if swimming out of himself. "That's fine," he said. "As long as you cook me something else." Then he sat up, more animated than she'd ever seen him. "I'd love one of your muffins, Hester."

She grinned at him, his excitement amusing her. "Muffins?"

He threw his withered hand to his heart. "They were your specialty. Oh, they melt in your mouth. How I've missed them . . ."

Meghan laughed, warmed by him. "Done. I'll make you some muffins."

TWENTY

"What's all this?" Tess said with a yawn as she padded into the massive kitchen and sat down in front of the row of muffins Meghan had made for Rupert, giving Charlie's side a pat.

"I've been up since 4 a.m.," Meghan replied, holding a heavy bowl against her chest as she mixed the ingredients, the sugary scent filling the space around her. I've been to the market already this morning, and I've been testing recipes for the last hour and a half." She stuck her finger into the batter and tasted it. "This one needs more salt."

"I'm not complaining, but what's going on?" Tess asked.

Rupert's advice had whirred in Meghan's unsettled mind all night. She'd barely slept, the idea of finally knowing something she could do that excited Rupert making it difficult to sleep. For the first time in ages, she was driven and eager to get up and get started. She had no idea if her recipes would work or not, but she could take the first step and let it lead her, like Rupert had said.

"I want to create a few recipes that are mine specifically." She pointed to each of the muffins in front of Tess. "I've made banana nut truffle, pecan glaze, ruby chocolate with raspberry, maple oat, and the ones with the frosting are bow-wowzers for dogs, made with peanut butter and banana. Charlie loves them already." She lifted a spoonful of batter from the bowl in her hands. "These are going to be butter popcorn. In honor of Hester's movies."

"Oh my gosh, Meghan," Tess said, wide-eyed. "That's incredible. How did you come up with all these ideas?'

Meghan shrugged, unsure herself. "They're just coming to me."

"What are you going to do with all of them?" Tess asked excitedly, wriggling on her stool to reach a doggy muffin to give to Charlie.

Meghan spooned the batter into one of the muffin tins. "I have no idea," she replied, amused. "I started by making a few for Rupert and I couldn't stop myself." She took in the kitchen counter, filled with rows upon rows of all the delicious recipes she'd created. "Maybe I could offer some to people at work."

Tess got up. "Oh . . . You could have them test out different samples and we could see which one is the favorite! I'll be your first tester."

"Go for it," Meghan said, sliding the final trays in the oven as Tess grabbed one of the pecan glazed muffins and unwrapped the paper cup, taking a bite.

Tess slid down into her chair, her eyes rolling back in delight. "Oh my . . ." she said with her mouth full. "This is incredible . . ."

A tingle of purpose spread over Meghan's skin. "Really?"

"Yes," Tess said, taking another bite.

"I just wish Pappy could see it," she said, putting her hands on her hips and surveying the batter-filled bowls and dirty dishes.

"Yeah. He left before the loose ends were all tied up and never got to see you doing what you were supposed to be doing in life. But I'm sure he's somewhere watching," Tess said, looking around as if she'd find him.

The idea of loose ends reminded Meghan of that final day with him once more, and the complete focus he'd had when he'd grabbed her arm and said, "Go to Ricroft." Whatever the mystery was (or wasn't), it was in the past, and she was ready to focus on the present. She reached over and pinched a blueberry sugar crumble muffin, holding it up into the air. "Pappy, I hope you can see all this. It sure feels like a start."

"I'm certain that he can. And he's beaming down at you." Tess reached over the bar where she was sitting and snatched another muffin, unwrapping it and taking a bite. Shaking her head in ecstasy, she said, "Wait until the people at work taste these..."

The idea that Meghan would soon be sharing her own recipes with others suddenly filled her with anticipation. "I'll make us coffee. Then, we can take a bunch with us and taste test while we unload Pappy's closet."

"Sounds like a plan."

Pappy's house looked darker, much smaller, and its age was more evident after spending a night in The Seabreeze. It felt less like a place of refuge and more like a sidenote to bigger things that were on Meghan's horizon. She could suddenly feel Pappy's presence everywhere. It was as if he were telling her that this cottage hadn't been the destination at all, but rather a vehicle to get her to where she really should be.

The humid heat hit her, the air so wet that she struggled to get a deep breath, and she wondered how she and Tess had put up with it for as long as they had. Meghan twisted her hair into the clip she'd brought and turned to Tess. "Let's just pile everything in your bedroom."

Tess slipped off her flip-flops and stood barefoot, as if even the tiny strips of plastic on the tops of her feet were too hot.

With a click of the radio in the bedroom, Meghan and Tess began to empty the closet. Meghan grabbed an armful of Pappy's clothes, and for just a second, the feel of the massive pile, mixed with the faint scent of him, felt like a warm hug within her arms.

She breathed it in and hoped it was his way of telling her that he was there. She lumped them on the bed in Tess's room and came back for the next load, she and Tess working easily together, the two of them making trip after trip, the whole ordeal of moving Pappy's things feeling easier this time.

When they'd gotten all the hanging clothes taken care of, Meghan began moving shoes while Tess grabbed the items from the shelves, setting them neatly on the dresser in the other room. Meghan grabbed the lockbox, the little door swinging open, the small piece of paper fluttering to the floor below. She reached down and scooped it up. "We must not have latched it back last time," she said. "Good thing the earrings weren't in it." She wadded the scrap of paper and went over to the trashcan to toss it in, but something inside her told her to take one last look at it. She smoothed it out in the palm of her hand.

"What're you doing?" Tess asked, coming over to her with a pair of Pappy's church wingtips in one hand and his work boots in the other.

"Looking at that little piece of paper that was in the lockbox," she said, squinting down at it, confused suddenly. "This handwriting doesn't look like Pappy's."

"How can you tell? It's three numbers and a few letters."

She zeroed in on the letters that were legible: Pi . . . s. "Look at the S. It's too curly to be his."

"If you say so . . ." Tess said, clearly unconvinced. She clapped her hands together and snagged a muffin from the bag they'd brought with them. "Could it be your grandmother's? It was in with her earrings, after all." She unwrapped one of the cinnamon ones and took a bite.

The lightbulb went off. "That makes total sense," Meghan said, moving over to the closet and pulling out the old cardboard box that had held her grandmother's dresses. She fumbled through the items inside until she found the note. She compared the smudged slip in her hand to the lettering on the note: *One day, I'll come back. I promise.* "Yes! You're exactly right. The S's are carbon copies."

"So, they were your nanna's Pick-3 numbers?" Tess teased.

Meghan laughed, reaching into the bag and pulling out a maple oat muffin. She took a bite, something feeling very different for her this morning. She set the muffin down on the table and inspected the two pieces of paper again, feeling as if she'd been given something wonderful today but not sure yet what it was.

She slipped the only two remnants of her grandmother's writing into the pocket of her work trousers, deciding to keep them. "You know, I feel Pappy here, but maybe Nanna's here too."

Perhaps it was just her little start with the baking this morning, but Meghan suddenly felt like there was something she was supposed to learn by returning to the Outer Banks this summer.

"The butter popcorn muffin is my favorite," Meredith said, as they all began to collect their things to leave work for the day. The Mariner's team had gathered in the small staff room after their dinner shift, all of them abuzz, nibbling the muffins that Meghan had brought to the inn. They'd all stayed longer than she'd ever expected, and they were gushing over her creations.

"Your flavor pairings are spot on," Darren the chef told Meghan, to her absolute elation. "Maybe we could collaborate on some ideas for the holiday season this winter."

"See?" Tess whispered. "You're not mediocre. Vinnie's an idiot."

Meghan was unable to hide her smile. Rupert's words floated into her consciousness: *Take any step as long as it's the first one. And then take another one after that.* "I'd be honored," she said, collecting her things to go home.

"We should celebrate," Tess told her. "Let's take two of these muffins, go to Lost Love Coffee, and get the most decadent drink on the menu."

"You're on," Meghan said, slipping her handbag onto her shoulder and waving goodbye to their coworkers as she and Tess headed out into the late afternoon sunshine.

All the way to the coffee shop, they brainstormed more muffin flavors. "Maybe I could try making a few recipes at a time," Meghan suggested as they walked up to the coffee shop's door.

"Nightly desserts, handcrafted by the one and only Meghan Gray? I can't think of anything better," Tess said, linking arms with her and opening the door to head inside.

During off-peak hours it was quiet, with Chloe perched on her stool, reading a novel. "Well, hello," she said as they came in.

"Hi, Chloe," Meghan greeted her, approaching the counter. "We're celebrating, and I'd like to get your most indulgent coffee. Decaf. What do you recommend?"

Chloe looked up at the ceiling through her lashes in thought. "We have our double chocolate tiramisu with whipped cream, caramel drizzle, and white chocolate espresso crumbles."

"We'll take two," Tess said over Meghan's shoulder, before handing Chloe her credit card.

"I can pay," Meghan said, pawing at the card.

Tess held it out of her reach and gave it to the barista. "I'd like to do something nice for you. It's not every day that you decide to take your destiny into your own hands."

"I made muffins. I hardly think that's finding my destiny," Meghan teased, as they walked over to an empty table.

Tess playfully punched her arm. "It's a start!"

While they waited, Meghan lingered along the side where the memorabilia were displayed and peered down at the old journal once more, the writing taking on new meaning. But this time, as she stared at the words, something new caught her eye. She squinted at the page. "Look at this curl in the Y right here," she said to Tess, tapping the end of one of the words.

"What about it?"

Meghan stood there dumbfounded, before she remembered

that the notes were still in her pocket from this morning. She pulled them out, her pulse racing with the revelation. "Look," she said, flattening the sentence out over the top of the glass to compare as the espresso machine squealed across the room, the rich smell of coffee wafting toward them. "Nanna didn't write these. *Hester* did."

"Are you sure?" Tess asked, craning her neck to get a better look at both specimens.

"They're exact matches. I never noticed until now."

"Your grandfather knew her, right?"

"According to Rupert," Meghan replied. "Maybe the promise to return was made to my grandmother. Maybe *Nanna* put the box in the back of the closet, not Pappy."

"That would make sense if they were, in fact, best friends."

"Wow," Meghan said, their histories coming together. "But Rupert said Hester came back to be with *him* and when he was already married, she left. I wonder if she went to see Nanna before she disappeared."

"We'll never know."

"Two double chocolate tiramisus," Chloe called from the bar, sliding the porcelain cups overflowing with whipped cream and toppings toward them.

Meghan took a seat at the table, still thinking about Hester while Tess offered to go over to the bar to retrieve their coffees.

"I can't help but wonder if all of this was meant to be..." Meghan said, when Tess returned, still trying to get the whole story together in her head, filling in the gaps with what-ifs.

Tess set the coffees down with a grin. "You mean *destiny*?"

"Oh no," Meghan said, snapping out of it. "I'm turning into you!" But she couldn't help but feel it now. Something was indeed happening.

Tess laughed, and swirled the whipped cream and espresso sprinkles with a plastic spoon. "Would it be so bad to be optimistic for once? To feel like there's some grand purpose in your life?"

"I suppose it wouldn't," Meghan replied, for the first time understanding just a little how her best friend saw the world.

Meghan emptied her pocket before slipping off her trousers, Hester's two mysterious messages lying on the designer drift-wood paint-washed dresser of The Seabreeze. Curiously, she stared at them, wondering if Pappy or Nanna had meant to give her the one with the numbers on it. Had they just been in the box when he'd put the earrings inside, and he'd only been trying to keep Nanna's jewelry secure? Or was there something more to it?

Speaking of Nanna's earrings, maybe she should put them in the room safe . . . She walked over to it and stared at it, immersed in her thoughts. Then, suddenly, an overwhelming wave of rec-ognition crashed upon her. "Tess!" she called, unable to move, her heart beating so wildly that she was sure someone could see it if they were standing next to her. "Tess!"

"Yeah?" Tess came rushing in from the other room, her hair in a towel. "What's wrong?"

Meghan pointed to the safe. "Look."

Tess inspected the box. "What am I looking at?"

Meghan snatched the slip of paper with the numbers from the dresser and pressed it to the front of the safe, reading the smudged letters in Hester's handwriting. "Pi . . . s." Then she touched the insignia on the room safe. "Pinetop Securities."

Tess gasped.

Meghan pulled all her thoughts together, the picture becom-ing murky but still not clear. "And Rupert had been staring at the safe, saying he believed it was Hester's."

"See if the combination works."

"It's unlocked after the last tenant and ready for us to set it, so the combination wouldn't do anything, and the safe is completely empty."

Tess's face crumpled. "This house wasn't here when Hester was around. The safe is brand new."

"But is Pinetop Securities brand new?" Meghan grabbed her laptop, taking it into the grand living room and settling on the oversized white sofa. Tess sat down beside her, eagerly looking on as Meghan typed the company into her search bar.

Pinetop Securities offers first-class security to meet your corporate and residential needs. The longest-running securities company in the Outer Banks, we offer a proven track record of securing valuables for over 150 years . . .

Meghan looked at Tess, the thrill of finding another bit of the story bubbling up. "I'd say they were around back then." She returned her gaze to the computer, but her mind was elsewhere. "Hester left behind a combination to her safe." Then the enormity of what they faced hit her. "But how do we know which box or where?"

"Simple," Tess said.

Meghan waited, wondering how it could be, in any way, *simple.*

"You ask Rupert."

TWENTY-ONE

"Hi," Toby said, bumping into Meghan at the entrance of Rosewood Manor the next morning. His hair was slightly disheveled and his shirttail was untucked from his jeans.

"Hello." Meghan stopped, holding the bag of muffins she'd brought to surprise Rupert, shocked to run into Toby so early.

"I'm glad you're here," he said. "I'm just packing up Gramps's things. They had to rush him to the hospital last night."

"Oh no. What happened?" she asked, her heart racing in panic.

"He's caught a virus of some sort, but it's running him way down. He was dehydrated and he was having trouble breathing, so they wanted to get him in before he showed any symptoms of pneumonia. It came on really quickly."

"Is there anything I can do?"

Toby looked completely distraught and helpless as he shook his head, clearly unable to answer her question. With Rupert's age, this wasn't good.

"I'll come with you so you don't have to deal with it alone." She peered down at her phone for the time. "I've got two hours before I have to be at work."

"All right," he relented, but his distress was evident.

She followed him to Rupert's room, the silence of it settling heavily on her chest. She peered around at the movie memorabilia, all of it having new meaning for her. Now, it wasn't the work of a delusional old man, but rather the outward expression of someone struggling to keep hold of his life so it didn't slip away.

"What do we need to get?" she asked.

"A change of clothes for when he's discharged," he said, his gaze barely meeting hers, and she knew that he was worried about how this would all go. "And his toiletries. I thought maybe we could take one of his books for him in case he wakes up." He opened the closet door, and pulled out a pair of trousers and one of Rupert's button-up shirts.

As she looked through Rupert's book collection to find a good one to bring, Meghan knew Rupert's life couldn't end yet. Hester wouldn't allow it. He'd been Hester's rock, and Meghan was convinced that he had more to say about his life.

"He'll be okay," she said, more hopeful than anything else.

Toby nodded, not saying a word.

Meghan stood outside Rupert's hospital room, peering in through the little window beside the closed door while Toby went in and set the man's things down on the open closet next to the sink and counter that held cotton balls, antibacterial gel, and a box of tissues.

Rupert lay quietly in his hospital gown, his eyes closed, IVs in his arms that were lying motionless on top of his blanket. She wanted to burst in there and tell him she was by his side, but the staff had advised that only immediate family go in. They'd told Toby not to stay terribly long, to allow Rupert to sleep.

When he'd gotten Rupert's things situated, Toby stopped and stood near Rupert's bed, his head hung low as he reached out and touched his grandfather's hand. Then he turned and met Meghan's eyes through the window, the fear evident in his gaze.

The two of them walked together to the lobby, where they both sat down, neither of them knowing the next step. Meghan wanted to stay there all day to provide silent support for Rupert, but she knew that sitting there worrying wasn't going to do anyone any good.

"We should probably go," Toby suggested. His gaze flickered over to a middle-aged woman who shifted in her seat across from them, leaning tiredly on her hand while the book she was reading was turned over on the magazines that covered the coffee table between them. "He's not coming out of sedation anytime soon."

Meghan winced when he said it. She hadn't liked the idea of sedating Rupert, but he'd been giving the staff a difficult time, telling them all that he was fine. The same way he'd seemed to be fighting his dementia, struggling for a foothold in his own life, he was fighting this virus.

Toby stood up, so, without anything else more she could do, Meghan followed suit, and he took her hand. His touch gave her a sense of calm, and the way he gripped her hand, she knew that he was telling her that they were facing this together. Without a single thought, she followed him to the parking lot.

"Where are we going?" she asked, climbing into his Range Rover.

"I have no idea, but I can't sit here," he replied. "Anywhere you need to go?"

Meghan looked at her watch—she still had an hour until work. She thought for a minute, wishing she could do something for Rupert. But then it hit her. "Actually? Yes."

"Okay," he said, starting the engine. "Where to?"

"Pinetop Securities."

"If Hester did, in fact, give my grandmother a combination to a safe, there might be something of value in it," Meghan explained to Toby, as they waited for the salesman who was pitching the latest in-home security to a potential buyer.

"You can access the code via your mobile phone," the man said animatedly, while showing the woman how it worked.

"But even if Hester did have something in a safe," Toby said, "you probably won't be allowed access to it."

"Unless it's her home safe and it's hidden somewhere ..."

He allowed a tiny smirk. "You're getting as interested in Hester as Gramps."

"It's easy to do with Hester Quinn. She's so fascinating, and not only is she tied to Rupert but she's tied to my grandmother, whom I didn't know very well, other than the stories my mother told me. So learning about Hester helps me to know more about Nanna."

"May I help you?" the salesperson cut in.

"I hope so ..." Meghan replied, taking a deep breath and explaining her story to the man.

"Hmm," he said, going over to the computer behind the counter. "The only boxes we still have from that time period," he said, clicking keys, "would be at a small bank that's been open since 1949 called Wells Rycroft Savings and Loan." He turned the screen to face her. "You could try there."

Every nerve in her body prickled as the memory of Pappy that last day in the hospital floated into her consciousness. *Go to Rycroft.* Rycroft with a Y. She turned to Toby, speechless, and then back to the man, her body trembling. "What's the address?" Meghan asked, trying to keep herself from losing it.

"It's off of Beach Road, just before you get to Kitty Hawk."

"Thank you," she said, restraining herself from hugging the man.

Toby opened the door and the two of them walked out into the warm summer air. "Where to now?" he asked, questions written on his face. "Beach Road?"

She looked at her watch and gritted her teeth. "I can't yet. I have to go to work."

"All right," he said, something lurking in his eyes. "I'll take you back to get your car."

"Promise me you'll let me know if Rupert wakes up or has any change?"

"Promise," he said.

"You missed all the gossip," Tess said, tugging on Meghan's arm the moment she arrived at Mariner's Inn. "I have some details on your guy that you might need to hear."

Meghan grabbed her apron and tied it around her waist, tucking the leather server's book into the pocket, still stunned and on autopilot, trying to keep herself together after learning about Wells Rycroft Savings and Loan. "My guy?" she asked, her mind elsewhere.

"Toby." Tess pulled Meghan aside. "Meredith told us that the latest is that the other day, Toby tried to pay off a few of the zoning board members to get them to rezone so he can expand. He's *bribing* them. The other members found out somehow, and they're all up in arms. They're talking about trying to shut this place down completely."

"What?" Meghan said, flabbergasted. She chewed on the inside of her cheek, thinking. "That just doesn't sound like him," she said, remembering the sincere look in his eyes whenever he looked at her. Did she have him all wrong?

"Maybe it doesn't sound like him because he isn't showing that side to you." Tess grabbed a handful of menus in preparation for a few of the tables that were already filling up. "If this does get shut down, we might be looking for another job."

Considering that not a single place had called them back after they'd dropped off their résumés, that idea was terrifying.

The rest of the day, Meghan's thoughts were consumed with Rupert, Toby, and getting to the bank, none of it adding up.

After work, she'd filled Tess in on everything that had happened, and the two of them had stopped at home quickly to grab the paper with the combination on their way to Wells Rycroft Savings and Loan.

"Are you a direct descendant of John Gray?" the woman at the bank asked in awe, confusing Meghan.

"Yes. I'm his granddaughter." Her heart felt as if it might explode.

"May I see your driver's license, please?"

Meghan pulled the card from her wallet and slid it through the small opening in the plexiglass separating her from the bank employee.

"We've all been waiting for this," the woman said. "A few of us believed that it was just an urban legend and there was no owner that would come forward." She slid the license back through to Meghan along with a form. "Could you just sign here, please?"

"So, you have a box that belongs to Hester Quinn?"

Tess looked over at Meghan, the suspense clear in her rounded eyes.

The woman nodded. "Mm-hm," she said, pulling a key from a drawer and walking around through the swinging half-door to their side. "Come with me." She led them through a large entry into a room with locked boxes covering the walls. "For years, we've been told that the great Hester Quinn has a box here, and she's allowed access for anyone in her or John Gray's direct line. We called him years ago, and he said that either his daughter or granddaughter would probably retrieve the contents." She went over to the box. "If you have the combination, you're welcome to use it, or I can use the master key. I'll be outside."

As the teller left, Meghan stared at the box in disbelief. Pappy had been trying to tell her . . .

"Oh my gosh, Meghan!" Tess said, bouncing beside her. "Open it!"

With shaky fingers, Meghan moved the three small dials, lining up the numbers: 34-26-19. *Click.* The door opened. She reached in and pulled the small metal box from the interior, setting it on the counter in the middle of the room and opening the lid. Inside was a leather journal. Meghan peered over at her friend.

Tess clapped a hand over her mouth.

Meghan opened the book and gasped. She ran her finger down the bumpy ridge inside the journal where pages had been torn out, noticing that the color of the paper within and the thinness of the writing lines looked exactly like the ones she'd been reading at Lost Love Coffee. "That's my mother's name," she said, as she tapped the top of the note inscribed on the first page, the swooping letters blurring in her tears. She cleared them enough to read:

My dearest Jacqueline,

Audrey was the most grounded of the two of us. She was the one who was meant for a family, the one with the highest capability of real love. At the time, neither of us knew that she couldn't have children, so it made all of this a bit easier to bear once we found out.

When I first met your father John, I fell hard and fast for him. It was like free-falling off a cliff, scrambling to reach the ledge for safety, only to realize there was no return. That last night of summer, under the stars with him, I let myself go and gave in to my impulsive spirit. I never regretted it because if there was one truly great person in this world, it was him.

That night, I told him that I couldn't imagine a better place to live than Hatteras, but I think we both knew deep down that I wouldn't survive there. I needed the city lights, the buzz of the crowd, and the energy. In the end, that was my true love. By the next day, I had told him that last night had been wonderful but the daylight revealed that neither of us would be happy with one another. The best of both of us together had been that one night.

*I want you to know, my dear girl, that I adored him. I loved
him, and I love you. When I realized I was pregnant, I knew
that I wouldn't be able to give you the life you deserve . . .*

Meghan wiped the tears that had spilled down her cheek,
unsure if she wanted to read any more. "Hester is my *grandmother?*" she said into the air, unable to focus on Tess.

"No wonder you look like her," Tess said in barely a whisper.
"Read more."

Her stomach in knots, Meghan continued.

*In the nine months that I was away, trying to figure out what
to do, John and Audrey had begun a sweet friendship that
had blossomed into romance. Audrey had said that she didn't
want to be anywhere except with John, and she'd stayed, giving
up all her upbringing for the man she was wholeheartedly in
love with.*

*Audrey was the best friend I'd ever had, and for some
unknown reason, she stuck by me, when I wasn't capable of
being the kind of friend anyone would ever want. She offered
to adopt you, and she and your father raised you as their own.
They wanted to tell you about me, but I made them promise not
to because I never wanted Audrey to be less than what she was:
a mother. She was your true mother. I just brought you to her.*

*Every so often, when you were a baby, I'd come to see you.
But as you grew, it became too difficult for me to see the life
I could've had with my own child and a wonderful man. I'd
even come to the realization, years later, that there was, in fact,
someone I did love as much as your mother loved your father.
But that, too, was out of my reach.*

*The last time I was there, I left a note for your mom and
dad, telling them that I promised to come back, but I didn't. I
tried—believe me, I tried. But you'd gotten older and I didn't
want to have to explain why I was a sniveling mess. When I*

told your parents that I'd left you this journal, it was my wish
that they tell you, but only after you'd led a full and happy life.

Meghan stared at the words, wishing her mother could've read them. But she'd never been given the chance. How heartbroken Pappy must have been over it. "I can't believe this," she said, flipping the page to find more writing.

"Keep reading," Tess urged her.

But now, it's time to tell you the one thing I need to say. If he
isn't already in your life, Rupert Meyers is someone you need
to know. He was my best friend and the one person who kept
me sane most of my life. I've left your inheritance with him. He
has family overseas and I thought he might know better what
to do with that amount of money than your father would. This
journal was to be my fresh start. I ripped out my old life and was
ready to make a new one with Rupert, but I was too late. By the
time I realized that I could love the man who'd been in love with
me my whole adult life, he'd already moved on. In a note, I've
told your dad all of it, explaining to him that he's to give the
inheritance to you when the time is right. Rupert has my will.

Every paycheck I received, Rupert handled, paying my bills
and putting away the rest. Rupert's currently holding $45 mil-
lion of my money in his name, in off-shore accounts. I told him
to keep it until you come for it. I know it isn't the love that you
deserve from me, but it's everything I've sacrificed and worked
for. And in my lowest moments, once I realized the years of love
I'd never had, the idea of giving it all to you was what kept me
going.

"Forty-five *million?*" Tess asked, her eyes rounded, her mouth hanging open.

Meghan looked up from the letter, Toby's comment coming back into her mind with the speed of a freight train, causing her head to pound. *We knew he had off-shore accounts, and inheritance from our family overseas, but we had no idea just how much until he gave me full access to his books.* "If Hester left it to Mom and Mom left her inheritance to me . . ."

"I think you can get that comforter set you wanted now," Tess said, a glimmer in her eye.

"Oh my goodness." Meghan struggled to stand, her knees weak. "What if Toby has been using *Hester's* money?"

"What do you mean?"

"He told me that Rupert had off-shore accounts. And what about the rumors that he's going to steal it all to build onto Mariner's?"

"Well, if he is, it's yours, so he can't steal it."

Everything now a muddle in her mind, she continued reading, hoping to get more answers.

I can't say I was great at figuring life out. I was a bit of a disaster. But what I hope to leave you is something I never had: a clean slate. Fill this journal with your own story, and use the money to take you wherever you want to go. Just don't let it take you too far away from the people you care about the most. I spent my entire life chasing happiness, and I didn't know it was right in front of me the whole time.

Be ruthless in finding your own.

All my love,

Hester

Meghan closed the journal and held it to her chest, her entire life flashing before her in snapshots. "I ran to New York in search of a more glamorous life. I've spent all my time working, never settling down. I'm still struggling to find my own happiness . . ." The silence buzzed in her ears. "I'm just like her," she whispered, sliding down to the floor, pulling her knees up and pinning the journal to her heart.

Tess lowered herself down beside Meghan. "Yes," she said. "But your lives could be very different if you want them to be."

Meghan nodded, Pappy's words coming to her: *Your dreams are just your future stretching out in front of you. It's up to you to act on them.* "You're exactly right." After today, her life was about to change.

"I've left two messages for Toby, asking him to call me back," Meghan said, falling down next to Charlie on the plush sofa at The Seabreeze, her gaze falling on the journal sitting on the glass coffee table in a beam of light coming in from the back wall of windows.

Tess brought two bowls of soup over, setting them down in front of them and plopping onto the sofa beside Meghan. Charlie perked up, his nose twitching at the savory scent from the steaming bowls. "What do you think he's going to say?"

"I have no idea." She prayed that he'd totally understand and they'd figure it out together, but she wasn't so sure things could go that smoothly if he was, in fact, using the money and if the account was in Rupert's name. "I should probably contact a lawyer. I don't have Hester's will, and Rupert isn't of sound mind to confirm this."

"Talking to Toby would be your best option, but it wouldn't hurt to get a lawyer."

Meghan nodded, thinking, and then got up, grabbing her laptop. "Happen to know any lawyers in the area?"

"Fresh out," Tess teased, wriggling next to Meghan as she sat back down and picked up her bowl, spooning out a mouthful of soup.

With a quick search, Meghan had a list. "I guess I'll just call one."

Tess grinned. "You can do anything you want once you have the money. What are you going to do with all of it?"

Pulling her from her questions, Meghan threw her fingers to her mouth in utter disbelief, all those days of not knowing how she'd pay for even little things nearly behind her. She looked up at their lavish surroundings in The Seabreeze. "Like you said, anything I want." She let out an excited giggle.

Meghan's phone went off on the table, making her jump. "It's Toby," she said, looking at Tess.

"Get it," Tess urged her.

Holding her breath, she answered the call. "Hello?"

"Hey," he said, and she bit her lip, wondering how to even approach any of this. "You called?"

"Yeah," she said, her breathing shallow with her nerves. "Can we meet for a coffee tomorrow? I have something I need to show you."

TWENTY-TWO

"There's a pretty big issue in the wall behind the stove," the electrician said, wiping sweat from his dirty face as he stood opposite Meghan in Pappy's kitchen while the other men continued to work on old wiring throughout the house.

The cottage was scorching and full of dust again, the wood floors covered in dirty work boot prints. The drywall she and Tess had just painted had been cut into all over the house, leaving large places where they'd have to be patched and repainted. She'd basically be starting over, and much of the money she'd spent on painting seemed to have been lost. The heating and air company she'd hired to put in central air had already cornered her to choose the equipment she'd wanted installed and they were busy taking measurements.

"It looks like you've had two or three different owners wiring on top of each other," the man said, tugging on a massive knot of different types of wires. "No wonder you had problems. This is going to take a while to sort out."

"How long?" she asked.

"About a week or two longer than we'd expected. We're looking at a good month."

"A month?" She didn't know if she could stay in The Seabreeze for an entire month. Not to mention that she was living out of a suitcase . . .

The electrician grabbed the ball of wire. "Up to you. You wanna leave this here or fix it?"

"Okay," she said, relenting.

"It'll probably add another seven hundred dollars in labor."

What was she supposed to do, leave the holes in the wall and live in Pappy's cottage with no electricity? "All right," she said, having literally no other option but to agree. Right now, she didn't have that kind of money to throw around. All she could hope for was that Toby would come through for her quickly and locate her inheritance.

The ocean swelled and crashed against the shore on the other side of the wild grass-covered dunes behind Meghan, as she and Toby sat at one of the bistro tables on the deck of Lost Love Coffee after her shift at work. Meghan anxiously twirled her straw in her iced coffee, her heart in her throat, her eyes on the open journal in Toby's hands. Toby closed the journal slowly and set it down.

"How can you prove this is real?" he asked, folding his hands, the calmness a little too steady for her liking.

The buzzing of anticipation came to a screeching halt. She'd just assumed that after everything they'd learned with Rupert, she wouldn't have to prove this to Toby. But just like he'd done early on, he was doing it now: brushing off coincidences that were too obvious to her to ignore.

"My grandfather had the combination for the lock. Isn't that something? The bank people said they'd been waiting to see who would finally come get it."

"We don't know anything about the origins of this," he said. "And if it was Hester's, how do we know she wasn't completely off her rocker when she wrote it? She didn't strike me as the most stable of people."

"She left her money to her family," she said, having no idea what other words to tell him. "*I'm* her family."

"Meghan," he said softly, shaking his head, bewildered, "I can't part with *millions* of dollars of my grandfather's money because you've found some notebook with a cryptic letter inside."

"It's not cryptic. It spells it out right here." She opened the journal and tapped Rupert's name with her finger.

His shoulders lifted as if he had no explanation for it. "Until I have solid proof in an official document, our legal team won't touch this. There are no last names listed, we have no idea as to the origin of this, and my father holds no accounts in Hester's name. My hands are tied. You have to understand that. Do you have any legal proof at all besides this journal?"

"There's a will." She ran her finger under the words on the page stating it. "Rupert has it. Hester said it herself."

Toby shook his head, that sparkle she'd seen in his eyes now a cloud of disbelief. "I've been through all my grandfather's paperwork and I've never seen a will of any kind."

She knew that without a will, she had very little to prove her case. She wanted him to tell her they'd figure it all out, but she understood how massive this was, and she knew he needed time.

"I should go," he said, thoughts written on his face, his response telling her he was as confused as she was by the whole thing. "I'll see if I can find anything that would substantiate this, but I doubt I will."

"Okay," she said, not knowing what else to say to him, suddenly feeling like they'd drawn an invisible line between them in the sand, her heart breaking. Should she just let it go? She knew she couldn't. If that money were meant for her, it could change her life.

He turned to leave and she was glad that her back was to him so he couldn't see the unexpected tears that had welled up in her eyes. The last thing she wanted was to cause a rift between them over money, but if it was meant for her and her family, what could she do?

"Should we continue to stay here at The Seabreeze?" Tess asked as she sat next to Meghan on the sofa after Meghan had gotten home.

Meghan twisted toward her friend. "Why do you ask?"

"What if you end up having to go to court over this? I searched online and you can use letters as a will and take him to probate court over it. They could contest it if it's vague or if there's no evidence to support it, but we could try if we had to. Should we use his money or goodwill right now? Would it be a conflict of interest?"

Charlie jumped up beside Meghan on the sofa, nudging her to give him attention. "I don't know," she replied honestly, feeling awful. The very last thing she wanted was to fight Toby in court, and she knew deep down that his legal team would eat her alive. "Let's just see where it goes in the next few days and we can figure out our next move then."

"Have you thought about what will happen if the rumors are true and he's already spent Hester's money? Would you go after him and make him pay it back?" Tess asked, her face racked with worry.

Meghan shook her head, looking up at the high living room ceiling with its track lighting around it as she rubbed Charlie's side for comfort. "I don't know," she said again, tears pricking her eyes. She blew out an anxiety-filled breath through her lips. "I can't imagine it coming to that." A lump formed in her throat, her heart aching. "And if it did, how would I even pay a lawyer so that I could get the money, when I can't even afford rent?"

"I could use my savings," Tess offered. "And if we're really careful with our tip money, we could do it if we had to."

Meghan pulled her feet up onto the sofa and put her head in her hands. "If we still have tip money."

"What do you mean?"

"Would I be allowed to work for a man that I'm suing?" She shook her head, squeezing her eyes shut. "I don't want to sue Toby. I didn't ask for any of this..." Hester loved Rupert and would never have sued Rupert's family. Meghan was nearly sure of it.

Tess fluttered her hands in the air. "Nobody's suing anyone," she said. "All we have to do is prove that there's a will of Hester's, right? If we have that, Toby will come around."

"And how are we supposed to do that?" she asked, rubbing her aching temples.

"We'll start calling lawyers in the morning just to get advice. There's nothing we can do tonight. Let's take a hot bath and relax."

"I like the sound of that," Meghan said, although she wasn't quite sure how she was going to relax, not with Toby on her mind... If she took everything from him, would he ever speak to her again?

TWENTY-THREE

"The ambiguity of this could be a tough battle, especially if there are, in fact, no accounts in Hester Quinn's name," the lawyer, Mr. Wilson, said from across his desk as Meghan and Tess sat together in the guest chairs on the other side. He closed the journal and slid it across his desk to Meghan. You could always see if the will was recorded in probate court."

With the day off, Meghan and Tess had gotten straight up and headed into the office of the first lawyer they'd reached, after they'd stopped in to Lost Love Coffee for a big dose of caffeine to see them through.

"Do you know where a copy of it would have been filed?" the lawyer asked. "It would be public record."

"I'm not sure," Meghan replied, not very hopeful, given Hester's track record, but perhaps Rupert had filed it for her. "Could it have been in California where she lived?"

"Yes. You'd have to find out the city where your loved one passed away."

"Brentwood," Meghan said, turning toward Tess. "Remember the article we read?" She addressed the lawyer. "You are a genius, Mr. Wilson!" If Rupert had recorded it, and she could prove the money was hers, she and Toby could hopefully settle this without things getting messier than they should. She prayed they could somehow both find a happy ending in all this.

Mr. Wilson smiled smugly and folded his hands on his shiny desk. "Glad I could help."

"So, how are we going to get to Brentwood, California?" Tess asked, as they let themselves out of the office, stepping under the shade of one of the large palm trees lining the sidewalk. She tugged at Meghan's shorts. "Got any free plane tickets in those pockets?"

Meghan wriggled away playfully while she tapped her phone, still thrilled from the lead, however small it was. "The documents are all available online," she said, turning the screen toward Tess to show her the results of the search. Then she swiped the screen away and slipped her phone back into the pocket of her shorts. "I don't want to look yet, though," she said, taking in a steadying breath. "I want to wait until we're back at the house so I can see it on my laptop." What she wasn't saying was that she wanted to make each step slowly, taking her time and focusing on the very best way to handle this. The last thing she wanted to do was to ruin what she had with Toby and risk not seeing him or Rupert again. She needed to think about the best way to handle this.

"Have you thought about what your next move is if there's nothing recorded in the Brentwood public record?" Tess asked, as the two of them walked past the bright umbrellas of the beachside ice cream parlor where Meghan had lost Hester's journal pages.

"Hester will lead me to it like she's led me to all the other answers," Meghan said.

Tess leaned in, bumping shoulders with her. "Are you saying that *fate* will lead you to the will?"

Meghan laughed, her eyes on the dune she'd tried to climb that day. "It was as if Hester knew that I didn't need those pages," she said, the memory of them floating in the air coming back to her so clearly.

"First the muffins, now this? I never thought I'd see the day."

"I came here, asking Pappy what to do. But it's like they're *all* up there together, trying to show me." She tipped her head up, a flock of seagulls soaring above them. "I'm just as lost as Hester was. But now I have her journal—a clean slate—and I just have to figure out how to fill it. Money or no money."

"And how are you going to figure it out?" Tess asked.

"One step at a time."

Meghan stared at the email on her laptop, a heaviness the size of a boulder in her gut.

"What's wrong?" Tess asked from the chair across from her in the living room of The Seabreeze. The large doors were open, the wind blowing in, but Meghan's thoughts were too preoccupied to notice it.

"I just saw the bills for the electrical and the central air on Pappy's cottage."

Tess leaned forward, her forearms on her knees. "And?"

"Combined, I owe them $8,275." Tears welled up in her eyes.

"No luck on finding the will?"

Meghan shook her head. "I can't find it in the Brentwood public records. I've checked all the nearby localities, and even the Outer Banks in case Rupert registered it here—nothing." She took in a jagged breath, her chest tight.

"I have some savings," Tess said.

"I don't want to do that—no way—but I have no idea what to do."

"Was Toby going to loan you the money?"

"I can't ask him now," Meghan said, shaking her head as she recalled their last meeting. She'd put him through enough with the journal. She didn't want to be any more of a burden.

At the very least, she didn't even know what to say to him if she called him.

"The money isn't due until the work is completed, right?" Tess asked, standing up and coming over to stand next to where she was sitting on the sofa. Charlie stirred on the floor beside them, getting up and walking out to the patio where he flopped down in the sun. "Maybe we can figure something out." She gestured toward the front door. "We should take a walk. It's beautiful outside. Want to go? We can run through ideas, and it might clear your head."

"You can go. Take Charlie. He needs a walk," Meghan replied, swallowing the lump in her throat, her stomach churning. "I just want to sit here for a while and think."

"You sure?"

"Yeah, I'll be fine. You go."

"All right," she said, eyeing her. "Text me if you change your mind." Tess turned to Charlie. "Wanna go for a walk?"

The dog hopped up, jogging inside, his tail wagging furiously.

After Tess and Charlie left, Meghan picked up Hester's journal from the table and went out and sat by the pool. She tipped her face to the warm sun and closed her eyes as she held the book in her lap. She lay there for what felt like hours, drifting off until her thoughts pulled her back to reality. The repairs for Pappy's house would set her back so far that she'd never get on her feet, let alone move her career forward. And while Hester's journal clearly stated that there was an inheritance, she had no way to get it. The worry about it all circled in her brain like a cyclone.

Finally, restless from her contemplations, she opened her eyes. "Hester, you've been in my position. You know what it's like to not be sure of your path," she said quietly into the air. "What am I supposed to do?" She listened for anything, a word on the wind, a sign from above—anything at all—but nothing came.

Meghan sat up, staring out at the Atlantic, processing none of the view as she swam around in her thoughts.

What did Hester learn from her life? she asked herself. She opened the journal, her gaze falling on the line: *I spent my entire life chasing happiness, and I didn't know it was right in front of me the whole time.* Pappy's words now made even more sense. "The only thing we really need is love."

"All right," she said to herself as she closed the journal. "What have I loved since getting here?" She loved seeing Rupert, making up the recipes for the muffins, and coming back to Pappy's. Unexpectedly, her mind went to Toby, but she wouldn't allow the thought to come through. She pushed it out of her mind and focused on the rest of it.

What was her first step? What was the first thing she could tackle? Toby aside, the more she thought about it, the more she realized that the things she loved weren't about money or fame. The things that made her whole were her relationships, following her heart when it came to work, and coming back to her roots.

Tess burst through the door, interrupting her inner dialogue. "Come with me," she said, jerking Meghan up by the arm, an enormous smile on her face. "Hurry! I want to show you something. Get your purse and your shoes."

Charlie hopped up on the sofa, watching them.

Meghan set the journal back on the coffee table inside, grabbed her handbag, and slipped on her flip-flops. "What's all this about?"

"Just wait!" Tess dragged her outside and locked the door, leading her down the massive front steps of The Seabreeze.

"Where are we going?" Meghan asked, shuffling up beside her.

"The Memory Box!"

They walked along the sandy sidewalk, past a group of tourists coming off the beach, and through the line of palm trees leading to the second-hand shop. "Did you find something else of Hester's?" Meghan asked.

"Nope," Tess replied, leading her around the corner. "Better." She pointed toward the building.

Perched beside it was an old wooden cotton candy cart with two large wheels on one end and pegs on the other, with a faded red exterior. "What's this?"

"It's your future."

A confused smirk wiggled its way across Meghan's lips. "What?"

"What if we convert this cart and set it up next to the beach access in the mornings? You can sell your muffins, do taste tests—we could even serve coffee."

Meghan stared at the dilapidated cart. She'd set her expectations a bit higher, but the idea wasn't so bad. While taking classes or opening a restaurant would take a ton of money, this would be an easy investment. "How much is Simp asking for it?"

"Forty bucks."

Meghan's mouth fell slack. "Forty dollars? That's all?"

"He said it's been here for years." Tess cut off Meghan's view of the old cart. "Because it's been waiting for *you*."

"So, I'd be like . . . the muffin lady?" she asked, trying on the idea.

"That's exactly what you'd be."

She stared at it. "You know it isn't as easy as painting this thing. And I'll have to get a business license, a seller's permit, a food-handler's permit . . . I'll probably have to get some sort of parking permit . . . Do we even know where I'd be allowed to park it?" The fear crept in—could she do this? But then, Hester's blank journal floated back into her mind.

One step at a time.

"You know what?" she said before Tess could respond. "Let's do it."

Tess threw her hands in the air and danced around.

They went inside and paid Simp, using the last of Meghan's tip cash. Then, the two of them went back outside and lifted the end of the cart by the handles, rolling it back to The Seabreeze on one tire, the other flat. As they pushed it down the street, while she had no idea how it would help to pay her bills or fix anything else, she couldn't help but feel like she was taking that first step in the right direction.

TWENTY-FOUR

The sun casting an early orange light on the sand under their feet, Meghan stood back to take a look at their progress, the bright white cart that they'd painted on the beach out back with their left-over house paint gleaming at her. That morning, she'd gotten straight up and started painting.

"I'm going to have to buy some exterior paint at some point," Meghan worried aloud next to Tess, "but this should make it through the summer."

"It looks gorgeous," Tess said, holding the piece of wood for the top of the cart that she'd just brought back from the hardware store, the salty coastal air swirling around them as she unpacked a saw, screws, a few tools, and some sandpaper.

"I managed to get the old cotton candy bowl and counter off the top," Meghan said, clapping the sand and dust off her hands.

"Wonderful." Tess handed her the saw. "We can cut the wood to fit and then affix it to the top." Then her best friend flashed a devious grin. "I got some other things too."

Meghan peered into the bag. "What else?"

"They're not in there," Tess told her. "Let's get the top on and then I'll show you."

With paint-splattered hands, Meghan pulled the measuring tape from the bag and measured the size of the counter she wanted to make, stretching the tape along the cart. When she had her dimensions, she marked them off on the board.

"Can you hold the other end while I saw?" she asked.

Tess grabbed the free side, keeping it still while Meghan began to move the saw back and forth along the line she'd marked. They worked together until the board was just the right size.

After the tedious task of sanding it, they both held the board, affixed it to the top with the screws, and then puttied over the holes. "This is going to be gorgeous once it's painted," Meghan said, wiping the sweat from her forehead with the back of her wrist.

"Yes," Tess agreed. "But wait here. I'll go get the things I bought. They're a congratulations present on starting your own business." She ran around to the front of the house.

Meghan viewed the cart. The doors would need new silver latches and hinges, but she could upgrade those when she got paid, and she'd have to see if she could replace the tires at the bike shop in town...

Tess came running back around the house hugging the pole of a giant red umbrella, with another bag slung over her shoulder. "Surprise!" she said, opening up the umbrella and showing off its bright color. "I bought brackets too, so we can fasten it to the side of the cart."

"It's amazing," Meghan said, astonished by the gesture. "You didn't have to do that."

"I know I didn't," Tess replied, digging around in the bag. "I wanted you to have everything you need." She pulled out a silver box with a lock on the front. "It's a cash box."

Meghan smiled, unable to hide her fondness for her best friend.

"And!" Tess held up a finger while rustling in the bag once more, then pulling out a bright red basket. "I got this to sit on top." She placed it on the counter they'd just made. "To hold your muffins."

"The red is so bright and stunning against the white," Meghan said, the color scheme inspiring her. "It just *feels* right." She reached over and gave her friend a squeeze. "Thank you. I couldn't have done this without you."

"Yes, you could have," Tess said, wrinkling her nose playfully. "But I'm glad I'm here with you."

"In a very weird way, while I have no idea where this little cart will take me, it feels so natural, like it truly had been waiting for me. And *you* found it, so I needed you here." Meghan came around the other side of the cart. "But not just to find me this cart. You've been amazing through all of this." She reached out and gave her best friend a hug.

"I still wonder if Toby's going to kick us out of here," Tess said to Meghan, as they floated on lounge-floats in the pool at The Seabreeze. The sun had dropped just enough in the sky to cause long shadows to stretch across the patio. Tess made little splashes in the water with her feet to get over to the side of the pool and pushed off, sending waves across the pool. "Have you talked to him at all since you showed him the journal?"

"No." She ran her fingers along the glassy surface of the water, focusing on the last remnants of white paint washing off her nails so she didn't have to think about Toby. "I miss Rupert. I want to see him."

Tess paddled over, lining her float up with Meghan's. "Then why don't you? If you don't feel comfortable running into Toby, he probably isn't there now. You could sneak in and say hello."

The float bobbed as Meghan swung her legs on either side and sat up. "You think I could?"

"Why not?" Tess urged her.

Meghan jumped off her float with a splash, the cool water

instantly refreshing against her warm skin. "Okay," she said. A buzz of excitement swelled within her. "You know how I said that the cart felt right?"

"Yeah?" Tess got off her own float and pushed it to the steps of the pool.

"I feel the same way about Rupert. It's like Hester wants me to take care of him. No matter what, I'm going to see him," she decided. "It's important to me."

Meghan made her way through the crowds of tourists that littered the sandy sidewalks, past the brightly colored storefronts, along the road that paralleled the ocean, headed for Rosewood Manor. She was happy to see Rupert, but she also thought that if she could just get Rupert to be himself for a few minutes to tell her the location of the will, she'd find it, and maybe she could convince Toby, and then somehow all this would work out.

As she paced quickly down the sidewalk, past the beach trinket shops and the island bookstore, she considered how she'd approach Toby if she did find the will. Would he be angry with her? Would it impact the inn if she was entitled to the money? She'd have to wait and see . . .

Within a few minutes, Meghan rounded the corner and headed up the walk to the complex. She walked through the doors of Rosewood Manor and smiled at the front desk receptionist. "Hi there," she said. "I'm here to see Rupert Meyers."

"Of course. Let me get you a door code." The receptionist regarded her with a friendly nod, but as she clicked through a few things on her computer, she stopped. "I'm sorry, Ms. Gray," the woman said. "It seems that you've been denied access."

"What?"

The woman peered at her screen. "Toby Meyers has put a stop to all visitation for his grandfather."

Stunned, Meghan leaned over the counter. "What?"

"No visitors."

Her mind raced with reasons why Toby wouldn't want her to see Rupert, and all she could come up with was that he was scared Rupert might tell her something that Toby didn't want her to know. Something like the location of a will . . . Her hands began to shake as she realized that the rumors could very well be true about him and the reality of that was crushing. "I just want to see him for a quick second, that's all. Could we meet in a common area or something?"

The woman shook her head. "I'm sorry. He can't have *any* visitors. No one may go in except for family."

"Okay," Meghan said, hanging her head, defeated, still wondering if there could be another reason why Toby would do such a thing, and coming up empty. "Have a good night." She turned around and left the building. All that she could think about was the fact that she'd put a wrench in that plan that everyone was talking about. But that aside, what if Rupert got upset? Who would be there to calm him down? She stared at the front door, knowing Rupert was on the other side, feeling hopeless. What was she supposed to do? As Meghan stood there, worrying in the parking lot, an idea suddenly came to her. She looked around to be sure no one had noticed her standing there. The lot was empty so she quietly made her way around the side of the building, keeping an eye out to be sure she didn't have any followers.

One, two, three . . . She counted the windows to herself, guessing that Rupert's was the seventh one, remembering the view from when she'd opened his blinds. She looked out for the oak tree that she could see from his window. When she got to the seventh window, she hurried up to it and tried to peer in, but the blind was down. She closed her eyes and sucked in a nervous breath, holding it in her lungs. Then, before she could think too much about the repercussions, she knocked on the glass. When there was no response, she put her ear to the window, suddenly wondering if Rupert would be strong enough to get out of bed after his hospital stay.

But then, she felt a ray of hope as the blinds began to lift and Rupert was facing her on the other side. Unable to stop herself, she broke into an enormous smile. "Hi," she said with a little wave.

His face lit up.

"Can you open the window?" she asked him, pointing to the latch.

He unfastened the locks and levered it the three inches that it would open. "What are you doing out there?" he asked.

"I can't come in," Meghan said, unsure of what her response would be as to why, if he asked. "I just wanted to see you."

He stared at her as if he were going through all the memories he had of her. And then a tear fell down his cheek.

"What is it?" she asked.

"I thought I'd lost you again."

She shook her head. "You'll never lose me."

He tipped his head back, letting out a chuckle of relief.

"How are you?"

He pouted, considering the question. "They gave me mashed potatoes," he said. "They were awful."

Meghan laughed, the elation she felt seeing him again bigger than any will she could be given. A clatter in the hallway inside, however, snapped her back to the task at hand. "Rupert, I need to ask you something. It's very important."

He leaned forward, his unsteady hands grasping the edge of the window. "Ask me anything."

She looked around to be sure she was still alone and then leaned in, putting her face near the opening in the window. "You know the money I left you in off-shore accounts?" she said, her voice low.

"Of course I do," he replied, giving Meghan goose bumps.

"Where's the will I wrote to leave it to my daughter?"

His eyebrows shot up and he leaned back, his gaze roaming the room as if he'd only just remembered she'd had a daughter.

The sound of the wind rustled the trees behind her, startling her, and she looked around again quickly to be sure no one was coming up behind her. "It's very important. Can you tell me?"

He paced around in front of her, as if sifting through years of memories that were locked behind closed doors, suddenly stopping cold. He put his hand over his mouth. "Oh, no," he said.

"What?" she asked, hanging on his every move.

"She told me where it was that day she showed up at my door, but in all the commotion . . . I never looked for it. Did I?"

"Try to remember," she encouraged him.

"It's still in the desk drawer." He looked around as if he'd find it there at Rosewood Manor.

Her heart plummeted into her stomach. There was no desk in Rupert's room, which meant that either she'd have to go through Toby to find it in a desk somewhere, it had been moved when Rupert had gone into Rosewood Manor, or it had been left in Hester's desk and who knew where that was now. Toby had said himself that he'd been through all of Rupert's documents. It had probably been left at her estate, but wouldn't someone have found it?

A light clicked on behind Rupert and Meghan darted to the side, pressing her back against the bricks of the building.

"What are you doing, Mr. Meyers?" a woman's voice sailed through the open window.

"I'm talking to Hester," he said.

Meghan held her breath as the voice floated out toward her. "I don't see anyone out here. You're letting all the hot air in." The woman shut the window and the blinds came down.

With her body trembling, Meghan slowly walked away, hugging the building so as not to be detected. Then, with a heavy heart, she got into her car and drove back to The Seabreeze.

With her food cart permits completed online, Meghan began sifting through all the ingredients she'd bought at the store, jotting down ideas in her notebook. She'd been doing anything she could not to think about Rupert and the fact that she'd had to sneak over to a window to see him. She'd opened a text to Toby a couple of times but then thought better of it. Clearly, he didn't want to hear from her; he wouldn't even allow her to see his grandfather.

"What are your favorite cake flavors?" she called over to Tess, who was sitting on the sofa, flipping through a magazine.

"Red velvet and spice cake."

Meghan stared at the empty line in her notebook, thinking. "What if I did a butter pecan spice cake in the shape of a muffin?"

Tess got up and tossed the magazine onto the table. "I'd buy them all and eat my weight in muffins." She climbed up onto the barstool and rested her chin in her hands.

"I want to think of something no one else has thought of," Meghan said, her mind whirring. "I need something to set me apart from every other bakery."

"Well, Hester Quinn *is* your grandmother. You could do an old movie theme or something."

Meghan squinted at the idea, letting it marinate. "Maybe . . . You could be onto something. I need to wow people. What could I do?"

"You could give some of the proceeds to charity?"

"Good idea, and I'll probably do that. But I need something new with the muffins too." Still thinking, she reached over and picked up a few of the vanilla muffins she'd made, slathering them with her vanilla icing. "Hang on," she said, grabbing a bar of chocolate sitting on the counter and rummaging in the drawers for a zester. After locating the tool, she covered the iced muffin with chocolate sprinkles. Then, she got another muffin, iced it, and went over to the fridge, pulling out Tess's chocolate sauce she liked for her ice cream.

"What are you doing?" Tess asked with a laugh as Meghan drizzled the muffin with chocolate sauce.

"I need those chopsticks that someone left in a drawer," Meghan said, pulling the takeout chopsticks and removing the paper covering. She jammed one into the first muffin.

"What in the world?" Tess looked on.

Meghan iced another muffin and then rolled it in crushed nuts. Then, she began to stack the muffins, making a tower. She topped them with a final iced muffin and arranged mint leaves and raspberries on the top. "This is just a prototype," she said. "But what if I could package all different kinds of arrangements like this for parties?"

Tess's eyes rounded. "And cater."

"Mm-hm." Meghan nodded excitedly, feeling more and more in her element. "The possibilities are endless. I could do cupcakes and muffins, and go wild with the toppings too: gold dust, silver sprinkles, little candy hearts . . . Glamorous."

"Just like you," Tess said with a wink.

TWENTY-FIVE

Before work, keeping herself busy since she was unable to see Rupert like she used to, and trying not to think about the fact that she missed Toby more than she'd like to admit, Meghan sat at the enormous kitchen island of The Seabreeze with her pen poised over the blank page in Hester's journal. The pressure of writing something worth telling Hester, something to give merit to the woman's struggles, weighed on her. With a wiggle of the pen, Meghan put the tip of it to the paper to write but stopped again.

She'd hoped to tell Hester how much she wanted to prove that her sacrifice had been meaningful in some way, that letting Nanna raise Meghan's mother had been the right thing to do, but in the end, she knew that Hester already understood that. Hester had wanted the pages to be filled with a new life. Meghan needed to write about the family she'd built and the love she had for them, the two things the actress never achieved. But they were just as elusive to Meghan. The closest she'd come to building anything was the muffin tower she'd constructed. She peered over at it, pondering the grand scheme of life.

"Morning," Tess said, padding in and making a beeline for the coffee maker. "Whatcha doing?"

"Apart from assessing my wasted life, not much," Meghan replied, closing the journal.

"It's way too early for deep comments like that," Tess said with a yawn. "Coffee first." She pulled two mugs from the cabinet and clicked on the coffee maker. "The only time you wasted was the time you waited for Vinnie to be a normal human being," she said, making them each a cup and sliding one of them over to her. Trying to find a good response, Meghan didn't say anything in return, and Tess kept going. "You're still young," she said. "You haven't wasted your life when you've got over half of it still to live. And you've made a good start with the muffin cart."

"It seems insignificant now," Meghan admitted. She looked into the black liquid in front of her, seeing her shadow in the reflection on the surface of it, surrendering to the fact that she didn't have a clue what she was supposed to do. "I'm going to get ready for the day," she said, pushing away from the island.

"You aren't going to drink your coffee?" Tess asked.

Meghan reached over and grabbed the mug, holding it up with a smile that she put on for her friend's benefit.

Tess was gathering menus for the staff, and making sure the tables were set with stemware and cups with saucers. Meghan looked at her phone as she tied her apron around her waist. She'd missed a call from the contractors. While checking her tables at the hostess stand, the lobby of Mariner's Inn beginning to buzz with guests huddled around the small seating area tables while they had their complimentary coffee, she put the phone to her ear and listened to the message. The contractors wanted to ask her a question about where to put two of the vents for the air conditioning at Pappy's, only serving to cause the knot in her shoulder to ache. They asked if she could come by this evening.

"Meghan." Tabitha strode up to her. "I'm so glad you're early. Got a second?"

Meghan dropped her phone into her pocket, turned around, and leaned on the podium to face the manager, attempting to push the worry about her bills for Pappy's cottage out of her mind. "Of course."

"I've had five of your muffins," she said, wide-eyed, with a grin. "They're incredible. I told everyone at the inn about them."

A surge of exhilaration shot through her, making her forget all about the phone call. "Thank you."

"If this is more work than you want to do, please just say so . . . Tess told me about your muffin cart. And I was wondering if you'd like to set it up outside the lobby for guests. We'd allow you the space rent-free, and we wouldn't take any of the profits."

She cleared her throat to stifle the emotion that had risen up at the idea that someone believed in her capabilities outside of waitressing, and that she might have the opportunity to make a little extra money.

The prospect of selling her muffins every morning in the hotel sounded amazing, but it seemed too good to be true. "Why would you offer that if the hotel won't benefit financially?" Meghan asked.

"They're so good, Meghan, that we feel just having them available will be great for business."

"Really?" she said, trying to keep the squeal of excitement in check.

"Really." Tabitha gave her an encouraging nod. "People want to stay where they can get the best of the best. If guests can buy a gourmet treat while they're waiting for breakfast to open, it might calm the crowds." She grabbed the table map from the podium and inspected it. "If it sounds like something you'd like to do, we can talk specifics about what you'll need later this week."

"Yes, I'd love that."

"Great, we'll catch up later." Tabitha eyed the growing line at the entrance of the restaurant as she set the map back down for the hostess. "Time to get to work."

With her head held high in pride, Meghan took her spot at the back wall, waiting for her first table, knowing those tiny steps she was taking might just be in the right direction.

Meghan and Tess arrived at The Seabreeze after work to change clothes before going over to Pappy's. When Meghan pulled the car to a stop behind Toby's Range Rover, which was sitting in the circular drive, her heart began to hammer.

"Did he find the will?" Tess asked.

"I have no idea," she said breathlessly.

As Meghan parked the car, Toby got out.

"I'll just go tend to Charlie," Tess said, shutting the car door and jogging up the steps to the house, leaving Meghan to face Toby.

He took a step toward her. "Hi."

She smiled up at him, all the saliva leaving her mouth. She hadn't realized until that moment how hollow she'd felt without those blue eyes on her.

"The security cameras caught you sneaking around the premises of Rosewood Manor," he said, although it seemed like there was much more he wanted to say.

"What are you talking about?" She played dumb, hoping he couldn't tell that she was lying through her teeth.

The corners of his mouth twitched upward. "I saw you on the surveillance video."

Meghan sucked in a tiny breath. *Busted.* "Well, I'm not a trained snooper," she admitted.

"Clearly not," he teased back. But then, he sobered. "Our legal team advised that you not speak to me or my grandfather until they can fully investigate the inheritance issue." He took a step toward her. "I wouldn't keep Gramps from you or you from him, but I'm caught in a very difficult situation." His eyes found hers, a storm brewing in them, ripping her heart out.

"Please, tell me this has nothing to do with the rumors," she said.

He shook his head as if in disbelief and took a step back from her. "I need to go. I'm not supposed to be here." Without another word, he got into his car and drove away, leaving Meghan standing alone in the drive, wanting to run after him but not knowing how to make this all better, feeling utterly lost.

TWENTY-SIX

"We can route these vents to either wall," the contractor said over the buzz of a saw, pointing to the floor in Pappy's living room as Meghan attempted to focus on what he was saying. "Do you want them under the windows by the front of the house or on the wall by the kitchen, over here?" The man's boots made large dusty prints across Pappy's hardwoods, the house in complete disarray.

"Let's do it by the front windows," Meghan replied, shaking her head discreetly at Tess. Tess seemed to guess right away that Meghan was overwhelmed by the sight of Pappy's house and offered an empathetic smile.

"All right, by the windows it is." The man joined the others, who were all finishing up for the evening.

Meghan clicked a switch on the wall, and the lights to the kitchen came on. "Looks like the electrician's almost finished," she said to Tess, trying to look on the bright side, her pleasant expression hiding the stress that the bill would be due upon completion. She turned toward the front door, unable to look at it anymore. "We should check on Charlie."

Leaving the construction behind, Meghan opened the

door and led the two of them outside where Charlie was loping through the grass and onto the pier, kicking up sand.

"Look at him," Meghan said. "He worries about nothing."

"It would be nice to be a dog," Tess said. "Apart from having to do my business in the rain and snow . . ."

"Small price to pay for the rest of your life being like that." Meghan pointed to the dog as he sailed through the air after a butterfly, coming down with a thud.

Tess laughed, the two of them sitting on the front porch in silence for a while. The buzzing had stopped and the trucks were pulling away, the last of the contractors letting themselves out the back to go home for the night.

"I really don't mind fronting the money for the repairs," Tess said. "You can pay me back. I know you're good for it." She twisted around to face Meghan. "And if you don't, I know where you live," she teased.

Meghan rubbed the knot in her shoulder. "I hate to ask . . ." The truth was, she'd do everything in her power to pay her friend back, but it would take time, and she was nearly sure that the bill would drain Tess's savings. What would Tess do if *she* needed the money for something? Meghan would feel terrible.

"You've gotten nowhere with finding Hester's will?"

Meghan shook her head and let out a loud breath. "No. All I have to go on is Rupert's recollection that it's in a desk, which doesn't give me much."

"It's too bad that you can't see Toby. As much of a headcase as I thought he was, something told me the two of you would somehow find your way to one another."

"It's the romantic in you," Meghan said, although she couldn't deny the loss that swarmed her when she considered that she wouldn't be spending time with Toby anymore.

Charlie bounded up to them with a piece of driftwood in his mouth.

"What did you find?" Meghan asked, allowing a little grin of affection to surface through her tension. The dog wagged his tail furiously, pulling away when she tried to grab it. He dodged her once more and ran back off, all the way down to the beach where he dove into the waves.

"That looks like a great idea," Tess said.

"Running with a stick?" Meghan asked.

"No," Tess said, poking her playfully. "Swimming in the ocean. Do you have a swimsuit inside?"

"Yeah," Meghan replied, remembering the yellow bikini she'd left behind when she'd decided to pack the pink one instead. "It's in Pappy's room. Do you have one?"

"Yep. I have two here and one at The Seabreeze." She stood up, brushing off her bottom and then reaching for Meghan's hands. "Let's go join Charlie and forget all our troubles."

"I'm totally up for that," Meghan said, rising and following Tess into the house.

"I'm starving," Tess said, as she picked up the large plastic sheet covering the furniture and took a towel from the trunk she'd brought for the summer. "Should we call in a pizza?" She tipped her head to the side, toweling off her hair.

"Where would we eat it in this mess?" Meghan asked, buttoning her shorts and draping her wet suit over one of the plastic-covered dining chairs. "There's nowhere to sit."

"True . . ."

The sound of crunching gravel under tires outside stopped their conversation.

"Did one of the workers forget something?" Meghan asked, drying her hair and lumping the towel on the chair with her suit.

A door slammed and steps clambered up to the door, Meghan and Tess staring at each other, neither moving. Then, both of them jumped with the sound of a knock.

Tess went over to the window. "It's Toby."

Meghan opened the door.

"You said there's a will," he said, his blue eyes focused on her.

"Yes," she said.

"Gramps told me too. He said it's in the desk."

"Yes," she said again. "He told me that as well."

Tess stepped forward as if in solidarity with Meghan—two to one—but something told Meghan that they weren't necessarily on opposing sides this time.

That was the first time Toby regarded her. "Hi, Tess," he said. "Can we have a minute?" He waggled a finger between himself and Meghan.

Tess silently asked if Meghan would be okay without her, and Meghan nodded.

"Come on, Charlie," Tess said. "Let's go outside."

Charlie hopped up and ran to the door ahead of Tess.

In the quiet that was left between them, Meghan caught the slight scent of Toby's woodsy aftershave through the dust, every nerve in her body on high alert as she stared into his blue eyes.

"Want to tell me what's going on?" she asked.

He sucked in a tiny breath but then stopped, his brows furrowing as he seemed to wrestle with his thoughts. "I don't know where to start."

"How about the reason you came knocking on my door?"

Toby looked deeply into her eyes, taking her hand and leading her into her bedroom. With no explanation, he located Hester's table and pulled off the plastic. "Know what this is?"

Confusion swam around inside her. "It's Hester's dressing table."

He shook his head. "It's her writing desk."

It took her a minute before she connected the dots. Then, suddenly, the memory floated back into her mind: *She'd shown up out of nowhere, with a driver who'd filled a truck with her furniture—the pieces still full with her things, her personal items in all the drawers—and driven all the way from her house in New York.*

Writing desk. Still full of her things. It's in the desk. She stared at the single drawer, knowing they'd already opened it to look at the engraved branding but somehow hoping for a miracle.

Open it. All the way, she heard in Pappy's voice. Meghan looked up at Toby, her pulse racing, her hands trembling.

Slowly, he reached out and hooked the circular drawer pull with his finger, tugging gently as Meghan held her breath. The drawer inched its way out, empty, and her heart fell into her stomach.

Meghan reached into it, pushing her hand all the way to the back, moving her fingers around. "There's nothing in here," she said.

Toby stared at the drawer, but he was clearly thinking of something else. "Gramps said, 'I need you to find Hester and tell her that the ledger paper she was looking for is in her writing desk.' I thought maybe he meant the will, but I guess it was nothing."

She looked up at him in awe. "You'd help me find the will?" she asked, wondering why he would do something so kind.

He led her over to the bed and moved the covering, taking her hands and gesturing for her to sit. Then he lowered himself down beside her, breathing in a long, slow breath as if he were centering himself for what he had to say. "I built Mariner's Inn because I was grieving and Mary had wanted it. I channeled all my grief into building the inn, making it the best it could be. And I couldn't set foot on the premises. It was too hard because it was Mary's dream. Just having meetings there took all my energy and I'd rush through them."

She was curious as to why he was telling her all this now. "But you came to the party," she said, the recollection of his touch during their dance prickling her skin.

"Yes."

"Why did you come?"

He stared at her, fondness showing in those eyes of his, his chest rising and falling with his thoughts. "Because *you* were there."

Surprise raced through her veins, her heart slamming around in her chest.

"I tried to push you away because the feeling terrified me. I've never felt that way since Mary, and I didn't know what to do. And when the lawyers suggested I stay away, I tried, but it was impossible. I can't do it."

She reached over and took his hand.

"I didn't know if I was ready to feel this way about someone. And then when Gramps took to you so easily, it was even harder because I also didn't know if I'd ever find someone who would understand how my time would be split with caring for him. But you do."

"I do," she agreed. "And I love being around you," she said, taking his hand and placing it on her pounding heart. "You make me feel alive."

"I didn't explain fully when you thought I stole money from Gramps and paid people off because I thought it might be easier to let you go if you believed it."

"You're not stealing money from Rupert?"

"No. Before his memory completely went, he was worried about losing control of things. He gave me access to all his accounts and power of attorney for his legal and financial matters, telling his team I was in charge. And then he told me to take whatever I need and follow my dreams."

"I had you all wrong," she said in almost a whisper. "But what about the rumors that you paid off the board members for the zoning?"

"After I had dinner with you, I was terrified at my feelings for you and I turned all my focus back to Mariner's Inn for Mary. I was so desperate to make the inn perfect to honor her memory that I offered to donate funds to anything the board wanted if they'd just grant me the zoning. It ruffled a few feathers, but most of them understood."

"I'm so sorry," she said, shaking her head, her heart breaking for him.

"I'm not," he said, that wonderful smile of his that warmed her emerging. "It forced me to realize that yes, I loved Mary— I always will. But she's in my past and I'm still here." He took Meghan's hand and mimicked what she'd done with his, placing it on his heart. "I'm alive. And I feel it, too, every time I'm with you." He let go and put his hands on her face, cradling it. "Want to be alive together?" He offered her an adorable smirk that sent her stomach flipping.

"Yes," she said, feeling like her heart would burst.

He caressed her cheek, his gaze swallowing her in that way that made her melt. He leaned in and pressed his lips to hers, and it was as if everything she'd done in her life had led her to this moment. His warm breath mixing with hers, the way his hands worked up through her hair and down her neck, the gentle touch of his fingertips against her skin—it was all absolute perfection, and she couldn't have imagined feeling this way with anyone else.

When he finally pulled back, he was smiling.

"You're happy," she said, elation filling every cell in her body.

He nodded, his blue eyes sparkling.

"So am I," she said.

He let out a nervous chuckle.

"Knock, knock," Tess's voice sailed through the room. "Sorry to interrupt you two lovebirds..." She eyed Meghan, her eyebrows bouncing up and down, making Meghan's cheeks burn, wondering how long she'd been lurking by the door. "Whatcha doing?" She pointed to the open drawer in Hester's desk.

"Looking for the will," Meghan said.

"It wasn't in that drawer so you decided to frisk Toby for it?" Tess flashed a bold grin.

Toby laughed, only making the heat in Meghan's face worse. "My grandfather thought it was in that drawer," he said.

Tess went over to it and looked inside. "Hm."

Charlie sauntered into the room and followed Tess over to the desk, sniffing it.

Tess reached her hand into it.

"I did the same thing," Meghan said. "Nothing."

"Wait." Tess leaned in, shoving her arm all the way to her shoulder. "There's something stuck at the very back between the drawer and the wooden bottom."

Meghan stood up and ran over to it, dropping down and peering underneath it. "There's no way to get to it if it is behind the drawer. Can we slide it out?"

Tess tried to pull the drawer from its case, but it was secured with tracks on either side and it couldn't be removed. Toby fiddled with the metal rails. "It's permanently attached to these," he said. "We need a screwdriver to see if we can remove the metal from the wood."

"Hang on," Tess said. "I almost had it." She slid her thin arm into the drawer again. "I'm so close."

"Let me try," Meghan said, stepping up beside her.

Tess stepped back and let Meghan attempt to reach whatever it was.

Sliding her arm into the drawer, Meghan leaned as far as she could until her fingertips brushed what felt like papers, and her breath caught. "I feel something." She wriggled to see if she could get a hold of them, the tips of her fingers brushing them but not able to reach them. She strained, pushing her arm as far as it would go.

Pappy's voice filled her ears. *Almost there.*

She pushed herself as hard as she could, and then squeezed her two fingers together around the papers, pressing them to the bottom of the drawer as she pulled them forward. "I got them!" She dragged the pages into view and got hold of them, her pulse in her ears. "It's ledger paper," she said, her mouth drying out. There, on the ledger paper, scrawled over the pink vertical lines that usually set off the financials, was the same curling script from the journal. She read the first few lines aloud:

I, Hester Elizabeth Quinn, resident of Brentwood, California, being of sound mind and not acting under duress, hereby declare this document to be my last will and testament. I appoint Rupert Edward Meyers as personal representative of my estate . . .

Meghan lost her words, her eyes scanning the text, completely disbelieving what she was reading.

"What does it say?" Tess whined.

Toby leaned in, putting his arm around Meghan as she read the next paragraph.

I bequeath my property as follows:
   Beneficiary: Jacqueline Ann Gray or her direct descendants to receive the following property: $45,035,350.00. International Bank Account Number: 29-76-MBC7 . . .

Meghan stopped reading, all of it blurring with her tears. She was a *millionaire*. All her worries about paying her bills and investing in her dream job—all of them were gone in an instant. Then, she thought about Toby. "If this is one of Rupert's accounts, I'll help pay for the expansion of the inn," she told him, still breathless from it all.

"No," he said. "I wouldn't let you do that."

"Will you have a way to pay for it?"

"When I first got it up and running, I wanted to sell it and run away. I'd thought about taking the money and making a brand-new start somewhere like Florida where I had no memories of my former life, because it was all too much emotionally, but I pushed through for Mary. Now, I think she'd be ready for me to sell it."

"What will you do once you sell it?" she asked.

"Oh, I don't know. Maybe invest in a muffin business or something." He gave her a wink.

Meghan laughed. "*You* know about my muffin business?"

"Apparently everyone does," Toby said. "I heard about it when I stopped into the inn. They were all raving about them." He leaned in, so close that his lips almost touched hers. "Think I could try one sometime?"

Meghan closed her eyes. "You could try one tonight. I've got a bunch over at The Seabreeze." She leaned forward, her lips brushing his.

"I'd like that," he said, kissing her.

"Hello?" Tess's voice cut through the moment. "Person and dog in the room."

Their lips still together, Toby laughed, and the feeling of it was something Meghan knew she could never live without.

EPILOGUE

"I'll be just a few more minutes," Meghan called to Toby from the bedroom of their new farmhouse that they'd built on Pappy's land. With the funds from Hester's will, they now had a full-time nurse for Rupert named Penny, they'd renovated Pappy's cottage for him, and he got to take walks on the beach and look at the stars every night.

Meghan sat at Hester's writing desk with the journal. She taped in a photo of herself, standing behind her muffin cart that had a brand-new logo for The Muffin Lady on the front. While the little cart wasn't her main means of income, her muffins having gone national with production in four nationwide facilities with distribution to forty-three of the fifty states, she still set up there every morning at the inn that Toby had decided to keep running, with Meghan at his side.

They'd opened the new wing they'd bought themselves, with no outside investors, and built an enormous courtyard full of palm trees, bright pink bee balm flowers, and blue flag irises. They'd named the courtyard Mary's Corner. Mary had been with Toby to create the idea for the inn and Meghan had helped him carry it through to what it was today.

All of this was written in the pages of Meghan's journal, and now, she was about to write the next entry with Charlie curled up by her feet.

Oh, Hester, so much has happened that I can hardly write it all. My old boss Vinnie called today and told me he'd bought one of my muffins at the market up in New York. He apologized, telling me how wrong he'd been, and asked if I wanted a chef's position, but I turned him down. My life is here on Hatteras Island. What began on one "island summer," as someone special once told me you'd called it, Toby and I have now continued. Our families' lives have carried on in the place you wanted to be in the end. I hope that you can see it all and you're sitting next to Pappy cheering for us.

Sorry it's been a little while since I've written. Toby asked me to marry him and we said our vows on the beach outside our new home. With the help of his nurse, Rupert walked me down the aisle. I didn't have the heart to tell him that I wasn't married to him; his joy was overwhelming for us all. He really misses you. He shows me how much every day by the way he lights up when he thinks he's seeing you . . .

"Toby's too patient," Tess said from the doorway. "Hurry up! Alex wants to go down to the beach and I'm trying to convince him that Hatteras Island is a wonderful place to live. Our best friends are millionaires and one of them is the granddaughter of a famous film star! It's literally the perfect place for an up-and-coming actor."

Meghan laughed. "Sorry. I'm just writing in Hester's journal. I'll finish up and be right down."

"I'll be back in two minutes with cocktails to entice you if you're not," Tess told her as she headed back down the hallway.

"That's fair," Meghan called to her, smiling adoringly as she thought about her favorite friend in all the world. Her pen poised, she finished her entry:

Tess was so inspired by my drive to run my own business all by myself and do things my way that she took it upon herself to call her old flame Alex Tisdale and ask him out. They'd met years ago, waiting tables together while he pursued his acting career. They're both staying with us for the summer, working at the beach bar down the road, and Tess is trying to convince him to stay and find a house to rent with her. What she doesn't know is that he's already told me he's planning to stay, and he's got a ring in his suitcase that he's planning to give Tess in front of us all tonight at dinner. I've never been happier for her.

"Hey," Toby said, setting a bright yellow fizzy cocktail down on Hester's table and kissing her on the cheek, his lips lingering near her ear, still causing happiness to bubble up, goose bumps on her arms. "Tess said to bring this up."

Meghan laughed. "That wasn't two minutes. That was about thirty seconds." She shut the journal and placed it in the drawer of the desk, standing and turning to face the man of her dreams. He kissed her, his lips warm and tasting of rum from the drinks he was most likely making for everyone.

"Gramps is downstairs, having sips of my pineapple juice and coconut rum," he said with a devious grin. "He says he wants one for himself."

"Does Penny know?"

He shook his head, making her giggle. "I'll make him a martini glass of pineapple juice so he thinks he's having a cocktail with us." But then his expression sobered, fondness for her sliding down his face. "You look beautiful," he said.

"Thank you," she said, her heart bursting with happiness. She reached out for Toby with one hand and picked up her cocktail with the other. "Come on, Charlie. Want to go to the beach?"

Charlie hopped up, rushing past them, sliding his way down the hardwood steps in a flash.

Together they went downstairs, with nothing but a sunny future ahead of them.

ACKNOWLEDGMENTS

I am forever appreciative of the steps Oliver Rhodes took to give me a chance and build me as an author. He set the bar for my creative journey.

I owe a huge thank you to my amazing editor Christina Demosthenous, who shaped this book right up. I couldn't have done it without her.

A big thank you to Nurse—and one of my best friends—Tia Field, and to Doctor Sarah Grayce, for lending their expertise in medical lingo.

And to my husband, Justin, who had to deal with me while I wrote two books at the same time, after promising I wouldn't do it again. I am blessed to have his love and support.

A LETTER FROM JENNY

Hi there!

Thank you so much for reading *An Island Summer*. I hope it made you want to run to the beach and explore all its historical treasures before rushing to find your own family and hold them dear.

If you'd like me to drop you an email when my next book is out, you can sign up here:

www.ItsJennyHale.com/email/jenny-hale-sign-up

I won't share your information with anyone else, and I'll only email you whenever new books come out.

If you did enjoy *An Island Summer*, I'd be very grateful if you'd write a review online. Getting feedback from readers helps to persuade others to pick up one of my books for the first time. It's one of the biggest gifts you could give me.

If you enjoyed this story, and would like a few more happy endings, check out my other summer novels: *The Summer House, Summer at Firefly Beach, Summer by the Sea, The House at Firefly Beach*, and *The Beach House*.

Until next time,

Jenny xo

KEEP IN TOUCH WITH JENNY

facebook.com/jennyhaleauthor

twitter.com/jhaleauthor

instagram.com/jhaleauthor

goodreads.com/7201437.Jenny_Hale

ABOUT THE AUTHOR

Jenny Hale is a *USA Today* bestselling author of romantic fiction. Her novels *Coming Home for Christmas* and *Christmas Wishes and Mistletoe Kisses* have been adapted for television on the Hallmark Channel. Her stories are chock-full of feel-good romance and overflowing with warm settings, great friends, and family. Grab a cup of coffee, settle in, and enjoy the fun!